OMG

OMG

Jenny Pivor

Merrimack Media
Salem, MA

Published 2019 by Merrimack Media

Contents

Acknowledgements

Inspiration and support come from many places. Thank you to my writer's group and especially Loren Schechter and his diligent red-pen, but also Mary Baures, Linda Malcolm, Diane Sharpe, and Dan Kaplan for their insight. A special thanks to Ray Daniels for his plot suggestions and SSA Jeffrey P. Heinze from the FBI Office of Public Affairs, who validated plot points and helped with proper terminology. Mark Malatesta was instrumental with editing as well as "getting" my story and helping me deliver it in concise terms. in Without the support of my late husband, Jay Pivor, who listened tirelessly to chapters, this book would not have been possible.

Dedication

To Jay

Prologue

There was nothing that anyone could have done. Natalie's coworkers looked over their cubicles with shocked faces, as the EMTs gave up on reviving her. They covered her with a sheet and wheeled her onto the elevator, and out the door. Her team came into the common area and stood as quietly as trees in a forest, with only soft whispers about the hideousness of what had occurred, shuddering between them like the wind. *My God. Did you see what she looked like?* They looked at each other helplessly, and then they were sent home, while the area was fumigated.

The ambulance drove silently from Visiozyme's prime Kendall Square location and over the river from Cambridge into Boston, where Natalie was taken to Mass General Hospital.

It had been just an hour before when Natalie had returned from weekly lunch with Gerry Fox. She'd started feeling odd was just a few minutes after she sat down at her desk, but dismissed it, thinking that she might be queasy from something she'd eaten or was coming down with a virus. Natalie had popped two Tums in her mouth from her top drawer and opened up a spreadsheet on her computer. As she waited for her stomach to settle, her skin began to tingle, as if her nerve endings were on fire. Then a nasty rash erupted on her arms and face. She touched her burning cheeks and was horrified at the new landscape of bumpy peaks and valleys that had formed on her perfect skin. She could feel her veins delivering acid throughout her body—her skin felt like it was melting her from the inside. She tried to focus on her computer, but the screen danced in circles in front of her eyes.

She watched her symptoms develop with a weird fascination. Had she been poisoned? Natalie knew that her colleagues called her a bitch behind her back. She also knew what she was getting into when she took the job as the only woman manager at Visiozyme, and figured that this came with the territory. But being poisoned was something else entirely.

Why would anyone want to get rid of her? As far as she knew, her only fault at work had been her enviable success. She was a prized member of the executive team, and very good at what she did. Natalie didn't think that her colleagues were bad guys—just clueless. Her stomach lurched off the rails in vile contractions, guiding her quinoa and kale salad towards making an encore. Of course, there was Gerry's wife who might want her dead, but Natalie doubted if she knew the extent of her relationship with Gerry.

Of course, there was the team of wild programmers that she managed, all male except for poor Bettina, the interface designer. Bettina was the butt of their jokes when they thought that she was out of earshot. This week's brand was a running competition to compare the size of Bettina's brain to her breasts. There was no good outcome for Bettina in these jokes since the consensus was that both were too small. Those morons were also clueless but in a different way. She'd already fired one them—Simon Whitehead. He was the only one who was just a shade more off-kilter, and just strange enough to try something so diabolical—but he'd been marched out of the building five weeks ago, and had no access. The rest of them were jerks, but probably harmless. Natalie had been a stickler for detail and pain, but who would want her dead?

She considered it ironic that she thought of her workplace as toxic. After all, Visiozyme, was a biotech company that specialized in anti-depressants. Wasn't the whole point of the medicines they produced to make people feel better? There was only one person who bothered to talk to Natalie at all. It was Gerry Fox, one of the board members. And he appeared to be very pleased with Natalie's performance.

She speed-dialed Gerry Fox. "It's me," she told his voicemail. "I'm feeling sick, and at first I thought it might be something that we ate at lunch. Do you feel bad too? It *could* be food poisoning, but this is very strange. I'm *trying* not to panic, but I think I might have been poisoned. Can you help? Gerry, where the *hell* are you?"

Natalie stood up, feeling woozy, and nearly passed out as she ran to the ladies' room. She glanced at her reflection in the mirror. Her dark frightened eyes looked ghoulish against her white skin. The blotchy rash that she'd sprouted on her arms was now on her cheeks and had erupted into tiny blisters. As her forehead broke out in a cold sweat, Natalie collapsed on the tile floor. Her hands slipped from her mouth that she'd been holding with both hands and the blood that she'd tried to contain spilled and spread into a sizable puddle on the floor.

Bettina's scream, upon finding Natalie on the ladies' room floor minutes later had set off initial pandemonium. The ambulance only took moments to whoop whoop its way to the front door of the Kendall Square headquarters of Visiozyme and then Natalie was gone.

Steve Hahn, one of the head programmers on Natalie's team, stepped outside onto Main Street and took out his phone and called Gerry Fox. No one picked up. "Hey, it's Steve Hahn. Sorry to tell you this, I thought you might want to know that Natalie is dead. Call me."

1

Simon Says

Jolt was Kylie's favorite coffee shop and the unofficial epicenter of the startup world in Kendall Square. As usual, it was humming with an undertone of excitement and productivity, and Kylie knew she could get inspired just by breathing the caffeinated air—the perfect setting to plan her new business, or what she hoped would save her from destitution. As she sipped her coffee, hoping the caffeine would help the headache brewing, a lanky guy approached her table. He looked unapologetically awkward, balancing a laptop and a cup of coffee.

"Hi. I'm Simon Whitehead," he said. "Can I sit down for a minute to talk?'

"I'm kind of busy. What's this about?" She gave Simon a once over. He hardly looked old enough to be drinking coffee. His baby face showed sparse whiskers reminiscent of stray weeds popping out of the sand. He had the look of a precocious and unkempt middle-schooler.

Simon slid into a seat anyway. "How's your business plan coming?"

Kylie sucked in her breath. She hadn't told anyone. "How do you know about that?"

"So, I consider it my job to know what's going on here. I picked it up on Wifi." He gestured wildly in the air with a hand as if her business plan were floating up there. "Looks to me, as if you're going to need a developer. And, this definitely looks like something that's right up my alley."

Kylie gulped and nodded. "Fair enough ... evidently, you've got some hacking chops. What are you, a hacking predator hanging out at Jolt looking for projects?"

He nodded and smirked. "Something like that."

Located at the edge of MIT, Jolt was where laptop-toting techies banged out code and salivated over venture capitalists who might fund their startups. She supposed it was the perfect place for a hacker to look for work, but it seemed he was pushing it.

She named her startup OMG. It would operate like a GPS, but instead of geographic directions, OMG would inform users of the turns they should take in their lives. Kylie assumed she wouldn't have to explain to anyone how OMG, stood for *Oh My God*, although she knew some people, like her parents, might not get it. She saw OMG as a Ouija Board on steroids, capable of accessing real information and applying actual data to assess the risks inherent to life's big questions.

Should you dump the girl who's been giving you the runaround?

OMG could search her emails and texts to tell where the questioner stood.

Kylie could have used OMG in college when Andrew left her to *meet new people*. She would have seen the breakup coming instead of being blindsided by his sudden disappearance. If only she could have accessed its power and checked, she would have known he was already dating one of her friends.

Besides its obvious advantages, OMG would be her ticket to living life her own way, without working a dreary job or whatever else her parents advocated as the good life that had nothing to do with her. Now that she'd dreamed it up, her entire future as an independent, solvent person would hinge upon finding a database superstar to bring her business plan to life ... versus her going broke, getting an actual job, and explaining her failures to her parents. All she needed was to find the right person to build it. It occurred to her perhaps the fates had sent a gift and it sat in front of her.

"Okay, Simon Whitehead. You've got my attention. Tell me about yourself."

"I will, but also, you can always check me out with your friend, Jared. You know him from grad school, right? He gave me a couple of freelance jobs and always swore I was genius."

Kylie shook her head in disbelief. *What else did this creepy kid know about her?*

"Go on."

"Okay. I've got a degree from MIT and have some great database experience."

"Like what?"

Simon's smirking pouty lips curled up at the corners as if he were in on some private joke. If he was like the programmers who she knew from grad school, she was probably the source of his amusement. Kylie knew some super-geeky guys were often uncommunicative; possibly even mutants who were more comfortable talking through their computers. But she didn't need Simon to be her friend, just to build her vision. Kylie gave him an encouraging smile. He only stared at her.

"Do you have some examples of what you've done?"

He rolled his eyes at the walls, where only the monthly art exhibits added some color, while the paintings were so disturbing. Kylie, who usually appreciated art, might have preferred them blank. His shoulders raised in an apathetic shrug.

"Mostly I've done some private projects, but I worked for Visiozyme for six months."

"When did you leave?"

"About six weeks ago."

"What have you been doing since?"

"Mostly freelance stuff."

"Visiozyme's a good company. How come you left?"

Simon removed four sugar packets from his pants pocket and added them to his coffee, stirring it before taking a big gulp. A strand of hair fell over his high forehead, enhancing his unkempt street urchin look. "So, it was okay for a first corporate kind of job, but I was the new kid on the block and everybody dumped extra grunt work on me." He drummed his fingertips on his closed laptop. "Guess I'm not a corporate kind of a guy."

"Besides being a hacker, what kind of guy are you?" She narrowed her eyes at him.

"Creative, I guess; visionary ... yes, definitely visionary." He punctuated it with a nod.

"What's your vision?"

"Mostly connecting various systems and artificial intelligences to make data flow smoothly from one to another."

"What did you work on at Visiozyme?"

"Not what they promised. They had me doing QA. You know, quality assurance? It's mostly testing."

Kylie jotted QA on a fresh page in her notebook. She did not like his galling assumption again that she didn't know anything. "I do know, but why did you quit?"

He shrugged. "Bored, I guess."

"But you do like databases?"

"They're my specialty. I like the logic and how they allow me to get creative in the structure."

"You have to test databases too, you know. As you obviously know from hacking into my computer, I'm looking for a visionary database specialist. It's possible you could be a good fit. Can you give me a reference or two and I'll get back to you? If I like the way everything sounds, we can discuss salary."

He made a sour face. "Look, you've already seen what I can do. I like the project and can work for just a deposit until its built, and then you can pay me the rest."

Kylie particularly liked his idea, but also added a note: *Very eager. Possibly desperate ....* Still, he could be her guy—with his apparently excellent skills and creativity. She would call Jared and see if he confirmed the high praise Simon had mentioned. She did want a Visiozyme reference since it was one of the leading biotech companies in Kendall Square. If it checked out, she was lucky to find someone almost immediately.

"Anything else you've done?"

"I volunteered for a while at a city program and taught old people how to use computers," he added as if remembering someone told him he needed to do some community service.

Could that possibly be true? Kylie couldn't imagine it, given how his eyes darted and how uncomfortable he appeared. She would see.

"Fine, for starters, just give me a reference name for Visiozyme and we'll go from there. Can you also write the dates you worked there?" She handed him a pen and flipped to a new piece of paper in her notebook.

Simon promptly printed the information in tiny, angular letters. His reference was for Natalie Saltz, his former supervisor. Kylie felt certain she had heard the name somewhere before.

"So, why did you become a programmer?"

For the first time since he sat down, Simon met her eyes fully. "My parents thought I was a child prodigy. When I was six, they sent me to computer camp where I wrote my first program. It was awesome. It had these airplanes bombing and chasing each other ... just kid stuff, but it was pretty cool. I realized how I could create this universe, and then I couldn't stop. Know what I mean?" His mouth curled into a smug look again, with a smirk growing in a diagonal line across his face as if he might be thinking ... of course she didn't know.

Kylie bristled inside. If she could code, she would not need him ... not that she'd had the slightest desire to build a computer program. She retrieved her notebook and jotted down on a new page: *Arrogant.*

"Go on," she said.

"So, I was always a wimp; one of those kids who was scared of everything."

Kylie's opinion of him softened somewhat with his self-depreciation. Maybe he had a human side after all.

Simon smiled and met her gaze. "I'm a bigger wimp now. "But I understand the power of code, so it doesn't matter anymore since ... in my world ... I control everything. The geeks shall inherit the Earth, right?"

Kylie noticed his slender fingers, which looked as if they'd never thrown a ball or gripped a hammer. "You're probably right."

His eyes flashed a shrewd glint. "So, can I ask you a question? What kind of boss are you?"

"I consider myself fair and I'm very collaborative. I have this idea of creating a computer platform to really help people, but I want to make some money, too. I'd want you to work independently, if this works out.

"Okay, then." He grinned. "Let me know when you want me to start."

"You're an operator, aren't you? I haven't agreed to hire you yet. I don't have a resume and I haven't checked any references. I want to think about this and check out a few things. Just write your contact information under your references." She flipped back to the page and handed over the notebook to him.

"You obviously don't know my value yet. You realize your project isn't just database integration, right? You need someone like me who also has AI experience. That's artificial intelligence, you know? You can't just get the information.

You need to have some assessment capabilities and intelligence to know what to do with it."

Kylie nodded, but gnashed her teeth as Simon complied and wrote down a name. He left her to finish her coffee and to resume her planning. Once he ambled off, Kylie realized she forgot to ask about his teaching the elderly. At that point, she was so dazed by his brazen behavior and obvious skills ... she didn't care if it was his grandmother he'd been teaching. She needed a developer. She didn't have time to lose. The balance on her trust fund was shrinking by the minute.

Kylie called the number he'd given her for Natalie Saltz, but was surprised to hear it was no longer in service. Maybe Natalie changed numbers? Kylie looked up the main phone number for Visiozyme on her smart phone, punched it in, and got a recording. No, she didn't know which extension she wanted. Yes, she could identify Natalie's name for the dial-by-name directory, and she carefully pushed the correct buttons. She heard back: *There is no such person in our directory. Please check the spelling and try again.*

Kylie scoured the Visiozyme website on her laptop, but was disappointed to find it had no contact information for its mid-level managers. Googling the name: *Natalie Saltz,* she hoped to find a phone number. Twenty-two pages with news articles on Natalie turned up instead. The first article stopped Kylie's breath. *Natalie Saltz, Manager at Visiozyme, Poisoned.* Kylie's fingers went cold as she clicked on it. *Executive Poisoned with Suspected Deadly Virus.* Kylie remembered the headlines and the TV coverage, thinking it sounded grisly, but nothing more had come of it in the news, and Kylie forgot all about it. No wonder Natalie's name had sounded familiar!

She studied Natalie's photos, noticing her clear, intelligent eyes, but found no answers. She checked Simon's dates of employment and he'd quit five days before it had happened. Possibly, enough time to separate him from anything to do with her death. He wouldn't have had access, but he'd left close enough to the day she died ... Kylie was a little suspicious. She wanted to hire someone who willing to take a risk—but not kill his boss. He obviously knew Natalie had been murdered. What was he thinking?

Who gives the name of a dead person for a reference?

Still, she had to see it through. She would call Jared and ask him about Simon. He'd already sent her some resumes for her first startup, but no matter what he said, Kylie didn't think she'd find anyone better, given Simon's skill set.

***

It had been earlier that morning when Kylie traipsed off to Jolt feeling stressed as a tightrope in the ninety-five-degree heat radiating off the pavement. Ridiculous. If she'd never listened to her parents, she could now be working in the mountains ... maybe doing summer stock. In the winter, the best part, she'd be hitting the slopes as a relaxed ski instructor. She didn't know why she hadn't paid more attention to what she really wanted, except maybe she was too scared to stand up to them. Now, she had to try to come up with a creative way to make it work on her terms.

Kylie skied as a child, and ever since, she fantasized about becoming a ski instructor. She loved flying down a fresh trail, the liberating speed freeing her from everyday problems, and through her own control, she alone, was responsible for her fate. She wanted that life where she would be outside in the fresh air with sparkling scenery. In that fairyland world, she'd be happy, doing something she loved. But according to her parents, her ski bunny idea was laughable, and by the way, if she did get a real job, how would Kylie ever make a living with just her BA in English? Predictably, just as her parents had been laying out her entire life, they'd given her the options they would be willing to pay for to continue her education and give her their support.

Since she did not have the gumption to cut the cord; Kylie chose getting an MBA over a law degree. She suspected: *starting a business would feel like the rush of a ski run.* It turned out to be true ... it felt similar to the beginning of hiking a trail, where the path was crystalline clear, with the world just waiting below for her to rush into it with the spray of fresh powder at her heels. Unfortunately, her business problems also felt as damaging and humiliating as her packed-powder wipe-outs.

She learned it just months after nailing her fresh MBA to the exposed brick wall of her tiny Back Bay apartment when her first startup began spurting money as if it were riddled with bullets and left dying in the street. Evidently, her ill-conceived idea: an app for corporations to support the homeless was more of a hit with her business school advisor than any business person in the real world.

It was finally pronounced dead by her during a sweltering week in June. Kylie went into mourning for her startup, and for her life that appeared to be over. The death of her dreams left her with no prospects, no ideas, no friends, and no boyfriends.

Kylie knew only one thing for sure: she definitely did not want a job. Working for her father's financial firm taught her that lesson. After a few days of stewing, she emerged from her air-conditioned apartment with her laptop tucked under her arm. She dumped her defunct business cards into the recycling bin and headed to the Copley T stop near the library. There was only one option ... success. She was determined to compose the next chapter of her life.

Walking to the MBTA, she descended into the Green Line station to catch the train where the stale heat in the station made it hard to breathe. Giant fans blew hot air around the platform, creating tropical winds whipping her hair as if she were a model in a high-fashion photo shoot. Within minutes, a clunky green train rushed into the station before screeching to a stop, and opening its doors. Why the city could not oil the trains, she could never understand. Still, she felt grateful to get a seat on the air-conditioned train.

Kylie rode to Park Street where she made the change to the Red Line and rode over the Charles River with a calendar-art-worthy view of the Boston Skyline as they crossed the Longfellow Bridge. She got off at Kendall Square and walked past the glass-walled tech companies to Jolt, to brainstorm another business plan.

Her second business could not fail. She sat there and opened her special moleskin notebook reserved for brainstorming and important to-do lists. In grad school, she became a star list maker, since it helped her think clearly and worked as a mind dump so she didn't have to carry everything around in her head all the time. She scribbled the business ideas down as they popped into her head:

1. An app to find the best ski trails
2. An app to remember where you put things

3. An app called OMG to help people make good decisions based on real data

OMG since it had the most potential to make a difference in the world. It could also make her the most money. Eagerly, she took the time to flesh it out with a detailed outline and workflow. Within a few hours, she felt bolstered with a renewed entrepreneurial high, and was ready to answer if anyone asked what had happened to her startup ... such as her snooping parents. She could say how she'd just pivoted ... moved on to a better idea, which it was a better idea. With that solved, her eczema magically stopped itching.

The more Kylie developed her idea, the more she knew everyone would want OMG. If it worked, it would tell the questioner whether he or she should take a certain job by reviewing the company's financials and the personality profile of potential managers. She could even have it research her father's bank balance when he vetoed family vacations, claiming lack of funds.

Kylie knew her vision was not legal, but its potential seemed powerful. She would have to make sure it would only be used to do good. She could see to it and only let select people get to use it. She did need to trust whoever she hired to build it. How can you ever know for sure who to trust? She already had enough people disappoint her to learn that valuable lesson.

Once she met Simon, Kylie remained at Jolt sipping coffee and wishing she already had OMG at her disposal, so she would know whether to hire him. Since she did not have the application OMG, Kylie would have to find out for herself.

2

Visiozyme

Kylie packed up her laptop at Jolt and walked two blocks up Main Street to Visiozyme's imposing glass façade, and through the doors to its marble lobby and a two-story atrium with a living plant wall. Dwarfed behind the reception desk, a small Latina woman in a black uniform sat engrossed in her cell phone. Kylie stood there waiting to be noticed, as the woman texted with rapid-fire thumbs. Kylie shot daggers with her eyes. Don't bother doing your job on my account, Kylie thought, plopping her purse on the counter, to get the woman's attention. Oblivious, the receptionist completed her text in maddening slow motion, only looking up when she was done. "Yes?"

"Excuse me, I know this is a bit unusual, but I'm here for a reference on one of your previous employees, and evidently, his supervisor has passed away. I'm not sure who to talk to. Maybe HR?"

"Who was it?"

Kylie told her. The woman had her sign in, then called HR. She hung up and pointed. "It's on the fourth floor. Elevators are that way. Ask for Susan Wynn."

Kylie's low-heeled boots clacked on the marble as she walked from the elevator and through the glass doors to the waiting room. The HR receptionist, a pink-skinned, preppy-looking guy in his mid-twenties—about her age—asked her to take a seat. Kylie felt jumpy and stopped in the ladies' room to check her hair. In the mirror, her reflection showed a trim young woman. Kylie thought she looked average, but admittedly had regular features and perfect skin. She had been called beautiful more than once, but Kylie thought people were probably being generous. She certainly didn't feel beautiful lately. She considered her dark eyes too intense and her look too tomboyish to qualify for that club. She combed her chin-length hair and sighed at the highlighted ends growing out. Hair salons, in general, weren't budgeted in her startup. She dabbed on some drugstore lip gloss, made a face at her reflection, and returned to the waiting room.

How much simpler her life would be if she could settle for a regular job, where she might work in a place like the corporate setting before her, with its standard industrial beige carpeting, and cubicles beyond another glass door. But then, there were the plastic plants. Ugh. Evidently, the healthy plant wall in the lobby was just for show. Upstairs, the actual workers didn't need the extra oxygen from the plants and got to breathe in plastic instead. She couldn't imagine conforming or fitting in here, although she wasn't sure exactly where else she'd fit in, except on a glittering ski slope with a big sky all around her, and where she wouldn't have to put up with anybody else's agenda. Then she remembered that this time, she was the one doing the hiring...not interviewing for a job. Still, numbing anxiety had settled in her stomach as if it were going on a long road trip.

As it turned out, Kylie had plenty of time to contemplate the fact she was not a corporate person. She waited, alternating between winding a few locks of her hair around her short, gloss-black fingernails and playing with her phone. What if Simon didn't work out and she couldn't find anyone to build her platform? Or worse, what if he'd killed his boss and decided to kill her too? Or maybe she'd first die of malnutrition from eating too many ramen noodles.

Her worst fear was coming up empty and having to tell her parents that she was about to become a pauper. They were already convinced that she was a failure; she could just picture how it would unfold. When she could no longer avoid it, she'd have to go home to their Lexington colonial where she'd grown up. It was located in a desirable winding street of similar homes, all with manicured lawns and trees behind that hinted of acres of conservation land.

Kylie pictured them seated for their dinner at the long table in their formal dining room with a long colonial table, surrounded by the ivy papered wallpaper that had always made her claustrophobic. She'd always hated the pretention of eating in there as if they were aristocrats or something. Her mother would sit at one end of the table and her father the other as if they were a king and queen. Kylie would be the poor chump alone in the middle as they ate warmed up take-out dinners that her mother had brought home from the specialty shop in town. They could easily have been seated in the cozy yellow breakfast nook just off the kitchen, where at least spatially, they'd look like a close family.

The conversation would start out congenially as usual, but would inevitably deteriorate from superficial comments about the weather and the Red Sox into direct questions about the state of her love life—or worse, the state of her finances. Kylie could picture her father's face, reddening as he warmed up. Eventually, upon discovering that she'd lost most of her trust fund on her first startup, he'd rant with rising volume and fury.

Not that he'd ever have done it, but his eyes would narrow into slits and he'd look as if he might smack her—she certainly wouldn't mention that she'd risked losing the rest on her next startup. He'd interrupt her useless attempts at defending herself with accusations of her immaturity and laziness. His complexion would deepen to the color of a rare steak, and he'd point a meaty finger at her face, insisting that she take a job at his financial firm. "Kylie, you've already interned there: That wasn't so bad, right?" She'd shrink inside, remembering the tedium and how she'd hated the pressure to produce leads from her endless list of cold calls. Ugh. She shuddered inside. They had no idea who she really was.

When his barrage would finally slow, Kylie imagined replying, "David, I'm not desperate, nor am I about to start wearing pantyhose and heels to some tedious job again, even if you are my father. I got an MBA for the precise purpose of learning how to do my own thing. I learned that when I interned for you."

"Show some respect. It's Dad to you, my baby girl, light of my life. Your internship wasn't so bad, if you recall. It got you into Harvard Business School, didn't it? We literally gave you that MBA. And, you're not desperate *because* of your trust fund. You're just lucky your grandmother left you this inheritance. I have no idea why she gave it to you so young."

"Grammy believed in me," she'd shrug.

The fantasy felt real because she'd heard it all before. She could imagine that he'd pull back his Queen Anne mahogany chair and walk over to her and touch her shoulder – his fatherly affectionate gesture of choice. Other families hugged. Other families accepted their children's wishes. His gestures never made Kylie feel like he cared at all. He would say in a quiet intimate voice that barely masked his rage, "Just remember, we paid for your so-called MBA. If you blow it, you'll have nothing. We don't get many chances in life. You've thrown yours away. Don't ask us to save you when it's all gone. That's all there is. Do you think Grammy would want you blowing through her money?" He'd head to the sideboard to pour himself a Scotch. Then he'd retreat to his den, the distant sound of ice cubes tinkling as he stomped down the hall.

Kylie's mother, Allison—a lawyer—would squint one of her smug everything-you-do-is- crap looks from behind her black designer photo-grays. Ugh. Kylie, as usual, would suspect her mother might be right. She just needed a little time and she would prove them wrong. They'd be very sorry. The mere thought of this scenario made her forearms itch, threatening another round of eczema.

Her parents had no idea how much trouble she'd gotten herself into, but failure had been an excellent teacher. Kylie was sure she'd learned the necessary lessons to make her dream a reality. If she could just get it going, her new business idea could make her a fortune. And when it did, she'd never need to have this dreaded conversation. It had to work. There was no other option.

A long half-hour later, Susan Wynn from HR finally appeared, startling Kylie from her daydream as she loomed over her. She was heavy, and wore a shapeless brown dress and carried a laptop under one arm. She extended a manicured hand to shake in one definitive downstroke before her cool fingers dropped Kylie's. "Nice to meet you, Kylie. We'll go into the conference room."

Kylie followed her past rows of cubicles to a room with four glass walls, so clean a person would have to be careful not to break her nose by walking out into an expanse of glass, thinking she was heading onto the floor filled with cubicles. From the wall of windows, there was a view of the subway station across the street where a homeless man stood, peddling papers just outside the steps—depressing. It occurred to her unless she got her startup going, she might end up joining him. No, she would probably just go back to being a snow bunny, which is what she wanted to do in the first place. Not such a bad choice, she thought, although humiliating at this point to choose it out of failure and have to admit it to her parents and the world. Susan sat Kylie at the end of a long glass table, taking the corner seat next to her.

"So, what can I do for you?" Susan asked.

Kylie offered her card with her regular company name instead of OMG since she intended to have more products. Why limit yourself? "I'm Kylie Maynard with Dogsled Media.

I'd wanted to talk to Natalie Saltz to check a reference on Simon Whitehead, but I discovered she's deceased. I'm sorry for your loss and to inquire so soon afterward, and I know this is awkward, but I'm just looking for some information on his performance, or possibly the names of some other managers to use a reference. I know this is an usual request, but since his supervisor is deceased, I was just hoping for a little information."

Susan nodded. "Yes, this is all very unfortunate. I'll see what I can do. Mostly, we're just able to verify employment though." She typed something into her laptop. "That's odd." Susan pursed her lips. "Simon's not in our database." She typed some more as her nostrils flared. "Maybe something's wrong with our server. How do you spell his name, just to double-check?"

Kylie gave the correct spelling, and Susan retyped it. "That's what I'd put in. Very strange. I remember meeting him once. I scheduled an exit interview when he left, but he never showed up."

"Do you know why he left?"

"Not entirely."

"If you don't mind me asking, since I know this is viewed as a homicide...well, Simon isn't a suspect, is he? I believe he left just a few days before this happened, but I'm thinking of hiring him, and just want to get a sense of his work style. Hopefully, that doesn't include killing off his supervisors."

Susan gave Kylie a blank look. "The police are investigating. I'm not able to discuss it."

"I understand. Maybe Simon had somebody he worked with I could talk to?"

Susan looked at her laptop again. "Look, I'm sorry. I can't let you upstairs, but sometimes some of the guys go out into the courtyard during lunch, around noon. I can't guarantee who's going to be out there, but it's a beautiful day. It's open to the public. You could go and get some lunch and hang out there, if you want. Just don't tell anyone how you found out." She smiled at Kylie.

"Thanks. Who would I even look for?"

"Possibly Steve Hahn. I think he shared an office with Simon."

"Thank you, thank you." Kylie did a slight karate bow in gratitude. She'd liked the symbolism of the left hand, symbolizing peace, always going on top of the right hand, which stood for war. She'd been doing these bows ever since her karate classes in high school. She'd loved her classes, but although she'd been great at the drills, she'd never was able to expel a loud and forceful kiai with her strikes. Her deepest voice had been locked inside of her like a secret, wrapped in a shroud of shyness. During the drills, she'd mutely ran through the blocks and punches while her classmates shouted explosive "huhhhs," which she learned were called kiais. Once when she tried the yell, she was mortified that she sounded more like a bleating lamb and was too embarrassed to try it again. She was much better at the bows, a formality to be delivered soundlessly and which marked the beginning and end of each set of moves. Convinced she'd never use karate anyway, the bow was her main takeaway and she still used it.

"How will I know what he looks like?" she asked Susan.

"Go." Susan smiled and pointed a mauve-tipped fingernail at the door.

Kylie stepped into the brilliant July sunshine and sat on a

bench near the T stop. She dialed Visiozyme again. This time, she punched Steve Hahn's name into the company directory.

A deep voice answered. "Yeah? Steve Hahn."

"Hey, Steve." She mimicked his voice in her lowest, business tone. "This is Kylie Maynard from Dogsled Media, and I'm looking for a reference on Simon Whitehead for a job at my new startup. You shared an office with him, right?"

"Yeah."

"So, what kind of work did he do?"

"He did a lot of QA. That's quality assurance," he explained as if talking to a moron. "He was okay."

"Did he do any database work?"

"Not really, but I think he can do that sort of thing."

"Were you guys friends?"

"No."

"Did he get along with people? Did he have friends there?"

Steve breathed into the phone for a moment. "Not really."

"About your boss. Did he get along with her?"

"Look, I've got a lot of work to do. Sorry. I really can't say."

"Okay, thanks. Is there anyone else I can talk to about Simon?"

Kylie rolled her eyes as she listened to more breathing.

"Not really."

"Okay, then." Kylie knew when she'd been stonewalled. "Thanks for your time."

She hung up, watching a hopeful pigeon bob its head at her, scoping her out for any possible snacks. The homeless man stood squarely at her boot tips, casting his shadow onto her legs. He was weathered and middle-aged, and wore camo fatigues. His cappuccino-colored skin was pockmarked and wrinkled under a ski hat topped with an electric blue pom-pom. He smelled like clothes forgotten in a washing machine...mixed with urine. He waved a newspaper in her face.

"Buy a paper, pretty lady?" His bloodshot eyes implored.

"No, thanks." He didn't budge, like a bad omen. Kylie slid to the side of the bench and stood up, bounding away as if his homelessness might be contagious.

There must be some way to find out what she needed to know. If Simon had hacked into Visiozyme's database and deleted his files, he may have proven himself as her rising star in the hacking department...but there was the minor detail of his dead boss.

Kylie mulled this over on the walk back to Jolt, where she bought another coffee. She opened her laptop and read more about Natalie Saltz's death. According to The Boston Globe, there were several suspects, but no arrests had been made as yet. She texted Simon. Can U meet me back at Jolt NOW?

Within seconds he replied, OK.

Only moments later, Simon slid into the empty chair at the same high-top table. He reeked of cigarette smoke.

"So, you rang?" His eyes were wide and innocent.

What a little weasel, she thought. Did he think she was an idiot? Trying to sound casual, Kylie leaned forward, lowering her voice. "You obviously know that you gave me the name of a dead person for a reference. What were you thinking?"

As Simon looked at his lap, his hair fell forward, obscuring his face. When he looked up, his brown eyes darted about like a pinball machine. "Are you serious? I'm a hacker. Nobody asks me for references. I thought maybe you'd figure that out, but you didn't. Anyway, I didn't know whose name to give you, so I used her's."

"You might have mentioned that she was dead. I can't believe you don't know anyone else. What about people you worked with?"

"So, the truth is, it was a sick joke. Look, I'm really sorry."

"Sorry doesn't quite cut it. Are you being questioned about her murder?"

He sucked in a long gulp of air and hugged himself. "So, yeah. The cops questioned me, but I was fired before it happened. They were just covering their bases."

Kylie held up her hand like a traffic cop. "Whoa. I thought you quit!" This kid was so far out of line he was in outer space.

He shook his dark, uncombed mop. "Actually, there was this problem with some of the software, and she blamed me. I got fired. I'm sorry I lied, but I never thought you'd check. Look, I have no idea what happened after I left. I mean, she was poisoned. I had no access. They wouldn't even let me in the building, so it couldn't have been me."

He had a point. Kylie softened a little with this rationale. "Tell me about Steve Hahn."

His eyebrows shot up in high arches with new appreciation. "I shared an office with him."

"Did you guys get along?"

"He was okay."

"Look, Simon, I'm really sorry. I'm sure that you're very talented, but I need to hire someone who can level with me. I've gone as far as I can with you. Thanks for your time. I hope everything works out okay for you."

Instead of getting up to leave, Simon lowered his shaggy

head into his long fingers. Kylie didn't know what to do. Meltdowns had not been covered in B-school. She looked around as if the weird art on the walls might hold an answer. It didn't.

"Hey, you'll be okay. I'm sure that you'll get a job soon." She had no idea if this was true. She felt like patting his head, but restrained herself. "Do you have anybody to talk to?"

Simon shook his head no. Kylie's heart turned a bit, and she didn't know what to say. She reminded herself the street urchin wasn't her problem. He was a mess. "I'm sorry, Simon. Maybe you should talk to your parents. I'm sure that they would help you out."

Kylie sat with her arms folded across her lap, watching him, for what felt like an eternity. Finally, Simon raised his head, as if he'd no idea she'd been waiting for him. He drummed his fingers nervously on his belly, just under the lettering on his black PHP Live T-shirt. Kylie looked around to see if anyone had noticed his behavior, which she considered bizarre, but everyone's eyes were glued to their laptops. Kylie was sure even if she ran through Jolt naked and stole one of the grotesque paintings, no one would notice.

"No, we're out of touch right now. So, I'm sorry for acting like such a dork. I don't know what got into me."

"It's okay. Good luck to you."

"Yeah, thanks." He got up, lumbered across Jolt with a long, lanky gait, and disappeared out the door. Kylie felt jumpy with a surge of anxiety. Maybe it was too much coffee or too much Simon, but she needed to be outside. She packed up her laptop. She would definitely call Jared now. She'd go to a park bench somewhere to dig up those resumes he'd sent her once and maybe he had someone else. She was certainly interested to hear what he had to say about Simon.

She left the café, gulped a deep breath of fresh air, then another, and another, until she started to calm down. Kylie turned away from Visiozyme to a side street, walking past the office buildings that contained booming tech businesses, full of people working. She overheard groups of programmers discussing their projects as she passed by.

After a brisk mile-long walk to the Charles River, up Mass Ave., and back to MIT, Kylie had refocused her thoughts. She'd always found being near the water was the next best thing to being in the mountains. It gave her clarity, just the same way her troubles started to fade in a ride up in a chairlift. By the time she reached the top, everything was clear and she felt at peace. Maybe she was just allowing herself to breathe a little.

As she calmed herself, she realized that she needed a plan. Her first and most important goal was to hire a developer. Simon was just a minor blip. Everyone in the Kendall Square tech world appeared to be smart. She was certain with all the talent around her, she'd find another developer in no time. That would be her goal for the week, period. Goals were everything. Without goals, she wouldn't get anywhere. That was the first thing she'd learned in B-school. Onward.

Kylie passed the T stop again, where the same homeless man in camo fatigues held up his newspaper, not remembering her. "Sure, okay," she said, thinking perhaps it might be good karma and if she could buy some of that, and help someone else, why not? She peeled a dollar bill from her wallet and took the paper, feeling magnanimous as she nodded pleasantly at him. He gave Kylie a big gap-toothed smile. Reading papers was not part of her immediate agenda, so as she walked on and tossed the paper in the trash before heading to one of the outdoor tables behind a high-rise apartment building across the street from Jolt.

Kylie opened her laptop to search her resume folder for the other candidates that Jared has sent her, but her folders were GONE—including all her work on her new business plan! So much for her epiphany of clarity and wisdom. Her momentary equanimity immediately dissolved into a high blood pressure tsunami that roared in her ears. Kylie remembered having viewed the missing files at Visiozyme, so she'd had them less than an hour ago. She would kill that skinny smart-ass geek.

Kylie swore to herself and conjured up all the karate moves she'd learned way back in those after-school classes, planning to find Simon and deliver a swift roundhouse kick to the lower end of his PHP Now shirt—somewhere he'd remember it for a long time. Then she exhaled loudly, recalling that her laptop was backed up every night. She might have lost a little bit of data—a minor inconvenience. That was another thing they'd taught in business school: back up, back up, back up. Evidently, they'd known what they were talking about. Kylie slumped with relief.

She texted Simon. Very cute trick. You are sick. Knock it off or I will call the police.

In a second, he answered. Will fix, but now you see how talented I am.

Ironically, she did—and felt a surge of excitement, realizing that he possessed exactly the skill set she needed. Then, out of nowhere, Simon plopped down on the bench next to her and set his laptop on his legs.

Kylie looked up, not totally surprised. This kid was crazy. "What are you doing, stalking me?"

"Yeah. No. So actually, I just tracked you on an app I designed. It told me where you were."

She shook her head. "You've got some balls, but deleting my files crossed a line. I could have you arrested."

Simon shrugged. "Hard to prove, right? Especially, if I fix it. Sorry I did it, but I wanted to show you I have the tools to find out what I want—and I will use them. Think about it. I saw your business plan, and if you hire me, I can build OMG. I'd be like your secret weapon—your private guerrilla database team. And I'm very loyal. It's a brilliant idea, by the way. I'm into it, totally. So, you can consider it like an audition."

"Yeah, but you're a spook. Who does that?" She was all at once furious, wowed by his audacity, and a tiny bit flattered. Still, he was a nut case. "How do I know you didn't kill your boss? You're just nuts enough to do that."

"Look, you've got to take my word on that one. I didn't do it. True, I didn't like her much, but I wouldn't have killed her."

"How do I know that for sure?" she asked, starting to realize he was probably a different kind of crazy.

Simon shrugged with his hands in the air: half-apology, half-nonchalant. "I may be a hacker, but I'm not a killer. It could have been anyone in the department, and who knows about her personal life, or if she even had one? She was a clueless bitch. Everyone hated her. Okay, maybe I wanted to show you what I could do, like kind of an audition. And I did. But I swear, I'll never do it again—but I'm not a murderer. Man, you've got a killer idea."

"Under the circumstances," Kylie remarked, "that was

probably not a good word choice. Actually, OMG could do a lot of good. I'm hoping it will help people in their lives."

Simon's eyes became round and sincere like a nerdy choirboy as he listened to her expound on how she was going to save the world. As she gave her spiel, her mind was spinning. Kylie had to admit she saw his point about being useful. Building OMG was going to require some amazing database work, and a fair share of hacking, too. Simon's hacking ability was what she needed to shape her entire vision—not to mention the fact he had enough charm to sweeten all the coffee at Jolt, if and when he decided to turn it on. Kylie didn't care who had killed his boss, as long as it wasn't Simon. She imagined what she could do with his talent behind her.

"Hey, look, I'm sorry about your computer. I'll restore it for you." He opened his laptop.

Kylie had always believed she should trust her gut. The kid was totally out there, but in some weird way, he was like a puppy up for adoption. She began to trust him, just a little. Kylie figured she must already know the worst.

Sometimes, it takes years to find out someone is going to screw you over, and Kylie didn't need those kinds of surprises. She studied Simon—from his wild hair to his sleek brown sneakers. He was just a crazy kid. Underneath it all, she thought, *how much do we really know anyone?* She could easily hire someone who wasn't as talented, who played it straight...and then BAM. She'd be done in for any number of reasons. Her stomach started jumping like a slot machine just hitting the jackpot.

Kylie nodded. "Okay, Simon. Let's see you restore my computer."

Simon opened his laptop in grand fashion, held his fingers over the keyboard like a magician about to perform a trick. He twinkled his fingertips over the keys as if he were distributing fairy dust. Then, he punched in a few commands. "So, go ahead and try it now," he said, peering at his screen.

She checked her documents on her laptop, and sure enough, everything was back and as it should have been. He watched her, nodding triumphantly.

Kylie nodded. "Alright. You win. Just don't disappoint me. I'm sure HR at Visiozyme would love to know who hacked into their computer—and if my computer is hacked into again, I will prosecute you. Now, let's get to work."

"You won't regret it."

Kylie shut her eyes, hoping beyond hope he was right. If she had been religious, she might even have called it a prayer.

3

The Western Edge

In the three intense months it took to build OMG, Kylie hardly talked to anyone except Simon and the nose-ringed, tattooed baristas behind the counter at Jolt who sullenly poured her coffees. There were two of them, but it didn't matter which one waited on her since they all wore the same scowl as if it were a requirement for employment. Kylie waited for her oversized cappuccinos, crafted with artistic designs of hearts or teddy bears on top as they slid them through the small space between the display of gluten-free pastry and the cash register. But Kylie's conversations with them were minimal, mostly about which muffins, which meant that in reality, she didn't actually talk to anyone but Simon.

Kylie liked it that way since she was laser-focused on reviewing Simon's workflow. He'd made her ideas come alive.

She even gave up the morning news. Instead, she organized her day over morning coffee and Cheerios in her small apartment. She liked making checklists on her computer of what needed to be done that day and took great satisfaction in checking each item off as complete before she fell into bed at night.

Once Simon created the first prototype, OMG's potential was obvious. In record time, the program exceeded her hopes. Simon connected her platform to every conceivable database in stealth mode...so much more than the powerful fortune-telling machine she'd originally conceived. Instead of providing "turn right" or "turn left" advice as she'd first envisioned, the app was capable of providing far deeper data. Its long fingers could reach into all aspects of a person or company—it was a massive spying machine able to reach in and pull out surprising information. If knowledge was power, her knowledge machine not only had balls, it was hung! In fact, Kylie had already used it to find out some fascinating, but troubling information on her parents...more than she'd ever dreamed of knowing.

Kylie and Simon could now see everything that was out there about anyone they chose. There had been meetings at what had become their regular high-topped table in a dark corner at Jolt where they'd reviewed designs for wireframes for the app. Simon succeeded at hacking into every major bank, as well as email accounts and cell phone records of anyone he chose, and he could retrieve scripts of texts. Afraid to leave any type of trail that could prove to be illegal, Kylie meticulously deleted any incriminating emails between them. She knew one thing for sure: OMG would need to be in the hands of the right people to accomplish good, or it could become a master tool of evil. She brooded over where to place that powerbomb.

While it was true Kylie wanted to make real money, it was equally important that her new platform be used to make positive changes in the world. She needed to determine how to screen its users carefully, and make sure it would be used to elect statesmen rather than power-hungry creationists who would start burning books and closing abortion clinics if elected. Kylie had never considered herself a political person, but was horrified at climate change or losing her right to choose, should it ever come to that. OMG empowered her...maybe she did have a chance to save the world by helping someone get elected who could make a difference. She would have a part in shaping a world where she wanted to live.

In the past months of building OMG, there had been umpteen unreturned voicemails and texts from each of her parents, who evidently were about to call Missing Persons. Kylie finally responded to a text from her father. *Are you dead or alive?*

Kylie texted "Alive." That singular word led to the dinner date she was about to be late for unless she left her apartment within the next two minutes. As usual, she was starving. At least she would get a good meal... there was only so much ramen a person could eat. Reluctantly, she shut her laptop and checked her reflection in the mirror on her bedroom door. Her black turtleneck, jeans, and boots would do. Kylie threw on her woolen pea coat and gray watchman's cap to hide all but the blonde ends of her dirty, shoulder-length hair.

Since there'd been no time or money for salons, she promised herself new highlights when she made her first sale on OMG. Until that happened, she would have to live with looking like a mutant skunk. She'd been snipping at her two-toned bangs when they began to fall below her eyes, leaving a jagged, mostly chestnut-brown fringe hovering over her eye lashes. She'd hardly worn make-up for months, so that wasn't even a thought.

Already late, she speed-walked across the Boston Common to Park Street. Breathless, she ran down the steps in the station to transfer to a Red Line train and boarded just before it closed its doors. Kylie dreaded the conversation and rode the two short stops considering how to respond to her parents' inevitable questions. Since her self-imposed silence with her parents, this was going to be their first actual conversation in months. So out of practice with communicating with them if she could ever call what normally transpired as communication, she might as well have been attending a silent meditation retreat.

After a brisk walk through Kendall Square, she reached The Western Edge, a trendy new restaurant, nestled in a courtyard among similar upscale eateries on Hampshire Street. Her parents were already seated at a table, drinks in hand, anxiously monitoring the door.

Kylie waved and headed for the table, cringing inside, knowing how they would undoubtedly grill her about her life—especially her finances. She had selected that bistro precisely for its function of insulation by sound. The space was beautiful, with white-painted brick walls, a wide-plank wooden floor, and twenty-foot ceilings with exposed beams, but it was an acoustical disaster. Conversations bounced off the bricks, blending into an unrelenting roar. A possible confrontation would not be easily overheard. Perfect.

The first half of the meal went better than Kylie expected. From across the table, her parents yelled their innocuous inquiries about her apartment and her health. Next, they asked if she had met anyone...specifically meaning someone who could support her in the type of lifestyle her parents enjoyed: country clubs, sailboats, and travel. Kylie fielded their questions from her arsenal of vague replies, but she knew it was just a warmup and would inevitably lead to the dreaded question. Her mother stabbed a piece of lettuce with her fork, lowered her photo grays down her nose, gave Kylie the look and shouted over the din. "So, how's your job hunt?"

Kylie regarded her grilled salmon, artistically stacked on a bed of kale and quinoa, and cut a bite. She dangled her fork midair as her mother's steely eyes held her speechless.

"Answer your mother, baby," prodded her father, taking a sip from his third glass of scotch as he waited.

"Okay, here we go. As I've been telling you, I'm not looking for a job. I'm developing a simple app and it's going very well, thank you." To prevent a barrage of questions from flying out at her like bats in a barn, Kylie decided to call it an app to her parents. That was vague and trendy. Plus, it sounded more innocuous than saying she was building a far-reaching and robust database program called OMG able to hack into banks, phone records, and email accounts.

Her father's forehead creased as he thoughtfully cut his steak. He took his time and drained his glass before speaking. "Baby, beloved daughter of mine, that's fine you've designed this new app. Trust me, we're thrilled you're such an entrepreneur...but how are you paying for this project, never mind supporting yourself? As far as I can tell, you have no income. Get yourself a job, and you can design this app thing-a-ma-bob in your spare time. You have an MBA from Harvard for God's sake. Didn't they teach you anything? Businesses take money!"

Kylie's salmon suddenly tasted like a wad of paper. What a waste of a good meal. She gave him a sour look. "I am very aware of that."

"Answer your father." Her mother's buffed fingertip pushed her glasses back up the bridge of her nose, obscuring her eyes.

"I just did. Look, I'm fine," Kylie snipped, already formulating her exit lines.

"What was that?" boomed her Dad.

"I'm fine!" she yelled. "You wonder why I don't call you? Maybe if you'd stop grilling me, I might want to talk."

Allison's thin lips clamped together, deepening the closed parentheses at the sides of her mouth. "What do you expect us to do? We're concerned. You're using your trust fund, aren't you? And what happened to that other app you designed in grad school?" A lock of her chestnut bob inched over her high cheekbone as she shook her head back and forth looking as sad as if Kylie just told her she had terminal cancer.

"I pivoted to a better idea, that's all. Look, don't worry! It's my money. In case you haven't noticed, I'm an adult. I don't need to answer to you. Why can't you leave me alone? You're always poking around in my life, but it is my life, not yours." Kylie looked up at the exposed wooden beams on the ceiling, choosing her words. Although her parents always said they loved her, she wondered? If they did, they'd leave her alone when she needed time and space; and be there for her when she truly needed them. Her hope had always been ... they might have the smallest clue about who she really was and what she was really trying to do. So far, she'd been disappointed. The ceiling held no answers. There were no words to make them understand what she was doing, let alone get them to approve.

In a rare fatherly display, David reached over and squeezed Kylie's hand resting on the table. His fingers felt warm as they covered Kylie's more delicate hand. "Baby, we just want to make sure you're okay. You know we love you. If you blow your money, that's it. We'd hoped you might have it to buy a house one day, or use it for when you have children. Unfortunately, what with the recession, I'm not able to support you anymore."

"I told you ... everything's fine. And I don't *want* children. Could both of you *please* leave me alone?"

She withdrew her hand to her lap, remembering how many drinks he had. At one, he was fine; at two, congenial; at three, sappy. She appreciated that at three drinks he was at his most emotional state, but Kylie hoped to be long gone before number four when *nasty* would kick in.

"It's okay to take your time, but never say never," he mused. "You're young, and I'll bet you'll change your mind someday. I know your mother would love to have grandchildren."

Kylie rolled her eyes. "Yes, since she's such a natural and wonderful mother."

Allison scowled. "What exactly is this app, or whatever it is you're doing? What's it called, by the way?"

"It's called OMG. Just wait until next month, and I can demo it for you. I think you'll find it pretty amazing."

"What does it do?"

"And why did you call it OMG? What is that?" asked David.

"It stands for Oh My God."

David's features curled in puzzlement. "Is this some sort of religious thing? I thought you had no use for religion."

"Dad, OMG is just an expression. It has nothing to do with religion. You'll see."

"You still haven't told us what it does," said her mother.

"You'll have to wait. I promise you will be amazed. I'll show it to you soon."

Kylie had tested OMG, querying the app using her parent's names, and felt astounded to learn her father, who had always pleaded near destitution when she asked for money, did in fact have have a multi-million-dollar stock portfolio and a Swiss bank account. She was also shocked to discover her mother was having an affair with a partner at her law firm, and they'd written some surprisingly juicy emails that made Kylie blush as well as feel nauseous. *So much for their self-righteous indignation.*

If they kept cornering her, she might consider giving them a demonstration they wouldn't forget. Then it would be their turn to squirm and make excuses. Kylie could picture her mother paling under her high-end, age-defying makeup, and both of them denying all of it until Kylie proved it with a jaw-dropping demo right after Thanksgiving dinner.

Payback time for making her live by their rigid rules and the boarding-school life they'd imposed upon her. Not that Kylie had not adjusted, even thrived, but it would have been nice to have a home where she felt loved for who she was, instead of one in which the very air smelled of their impossible expectations, where the dollar sign governed any sentiment.

All she ever wanted was for them to see her. And to love her. Already, OMG had proven invaluable to Kylie, showing her parents were the hypocrites she suspected they were all along. It explained a lot, and she was only beginning to grasp OMG's power. She didn't think she could gain their love with it, but it would certainly make them respect her.

Still, she couldn't picture her mother with another man. And her poor father! The thought of her mother's infidelity hurt Kylie's heart. But her mother had also been hurt. All of the times she wanted to take family trips and her father denied them, preferring to sit in his den with a bottle of Scotch.

Poor all of them, she let out a sad sigh, wishing she could make everything right and they could start over as a family.

"Why the big sigh? asked her father.

Kylie shrugged. "No reason. I've just been working hard."

"I have to say I'm intrigued," he said. "Still won't give us even a hint?"

"Sorry, but no. Let's just say OMG's a game-changer."

"That does sound intriguing," commented her mother. Then mercifully, Allison changed the subject. "What do you think about the election?" she inquired. "I met Bill Reinstadt at a Bar Association dinner where he spoke. I have to say, I'm impressed. Reinstadt has some good ideas for the economy and the environment, and I think he's a young man who's going somewhere."

Kylie felt grateful to her mother for bringing up the new subject; especially this topic since she'd also been following him. So far, she admired what she heard. "What's he like?"

"I'll tell you what he's like," interrupted her father with a scowl on his face. "He's another one of those know-it-all liberals who isn't going to get anything done except raise taxes, just like the rest of them." His complexion deepened to the color of his rare steak. He caught the eye of the waitress, pointed to his empty glass of Scotch, sat back in his chair, and folded his arms over his ample belly, anticipating his fourth drink.

"David, stop. That's not necessary. Her mother shook her head in disgust. "You might try keeping an open mind."

Kylie was always amazed how they wound up together since their politics were so different. She held up a finger to make a point, "Remember when I was an undergrad and was really into Khalil Gibran? There's this quote that you should hear. In fact, I think you should memorize it." She recited the whole thing while David blankly stared at her:

"Your children are not your children. They are the sons and daughters of Life's longing for itself. They come through you but not from you, and though they are with you, yet they belong not to you. You may give them your love, but not your thoughts. For they have their own thoughts. You may house their bodies, but not their souls, for their souls dwell in the house of tomorrow, which you cannot visit, not even in your dreams. You may strive to be like them, but seek not to make them like you. For life goes not backward, nor tarries with yesterday."

"What did you say?" yelled David.

Kylie glared at him. "You heard everything else I said."

David turned to Kylie and patted her shoulder. "Fine. Look,

if working with this guy will make you happy, then okay. Hopefully, it will lead to a paying job. I will keep my big mouth shut."

"Thanks, David," said Kylie, surprised. "That's a great idea."

Allison turned to Kylie. "Lovely we had an English major in the family. It comes in handy, evidently. Glad you can mellow your father. At least part of your education is paying off. As far as Reinstadt, sorry to say, I didn't get to say more than hello. He seemed pleasant enough, and from his policies, he appears to be very smart. And very good-looking. He had an entourage of women lining up to meet him. That's a winning combination in politics."

Suddenly, Kylie was absorbed in the conversation with her parents, maybe for the first time in years, or maybe in her entire life. She had been following Bill Reinstadt and was pretty wowed by him. He was the only candidate she'd ever heard of who had some viable sounding solutions on how to solve problems, like creating jobs. He was running for a Senate seat, and Kylie knew enough from her economics classes in college to understand what Reinstadt suggested made sense; everyone must give a little, and people, even corporations must play by the rules. He was a guy who might be able to save the country if he ever got elected. Kylie thought he was not only a statesman, but a champion for the world, and possibly could even be president. He was exactly the kind of candidate she could get behind; the medicine the country needed to heal. He'd be like JFK or FDR. As far as she could tell, Reinstadt seemed to be exactly the type of person she would want to use OMG. She just needed to be sure?

Of course, if Reinstadt was a rule follower, he might not want to use it at all, but Kylie suspected being a politician, he could be Machiavellian enough to see getting elected to do some good would justify using a powerful tool to insure his getting there. Once he got elected, OMG could provide the facts that would create realistic ways to influence legislation so he could accomplish something important. If Reinstadt was the man Kylie hoped he was, he would use the information wisely.

"Do you know anyone who could introduce me?"

"Now what are you up to?" Her father's eyes bulged with wild alarm. "Is my apparently independently wealthy daughter going to become a Reinstadt volunteer, or are you going to line up to be one of his women? Either way, I think this is the last thing you need." He threw his club tie over his shoulder for emphasis.

"Dad, calm down. Trust me, I have no interest in dating Reinstadt. That is so ridiculous. I do like his politics." Kylie turned to her mother. "Well, do you know someone?"

Amused, Allison scrutinized Kylie. "I could certainly get you a contact number, but you could probably get it from his website."

"Okay, fine. I'll do that."

"Just be careful, Kylie," said her mother. "You're an attractive young woman and very impressionable. I don't want to see anyone taking advantage of you."

"I can take care of myself. Don't worry. Besides, you like him too!"

Kylie excused herself after their plates from their entrees were removed from the table and her father was well into his fourth Scotch. "Thanks for dinner. I have a ton of work. I'll see you guys in a couple of weeks at Thanksgiving."

"Remember what I told you," warned David.

"How could I forget? Thanks for all the advice." Kylie quickly kissed her parent's cheeks before bolting to the door.

Outside, Kylie exhaled billows of condensation while putting on her gloves. She could not ever remember such a cold November. The solitary roses remaining on the bushes outside some of the buildings were defiantly hanging on but looked forlorn and not long for the wintry world. She headed up Hampshire Street to Main, where she passed the monolithic buildings similar to Visiozyme housing other biotech and technology companies. When she reached Kendall Station, she descended the steps to take the Red Line.

Bill Reinstadt stayed on her mind. She couldn't stop thinking about the man who would be a perfect fit for OMG. If she could get him elected, she would become his trusted advisor; a solid brick in the foundation of his team and it would be a giant step in her career. But first, she needed to learn more to make sure she wanted to support him.

At Park Street, she climbed the stairs to the Green Line platform and caught the first train to Copley. From there, she strolled down Dartmouth Street. Even though it was still a week before Thanksgiving, the twinkling white lights were already wrapped around the trees from the roots to the branches, lighting up the Commonwealth Mall and making it look like a fairyland.

Once settled in her tiny apartment, Kylie immediately opened her laptop sitting on the kitchen table doubling as her desk. She found Reinstadt's website, a predictable red, white, and blue affair. No surprises there. Her mother was right. He certainly was handsome. His close-up photo smiled back at her as he stood in front of a waving flag, his ultramarine eyes twinkling.

Kylie logged into the OMG development site. It was still only bare bones with simple text boxes and no graphics, but she knew it was functional enough to give her the information she needed. She typed **Bill Reinstadt** into the *find info field* and searched financials, personal relationships, religion, politics, and connections. Then, she waited for OMG to do its Magic. Within minutes, the app generated a report.

She was excited to read: Reinstadt was forty-two; a college football star at Newton South with a business major at BC, a graduate of Harvard Law, and a State Representative, who succeeded in some education reform in the Boston Schools. There were other common knowledge facts she just noted on his website. Comfortable, but not wealthy, he had received a sizable war chest from the DNC for his Senate Race and some interesting contributions from pharmaceutical companies. Aha!

What puzzled Kylie was personal data. He had a long-term relationship with Emily Wickland, owner of a Boston PR firm, *Making Faces*. They were together for eight years, which made Kylie wonder why they never married? She looked for some sparks when OMG brought up their emails and texts, but the messages to each other were dull. *Pick you up at eight. Looking forward to seeing you later.* Kylie wondered if this was the sort of thing that happened after eight years or if they had more of a friendship.

He was from a large Catholic family and appeared to be very well connected in Boston's political tapestry. His email inbox included notes from the mayor and top state and national committee heads. He had received two speeding tickets over the past decade, but nothing much of interest in that department.

Kylie speed-dialed Simon from her pathetic list of only four names. One was her mother, one was her father, one was Meghan, her old college roommate who she should call one of these days, and the other was Simon.

"Hey," he answered.

"Hey. I just searched Bill Reinstadt and got some info, but I'm curious about him. I want more."

"You mean the guy who's running for Senate?"

"Yeah, him. I'm curious why he never married his girlfriend, Emily Wickland, and I'm wondering about some political contributions he received from pharmaceutical companies. Can you see what you can find out?"

There was a silence, but he finally agreed with an odd hesitation in his voice.

"Which companies?"

"I saw one from Genzyme and BioMed. I'm wondering if there was one from Visiozyme."

"Why? What do you care?"

"I'm just nosy, I guess. I don't know, this is probably unrelated to anything, but still, it sort of intrigues me since your boss was murdered."

"What are you now, a private detective?"

"No. I think he's an honest guy and I want to validate that fact."

"Okay, fine. If you want, I'm on it."

"You're good, Simon."

"Yeah, I know."

"Can I say something?"

"What?"

"So, I think if you keep nosing around in people's lives it's just going to get you into trouble."

"This from you? Aren't you the super-hacker?"

"Yes, but OMG was your idea. I'm just sayin'..."

He was agreeable enough, but there was his hesitation and an odd edge in his voice making her feel uneasy.

4

The Meeting

Simon's advanced search generated a lengthy report on Reinstadt. It had Kylie hunching over her laptop for hours. She read the emails from his every-day-guy-account first with the address of go.pats@billreinstadt.com. The account seemed to be used to set up golf games and field dinner invitations and fundraisers. There were perfunctory emails from Emily, mostly to make plans.

Kylie still thought their relationship seemed unusually tepid, almost business-like. But what did she know? It had been over a year since she herself had gone out on an actual date, so she wasn't especially qualified to judge. Still, she imagined if one day she ever did have a relationship, she would want it to be a whole lot hotter than theirs. The way things were going with her love life, she could always become a nun if her business failed and solve two problems at once. Except for the religious part, she was practically in training for it now.

Kylie hoped to find some more interesting emails and was pleased to find a receipt for several large donations to the MSPCA. She loved animals, and always felt simpatico with the dogs running free in one of the fields at the Boston Common as if their souls were connected to hers. Reinstadt was a member of the Museum of Fine Arts and the Symphony and he had bought two season tickets to the Patriots and the Red Sox. The hundreds of emails from his friends negotiating giveaway dates for his tickets identified one possible reason for his popularity. There was a subscription to a fine-wine club, and he'd ordered wine from a different country every month last year. Apparently, this month was to be reds from Argentina.

His law firm account contained hundreds of emails to clients, many with pdfs of financial statements and divorce papers. Kylie dismissed those quickly since there was a limit to her capacity for snooping. Then she found some offers to fund his campaign she had not seen on the original list. One was from Gerry Fox, who according to the signatures on his emails, was a board member of Visiozyme, who had offered Reinstadt $1,000,000 for his war chest. *Visiozyme! Bingo.*

She speed-dialed Simon.

"You knew Gerry Fox when you were at Visiozyme, right?"

Simon kept breathing into the phone, long past when he should have given her an answer. "No, not really. Why?" There it was again... that weird catch in his voice.

Remembering what Simon had previously told her ... how Natalie Saltz had dated Gerry, the skin on Kylie's arms broke into goosebumps. Maybe it wasn't just her imagination how

Simon sounded nervous. Now that OMG was ready, she could use it to investigate him! She would also look up Gerry Fox as well as Natalie Saltz. The possibilities made her fingertips twitch. And then it hit her. Kylie suddenly was struck with the possibility Simon could be on the wrong side and he could read her thoughts. He also had OMG at his disposal. What a fool she'd been. What did she really know about Simon?

"Are you there?" his voice broke into Kylie chastizing herself.

"Yes." She paid him to create a power machine, but she was so busy worrying about who got to use it, when in truth ... Simon could easily steal the whole program. Her lame nondisclosure form certainly couldn't stop someone as devious as Simon. She'd been an idiot. Suddenly, she was desperate to see him. She had to know OMG was safe. "Listen," she said, trying to sound casual. "Can you come over now to go over a few things?"

"Now? Seriously? It's eleven o'clock."

Kylie checked her computer and was shocked to see it was so late. Generally, she might be reading herself to sleep by eleven. "I thought you were a night owl."

"Sometimes. What's this about?"

"I've had some thoughts about the program and wanted to go over some stuff."

"So, what kind of stuff?" he sounded suspicious.

"Just some possible bugs."

"Bugs? Now? At eleven o'clock on a Saturday night? Is this about Reinstadt?"

"Sort of. I just need to talk to you."

"I guess. Where do you live anyway? This isn't like, um, a

booty call, is it?" His question both chided and mocked her request.

"Don't flatter yourself." She'd never invited Simon over to her apartment, although with *OMG*, he surely knew where she lived. Better to meet him in a public place. "Actually, you know what? On second thought, I feel like having a beer. Can you meet me somewhere? How about Solas? You know, that cute little Irish bar on Boylston?"

"I can be there in about a half hour. Should I bring my laptop?" He sounded mystified.

"Of course."

She hung up. What the hell was she going to say? *Simon, you could steal my product, and I'm terrified?* How do you know anyone for sure anyway? She'd read articles by psychologists on reading facial expression. She was particularly interested in how to tell if someone was lying to her. Evidently, you could tell if someone's lying by how they raised their eyebrows or do not make eye contact. She thought if she were trying to hide something, she'd make sure to secure her eyebrows in their normal position, nicely arched over her eyes, which she'd widen and fix on her questioner with sincerity. If she knew this, surely Simon did too. He seemed to be steps ahead of her. He knew everything she did times ten, which scared her now. Besides, a skilled liar would know how to mask his dark side when he wanted to. His eyebrows were just a minor detail. And what about Natalie Saltz? She now sensed that somehow, even if indirectly, Simon might be connected to her death. But how?

Kylie jotted some notes about what to say to Simon:

It's time we talked about how OMG is going to be used.

Obviously, you have access to this entire program, and I want to know you are loyal. How can I know that?

She threw on her coat and headed into the cold night air towards Boylston Street, marching by some late night partiers and couples, bundled up against the frigid air. She was hoping for inspiration but was coming up blank. She would just have to trust that magically, some inspiration would give her the right words.

Solas, a traditional Irish bar in the Lenox Hotel, usually packed just after work, was surprisingly quiet on a Saturday night. The host, a lanky Irish lad, sat Kylie at a vacant table near the window, he gave her an admiring smile, but it was lost on her. She sat facing the door so she might get the first glimpse of Simon. When the waitress came over, she ordered a beer and she started an OMG query on Simon through her phone. She hoped it would be done by the time he got there. Ten minutes later with cheeks pink from the wind, Simon approached the table, just as the results appeared. She quickly slipped her phone into her purse.

"So, hey," he said, throwing his parka on an empty stool. "What's up?"

The waitress set Kylie's beer in front of her. "Anything for you?" she asked Simon.

He ordered an ale.

"I thought we should talk about the project," Kylie said when the waitress left.

His eyes narrowed. "So you said. It's a little late at night for a meeting. What about it?"

"When I asked you about Gerry Fox, I sensed you had this

weird hesitation. I'm pretty sure you know something you're not telling me. Am I right?"

His eyes had a strange golden glint, rounded to choir-boy innocent. They were fixed on her as he nodded. "Kylie, I probably know a lot of things I'm not telling you. Would you like a list of everything I know, but have not told you?"

"Don't be ridiculous."

"So, yeah. He was seeing Natalie Saltz, my boss. He came into the department a lot, and I met him once. No big deal."

She checked his eyebrows, which were in their normal position. She knew she was being dumb about such a ridiculous sign of honesty, but it still gave her small comfort. "And? What happened after that?"

"Nothing."

"What do you mean, nothing?"

The waitress brought his beer as Simon shrugged. "Nothing." He laced his fingers, stretched out his lanky arms across the table, and cracked his knuckles.

This kid was infuriating. "You never talked to him except for that one time?"

He shook his head no.

"Why did you lie on the phone? This seems to be a habit of yours."

Simon shrugged. "It's no biggie. I'd forgotten I'd met him is all. I didn't really know him well enough to even remember."

"How can I trust you when you lie so easily?"

Simon took a long sip of beer. "It's a little late now to think about that, isn't it?" He jerked his shoulders up into another maddening shrug.

Kylie wanted to kick him under the table but restrained herself.

"Do you think he was involved with her murder?" she asked, deciding to wait until she read his OMG report and get back to his lying later.

"How would I know? What is this anyway? An interrogation?" He crossed his arms around himself.

"Not really. Okay, maybe a little. Look, with all the investigative powers of OMG at our fingertips, can you tell me you never got curious to check on people you know?"

"Not really. I don't know anyone but you. What if I did? What do you care?"

"C'mon, Simon. I'm sure you know people. I don't want my program misused. We have a powerful thing here, and how do I know what you're going to do? For starters, you seem to have a real problem with the truth."

His brows knit with irritation. "So, what did you do, drink paranoia tea? C'mon, I work for you. I told you I was loyal. I don't use the program except for testing. This power thing is your trip, not mine. I'm just a programmer. I don't care what you do with this thing. I just liked building it."

Maybe he was right. She was an idiot to feel so paranoid. He'd done everything she asked, given her what she wanted, and more.

"And what about Reinstadt?" she asked. "What do you know about him?"

"Nothing. Although, I did wonder if maybe you're getting interested in him."

"What if I am?"

Simon shrugged while his brows shot up to his hairline.

From out the window, the dull glow of the street lights shone on his normally white skin that now turned piglet pink.

"Not that it's any of your business, but this isn't personal. I just like his politics."

"Whatever."

"Look, I think I need to be clear about OMG. I know you've worked hard on it, and you'll be paid the balance as soon as I sell it. Just to state the obvious; it's mine, and it's private until I say so. I don't want you using it unless I give you permission. This can't get into the wrong hands."

"And whose hands are those?"

Maybe yours. "Can you imagine what some evil politicians would do with this? It would make smear campaigns like child's play. If you must know, I like Reinstadt's politics. I love what he's saying about saving the environment. I want to check him out a little more. He might be just the guy to use OMG. It could help to get him elected and to help him stay in office."

"What's so great about him? He has a girlfriend you know."

"Come on, Simon. You're not listening. He's got something special, and I don't mean his girlfriend. As far as I can tell, he's different from the bozos who have been messing up our country. He has some great plans and from what I can see, he's got principles. I love what he says about transparency. At this point, we certainly need a leader who's honest. I think if he could get elected, he could save the country from the mess in Washington. He's got some great ideas about reversing climate change. He even supports animal rights. Who knows? He might even save the world."

One side of his mouth stretched into a smirk. "If you say so.

You certainly have him on a pedestal. You'll never get him, you know."

"Why would you think I'm trying to get him? Anyway, what do you know? According to you, you don't know anyone."

There was his infuriating shrug again. "Hey, I'm just a programmer. Anyway, I do watch the news occasionally."

Kylie had seen news photos of Reinstadt with a lanky blonde at his side, flashing a perfect set of teeth, but she didn't give it too much thought. Evidently, she was Emily Wickland, but so what? She wondered how Simon would know anything about his love life. Kylie did know she wouldn't get anything else from him. She'd have to wait until the OMG report revealed any new information. When she got home, she promised herself to also run a report on Gerry Fox.

"Okay, thanks. I think we're done here," she said before draining her beer.

If only there were a way Simon could not trace her search queries. He could easily find out she'd run one on him just by checking the log. If he was on the wrong side, she could just picture his smirk as he watched her searches stack up chronologically. Still, she had to do it. After paying the bill, Kylie bundled up and headed home, now anxious to get to work. Let him think what he liked about what she was doing. Why would she care? She was his boss, after all.

Back in her apartment, she resigned to an all-nighter and made herself a cup of coffee. She settled in at her table to review the report on Simon from her phone. It had some of the information about his past that was new. She fumed when she read that he'd dropped out of MIT, since he'd told her he graduated. He was such a lying weasel. She wondered how deep

Simon's dishonesty went. She hoped this was the end of it, but had a sinking feeling it wasn't.

He appeared to have no friends or family ties. There wasn't much of a social media presence, but he was heavily into online gaming. He was a sought-after Go player with what seemed to be a lot of international challenge requests. His father was a biology teacher and his mother was a psychotherapist. That sounded normal enough, but he'd had some problems with bullying in grade school and had his front teeth knocked out. That was the only personal information that gave her any insight into his personality. He'd already told her the rest.

With the exception of a few spotty job listings, his report looked as if it had been scrubbed. It showed only a few emails in one account and they all seemed to be with Kylie. It appeared he had only one bank account, and it had a small balance. She ran it again and the emails and text messages came up practically blank. It would be impossible for her to be the only one he emailed or texted. Kylie felt nausea coming on due to worry.

She looked over the Reinstadt report again. She had to be sure about him. She found another email account with thousands of emails to environmentalists and economists, asking for advice. Kylie scanned through it for hours. It reconfirmed her impression Reinstadt was squeaky clean and was indeed the man the country needed. She was now certain he was the man for OMG, if only he would see its potential and buy the program. Now she just had to figure out what to do about Simon.

5

Sly like a Fox

Sunday morning Gerry Fox parked his car in his particular assigned spot behind his office, just blocks behind the tall buildings of Kendall Square. He walked up Cambridge Parkway, the side street where he had arranged to meet Simon and chose one of the park benches overlooking the Charles River. Since he predicted Simon would be late, at least he could enjoy a moment of peace and admire the photo-perfect view of the dome atop the Museum of Science which seemed to emerge from its mirror-like reflection in the river.

Groups of gulls congregated on the silvery islands of ice afloat on the sapphire water. Seemingly, the birds were undaunted by the biting winds—but from their squawking, it appeared they were complaining about how it was way too cold for November. Except for a few hardcore joggers, anyone with any sense decided to stay inside. Gerry pulled his knit cap down over his ears, tucking his graying ponytail, now hanging over his scarf, inside the hat.

He took a sip of his herbal tea from his insulated commuter mug and checked his watch. Fox shook his head in disgust at his stupidity at making an early morning appointment with someone as young as Simon. Thirty years ago, when he hardly had a care in the world, Gerry would have slept until noon on Sundays after a Saturday night of drinking with his friends. But he doubted Simon had any friends.

After rubbing his hands together for warmth, he put on his fur-lined leather gloves. Thanks to his regular workouts, Gerry was a muscular guy, and the cold did not usually bother him, but its frigid grip began to penetrate his legs covered by his perfectly distressed jeans. *Maybe he was just getting old.*

Bleary-eyed from too little sleep, Simon crunched through the snow from the street and approached from the rear. He slid onto the bench next to Fox and brushed some snow off of his brown sneakers. His feet were already freezing. He'd snapped the fur-trimmed hood of his khaki parka at his chin, exposing only a small slit of his face where white puffs of breath escaped from his mouth. Simon set his laptop on his legs for warmth and scowled as the raw wind blasted down the river, freezing what was left showing of his face like nitrous oxide. It was just like Fox to plan a meeting in horrible conditions, like some cheesy spy movie.

"So, what's up, Fox? What's so damn important we had to meet at the crack of dawn on a friggin' cold Sunday morning? What's the big deal?" He watched some geese land next to the gulls and wondered if there would be a turf war, but the gulls stayed to themselves as the geese waddled off to their side of the ice.

Gerry cleared his throat. His voice was gravelly and strained. "It's not the crack of dawn. It's eight-thirty, a perfectly normal time to be up and about. You must know I'm a suspect in Natalie's murder?"

Simon blew a large puff of condensation. "I'm not surprised. You were dating her, right?"

"Not exactly. I *am* married, you know. We were just kind of friendly. I know the cops questioned you about why you were fired, but now they've started sniffing around about our *little project*."

Simon turned towards Fox, whose eyes hid behind his mirrored sunglasses and were unreadable. "How did they find out about that? I made sure it was super secure."

"I don't think they know much, but evidently they've been digging deeper into Natalie's records and found some notes referring to it in your employment folder. She'd seen you working on the project during company time and questioned you about it. She became suspicious when you wouldn't talk. The cops are now extremely interested in why she fired you. They now have the idea it might be related to what you were working on."

"What the FUCK? You said no one would ever know about it."

"I know. I'm sorry. Why did you work on it at Visiozyme? Are you that much of an idiot? It's your own fucking fault. They don't know the whole extent of it, just that there's something there, but it's enough to make us suspect."

"You're SORRY?" Simon's jaw muscles flexed. "You might be a big-shot board member at Visiozyme, but this was your baby. I TOLD you it wasn't a good idea. Biological weapons? What the fuck were you thinking? Look, man; I was just your flunky. YOU hired me to design the sequencing. I worked on it at Visiozyme since I was so fucking bored there."

"Unfortunately, that's not what the cops think. I wanted to let you know they're going to be questioning you again because they seem to believe it was your idea. I want to help you with what to say."

"Help me? I'll tell them the truth. Why, what did you say? You blamed this on ME?" Sweat appeared on Simon's forehead but quickly evaporated, making him feel colder. His teeth began to chatter. He wasn't sure if it was from the cold or his nerves. His stomach felt like a guitar whose overly-tightened strings were about to snap.

"They already know Natalie fired you when she found out about this freelance project. She didn't know I'd hired you outside of your job there, but she was starting to ask questions."

"Right. So, I suppose that's why you killed her?" Simon suspected Fox had killed her, but dismissed it since Gerry had always been friendly to him. He was the only one at Visiozyme who ever bothered to talk to him except for Steve Hahn, but they shared an office and communicating was sometimes unavoidable. They were never friendly except for when a tiny bit of bonding over jokes about Natalie Saltz. Fox had appeared every Friday and presented Natalie with a dozen yellow roses before taking her to lunch...including the day she'd been poisoned.

"You'll never know, will you?"

"So, you're pinning this on me?"

Fox nodded gravely.

"FUCK, man. I don't think so." Simon watched a medical helicopter land on the roof of Mass General just across the river, taking small comfort in the fact someone else was having a bad day, although he could hardly imagine it being worse.

Gerry offered Simon a shrewd-looking half smile. "Who's going to believe *you*? You're this crazy, dysfunctional programmer. Look, I'm just giving you a heads up. It's going to be your word against mine, but if you have any evidence on your computer, I strongly suggest you delete it, before we um, have some consequences. What do you say we peek at your laptop?"

Simon gripped the computer tightly. "That's not happening. Even if there's something on here, which there isn't, I still have the back-up if I ever need it. You would know that. You already have the folder anyway. I suggest you delete it from your computer. I'm not sure what you're looking for. What's the big deal?" His words shot out with small bursts of condensation.

"Look, I'm not just messing with you. Open the laptop." Gerry's hand started to reach into his pocket.

Simon panicked. "What the hell? You have a gun? Are you kidding me? Don't be stupid. You can't shoot me. Man, I'm your insurance policy. It would be obvious you did it, considering Natalie's death. If I am murdered, don't you think the cops will figure out who did both? You DID kill her, didn't you?" Simon's eyes blinked as if he'd swallowed a strobe light.

"Open the laptop, Whitehead." He slowly pulled his hand from his pocket just enough for Simon to see the pearly handle of a gun.

Simon gulped ... confident he deleted all his emails from the Visiozyme server with Natalie about getting fired. There was a chance the cops could have grabbed them from her computer before he'd gotten to them. The project with Gerry Fox, code name *Lily,* was still indexed on his server backup, and it wouldn't show on his laptop unless he logged in, but that would only be a problem if the police seized his server. It was encrypted at least, which would slow them down. It wouldn't show on Simon's laptop, but there was the more immediate problem of OMG.

The instant he opened his laptop, the program would spring to life on the screen.

Fox inched the .22 out of his pocket. "Open it, Whitehead." His low voice sounded flat.

"I don't know what it is that you think you're going to see. Frankly, I don't get how a slime-ball like you got to be on the board of a major biotech company?"

The revolver now pointed directly at Simon's crotch. "Open it, wise guy, or I'll shoot off those oversized balls you seem to have grown."

"Sure, man. Don't get so excited. What's the big deal?" Simon opened the laptop, and OMG's query page glowed back at them, complete with its new logo. Its categories for searches he'd coded were laid out neatly and ready to go. "There. Are you happy?"

Fox sniffed, leaning into the screen with a strange grin on his face. "What're we looking at here?"

"Sorry, but that's proprietary. I'm not at liberty to share it with you." He moved to click a key to change the screen, but Fox pushed his hand away and scrolled through the query page.

Simon groaned.

"I don't think you're in a position to be holier than thou. What is OMG?" The new logo was embedded in a drawing of a cloud, and it clearly floated over search fields for name, income, relationship status, emails, police records and more. "Well, well, well, Whitehead. When did you do this? You've been a busy boy. Looks like you might have some bargaining chips after all."

"It's not mine to give you. This belongs to my client."

"Who's your client?"

"I can't say."

"I never knew you had so much integrity." Fox's gun inched closer to his crotch. "Would you like to rethink your answer, my little nerd boy? I'm sure I didn't hear you right."

"Not really. What do you care? You own half the startups in Kendall. What's another little app to you? And a gun? Really, Fox?"

"Maybe I'm greedy. I want to know what my little programmer is into." He moved the gun even closer.

Okay, okay. Her name's Kylie Maynard." His words came out in squeaks since his throat was so tight. "You don't know her. She's a young entrepreneur who just got her MBA. Look, man, this isn't even finished. Don't even think about using it."

"I already thought about it. Let's say we take it for a spin. If this does what I think it does, it could be very useful. Sounds like you might be a little sweet on Miss Kylie."

Simon groaned. He typed Gerry Fox's name into it. "It's going to take a while to generate a report," he said.

"I have time."

"Look, man, it's freezing out here. My fingers are too numb to type. Can we at least go to a coffee shop or something?"

"I don't think it's a good idea if we're seen hanging out together, do you?" asked Fox. "How about you go home and send me the report. While you're at it, I'm sure you still have *Lily* on your server. Delete it as well as any records on your log. But before you do that, put it on a thumb drive and put it in a secure place, not in your apartment. Then, I want access to this OMG program. You are to meet me at four this afternoon at the Civil War statue on top of the hill on the Boston Common. Don't even think about going to the police. Don't even think about not showing up. I will find you. You think you have problems now? You haven't seen anything."

Simon looked up startled as if Fox had read his thoughts.

Gerry's voice had become an evil-sounding growl. "Look Whitehead; this is how it would play out. You go to the cops, and they will sniff around until they find out more about our little project, and then you will spend the rest of your life behind bars. Understand?"

Simon nodded slowly.

"Good. Four o'clock?"

Simon snapped his laptop shut and stared at the frozen ground, feeling sick. "Yeah, sure. Whatever you say."

6

Contact

Plied with caffeine, Kylie was still going strong in the early hours before dawn on Sunday morning. She sat cross-legged on her corduroy couch, a donation from her parent's basement, and kept pouring over the data on Reinstadt for hours. Most of it wasn't worth saving, but one piece of information puzzled her. Gerry Fox had made a large contribution to Reinstadt's campaign. She filed the receipt in a new folder on her computer named *Relevant Info* and then studied the results of her query on Fox.

Eventually, the effects of her tall coffee wore off and she became drugged with sleep, stretched out her legs, and gave into it. Her laptop toppled sideways on the couch as her hands relaxed and loosened their hold.

Kylie awoke just before the sun came up when she showered,

threw on a robe, and then moved her laptop to the table with a fresh cup of coffee. When she clicked her computer awake, the OMG report on Fox was there waiting for her.

It appeared as if Gerry Fox had his fingers everywhere. He had grown up in New Jersey and graduated from Columbia with a degree in business. He got his start in marketing at Seagram's before marrying Candice West, a French literature major and a debutante at Smith.

They lived in Weston, a very upscale Boston suburb, with winding country roads lined with McMansions mixed among the historic houses. Curious which kind he owned, Kylie Googled it. Sure enough, it was a smug-looking, oversized replica of a French chateau with a circular driveway to the front door. Their twin boys were in prep school at St. John. Candice sat on a variety of hospital boards, and Fox was active on the board of directors for two local startups. He owned a venture capital business called SeedStart, and based on the thousands of emails he received, he was sought after by what looked like every entrepreneur in Boston, sniffing around for funding. Kylie sifted through them by doing a search for Reinstadt and Natalie Saltz, names that might tell her more about Fox's involvement in anything questionable.

Buried in there were emails to Natalie. Fox had been pursuing her, and it appeared as if they had quite a bit more going on than a standing lunch date. Some of their less steamy emails mentioned Simon. Natalie discovered Fox was doing a little work with Simon on the side and she had been questioning Fox about it.

"It's nothing. Just a little freelance project," he answered.

Kylie searched Fox's email for any possible communications

with Simon and found only three. Kylie leaned into her screen. They were all about someone named Lily.

How is she? Wrote Gerry Fox.

Excellent, answered Simon. *I saw her yesterday, and she's really growing up.* Kylie was puzzled. Who was Lily? She'd have to do more searches.

She perused the rest of Fox's data. Fifteen years before, he'd been a CFO from an inbound marketing startup that grew to be sold for billions and that he'd invested in Visiozyme. OMG gave her specifics on his financials. The man could have bought the entire town of Weston, and she clearly saw the contribution to Bill Reinstadt's campaign for a million dollars, no doubt peanuts for him. He had funded half of the startups at the Cambridge Innovation Center and it looked as if he was starting to get some good returns on a couple of them.

Then she noticed a check written to Simon Whitehead for $250,000! The payment was made a month before Simon was fired from Visiozyme. The amount of the check was much more than she'd paid Simon.

Kylie froze. A little freelance project? What was Simon doing?

Kylie scanned Fox's hard drive. Her heart pounded when she found an encrypted folder there titled *Lily*. This mystified her because OMG was supposed to automatically open all encrypted files. Evidently, the program wasn't infallible, or Simon somehow coded it to keep some encrypted files exempt. To Kylie, lilies were flowers sent to a funeral, and whenever she smelled them, the overpowering smell always sickened her with their cloying sweet scent. Whatever Lily was, Kylie sensed it was not going to be good.

Realizing Simon would be able to see her queries in the log, even her attempts to open the encrypted files, she didn't care. It was too late for that now. She furiously typed in some commands and accessed Simon's hard drive through OMG. He too had a folder titled *Lily*. Somehow, she'd overlooked it before, since she had not looked for anything like that or even close. His folder was encrypted too, and yet Simon had assured her OMG would be able to read encrypted files and he even showed her how it worked. *Something was very wrong!*

Kaylie held her breath as she as pulled up the report on Bill Reinstadt once again, hoping she wasn't going to find the Lily folder. She did not know what Simon and Gerry Fox were into but prayed Bill Reinstadt didn't have it, no matter what it contained. His hard drive had lots of folders, but *Lily* was not among them. Kylie searched his emails for the word Lily but came up blank. She looked at his cell phone records and quickly did a search on his calls to see if Simon's number was there? When she did not find it there, Kylie felt relieved. He appeared to be squeaky clean. She jotted down his cell phone number. It was too early to call, and she had to decide what to say.

Kylie slipped into her jeans and sweater, contemplating how she would approach Simon about *Lily* and Gerry Fox. The little weasel probably already knew she was sniffing around about *Lily*, whoever or whatever it was. She had to be able to search without him knowing, but there was no way for her to do that since all he had to do was check the log and he could see everything she had done. Simon had all the keys to her castle. Kylie decided to call Jared, her old buddy from business school, for another referral.

It was almost nine in the morning, a marginal time to call people on a Sunday. She punched Jared's number into her phone. She considered her words, and how to delicately state the issue without giving too much away.

"Hello?" his voice sounded thick with sleep.

"Hey, it's Kylie. I'm so sorry to call this early, dude, but I might need your help."

"No problem. Anytime, Kylie. What's up?"

"Two things. One is that I've hired Simon Whitehead, to do a project for me."

"Oh?"

"I should've checked him out with you earlier, but do you think he's a good guy?

"Yes, as far as I know. Why? Is there an issue?" His voice sounded pinched.

"I'm not sure. He designed a database for a program for me. Brilliantly, I might add. The trouble is now he has all the access to this powerhouse program. While I want to be able to hide the log from him, I also have some encrypted files I need to open. Do you know anyone else who could help with that?"

"Yeah, maybe. Let me have some coffee and I'll think about it."

"Sorry if I woke you."

"No problem. I'll call you back in an hour."

What if Jared was friendlier with Simon than she'd thought? Her stomach lurched. *What if Jared called Simon?* The two of them might be talking about her that very minute. She must be the biggest fool in the world. She spent the next half hour peeling off what was left of her black fingernail polish, biting off her already stumpy nails, and chewing off a hangnail.

At 9:30, she held her breath and punched the number for Bill Reinstadt into her phone.

He answered on the third ring. "Reinstadt," he stated as if he were a conductor calling out the next stop on a train. His voice was so familiar from hearing it on all the media. Now, it seemed odd to hear it on the other end of the phone.

"Hi Bill. You don't know me. My name is Kylie Maynard."

"Hello, Kylie. What can I do for you?"

She sucked in her breath. At first, her throat felt tight and defied her voice to speak, but she willed herself to relax and let her words to come forward. Introducing herself, she launched into her pitch. "First, I'm sorry to call you on a Sunday, but here goes. I'm calling because I like what you seem to believe in. I'd like to help with your campaign to make sure you get to go to Washington. I have a startup with a new kind of platform I think will help you get elected."

He was quiet for a long moment. "I'm listening. Tell me more. Who are you?"

"I'm an entrepreneur. I grew up in Lexington and graduated from Boston College and then interned with a financial firm. Got my MBA from Harvard last year. I live in Back Bay."

"Yeah? I went to BC too as un undergrad also. Great school. What does this miracle program of yours do exactly?"

Buoyed by his interest, Kylie felt confident enough to continue and now her voice flowed easily. "Look, all I can tell you is that it's a far-reaching database, more powerful than anything you've seen before. Rather than explain it, I'd like to demo it for you."

"It sounds intriguing."

"Do you have some time soon? I could come to your office and show it to you."

"Absolutely."

They settled on a time for early the following morning, and Kylie made sure to get his office address. When they hung up, Kylie called Jared again. It hadn't been an hour, but she did not care. Getting his voicemail, her stomach dropped down to her feet.

Suddenly she had to get out of her apartment. She threw on her coat, grabbed her laptop, and headed to a Starbucks sandwiched in between a line of galleries and upscale boutiques on Newbury Street. Usually bustling with shoppers and tourists on Sunday morning, the street was quiet with only a few people meandering with their tiny dogs in fancy coats. She got a table and settled in with a cappuccino. Checking her watch, Jared had five minutes left to call before she would have to request a bag for hyperventilating. Her breath was already shallow; her palms were clammy. Miraculously, her phone vibrated on the table right on time. Relief flowed through her like an opened floodgate when Jared's name flashed on the screen.

"Hey, Jared," she tried to sound nonchalant.

"Hey. So, I did a little noodling. Do you remember Michael, that Russian programmer? He was working on Courtney's startup? He goes by Misha, I think."

"I don't think so. Is he good?"

"He does some pretty complicated stuff. I'll email you his info."

"Great. What do you know about him?"

"Not much. Courtney seemed to like him. He seems like a nice guy. He's kind of a dude. I see him around sometimes."

"Jared? I have a question. How often do you see Simon? Are you guys friends?"

"Not really. I just remember him from some startups. Why?"

"Just curious."

"Kylie, it's a little late to be checking him out, isn't it? You jumped in and he built your database. What difference does it make at this late date?"

"You're right, Jared. It is definitely too late to change now."

They hung up, and Kylie ran two searches while sipping her cappuccino. One was on Misha. The other was on Jared. She planned to be more careful.

1

Reinstadt

Reinstadt's downtown law office was on the top floor of a highrise on State Street with a toney conference room overlooking the copper-roofed rotunda of Quincy Market. Twenty minutes earlier, the receptionist deposited Kylie with a mug of coffee at the long table. Kylie chose one of the upholstered chairs near the window and looked like a lonely figure at the expansive walnut table, swiveling around in her chair to admire the view while rehearsing her words. The longer Kylie waited, the more nervous she became, and her fingertips were growing as cold as her coffee. She'd hardly thought of anything else since she called Reinstadt and scheduled their appointment. A meeting she hoped would change her life. Everything she had done since she conceived

OMG...all the planning, all the money, and all the work ... had led up to this opportunity.

In the hours before the meeting, she killed time checking in on her new searches, but she was too anxious to focus. Besides, there were no obvious red flags; only some emails revealing Jared was gay, which she'd always suspected. She'd read more about Jared and Misha later. *Focus,* she told herself. *This is your moment if the man ever shows up.*

Finally, Reinstadt burst into the room with an assertive gait, smiling with his hand extended. In person, his undeniable charisma radiated from his warm smile. Still, it was his clear intelligent eyes that could entrance anyone ... especially her. He exuded undeniable energy that made Kylie, and evidently lots of others, into believers. It felt as if they could grab some of his stardust and ride along with him. It wasn't just his looks, although she certainly agreed with her mother. He was as good-looking as any successful actor cast in Hollywood, a star on some BBC historical drama.

At six feet with an athletic build, he looked almost too robust to be contained in his grey pinstriped suit, white shirt, and club tie. His dark blond hair was side-parted, and a bit longer in front, slightly touching his eyebrows on one side. But more than that, there was just something about his face that looked so sincere. The flash of monogrammed gold cufflinks on his French cuffs caught her eye. He was definitely not a business-casual kind of guy. His handshake felt warm and firm; a pleasantly toasty grip around her own icy fingers.

"Hi Kylie. Cold hands, warm heart, right?"

She laughed, dismayed how her giggle sounded like a tittering pubescent. She summoned up her lower-toned, professional voice she'd practiced in business school pitches, and willed it to come out. "It's so nice to meet you. I've admired your policies for a long time."

"Thank you. So, what can I do for you?" He sat down across from Kylie.

She opened her laptop. "As I mentioned on the phone, I'd like to show you a new computer-based program I conceived, and I think it could help you get elected for sure. I will explain. Because it's very new and has not been to market yet, I'll need you to sign a confidentiality statement. It just states you will not be telling people about my product." She pulled out her nondisclosure form from her folder.

He looked it over. "Why the secrecy?"

"Again, since I haven't really taken this to market yet, it's best to be cautious, even with you." She smiled and handed him a pen.

He quickly signed her form with a tight illegible scrawl. "Okay, I'm all ears. By the way, why me?"

Her body could not make up its mind about temperature and depending on where you looked, it was either fire or ice. Her face evidently had become the equator, flushing with heat, and her hands were the artic. Her stomach was the ocean between, full of nervous acid. "You're someone I've been watching for a while. Basically, I like your politics. We need someone to save the environment and you're great on women's issues. It sounds like you're that person and I just want you to get elected."

"Amen to that," he grinned.

Kylie clicked a couple of buttons on OMG and retrieved her report on Gerry Fox. "Here, let me give you a demo. I'm going to show you how you can get elected. I know campaigns can be like bushwhacking through a jungle. Imagine a tool that could show you who is honest, who you can trust, and oh, so much more. You know Gerry Fox, right? He donated a million dollars to your campaign. And you returned his check?"

A vertical line between Reinstadt's eyebrows deepened as he squinted at her. "And you know that *how*?"

"Hey, I am on your side, don't worry. But here, take a look. Just scroll through it, and see for yourself." She angled her laptop so they both could see Fox's financials. Reinstadt's eyes narrowed as he scrolled through the report containing a list of Fox's expenses. It appeared Reinstadt was the only politician who had received money from him.

He shook his head in disbelief. "That's pretty amazing. Obviously, you ran one on me, right?"

"Of course."

"This isn't legal you know. Basically, you're a hacker."

"You could look at it like that, but isn't it mostly about intention? The fact is you could benefit from this and if you did, you could do some real good, so it would be justifiable. It's like doing a small bad thing to create a greater good. I like what you say in your speeches, and I love how you have all kinds of environmental programs planned, never mind you supporting women's issues. I believe if you got elected, you'd help people and the environment. I'd like to make sure you get there by helping you figure out who is really on your side and who has the funds to help you get elected. I like to think of this less as hacking, than as a tool to save the world. Now that I see its power, and I want to make sure that it doesn't fall into the wrong hands, and frankly, I'm concerned."

"I see." He nodded, frowning. "What do you call this thing?"

"I hope this doesn't offend you, but so far, I call it OMG, because it's kind of funny, but also because it's omniscient in its reach. I'm not religious or anything like that. Mostly, I believe in nature and kindness—which I guess are pretty universal. I want OMG to help heal the earth, so now that I think of it, it really does feel spiritual to me, but not really religious, if you know what I mean?

Kylie wondered if she knew what spirituality was any more, never mind religion. She used to pray when she was a kid. Every night she'd ask God to make her parents love her. She promised to be good and do her chores without complaining. She prayed not to have to go to boarding school. She prayed to have Andrew plead with her to take him back after he dumped her, but none of it happened. She was done praying. Now she just crossed her fingers and hoped. Even without religion, her life had become a series of *Hail Mary* maneuvers.

His frown deepened. "I do, indeed. The religion thing isn't a problem. Spirituality is good and sounds like you have your head on straight. Still, given that you ran this thing on me, I suppose you know everything, including my finances."

"Yes, I guess I do," Kylie said, knowing her face was flushing. "I looked because I wanted to make sure you were the guy who should be using this."

"So, you vetted me? And?"

She gave him a sheepish laugh. "You passed with honors. I do wonder about the million you got from Gerry Fox. How do you know him?"

"I don't really know him well, but he came to a fundraiser with his friend, Natalie Saltz, who you may have read about in the papers. Evidently, she was poisoned. That was terrible.

Since you ran a report and must know everything, you must have noticed that we refunded his check. Obviously, this was long before Natalie was poisoned."

"I didn't think there would be a connection. Why did you return the check, if I may ask?"

"It was too much. If someone gives you that much money, you pretty much belong to them. That's not how it's supposed to work. Anyway, there's laws against giving that much."

Kylie nodded and smiled. He was so honest; definitely the right guy for OMG.

"How did you know Natalie?" she asked.

"I didn't. She was a friend of the woman who hosted the fundraiser. Look, shouldn't I be asking you the questions? What's the price tag for this thing?"

"I was thinking $150,000 to help you get elected, and then another $10,000 quarterly for each year you hold office. It might sound like a lot, but it was expensive to build it. I know exactly how much you have in your campaign donations and I think you can see how handy this will be for you in deflecting the treachery in Washington. You can find out who is truly on your side. It can get you elected so that you can do some good. That alone is priceless."

For a long moment, Reinstadt regarded a gilt-framed painting on the wall depicting a schooner adrift with a storm threatening in the distance. Kylie followed his eyes, realizing she was adrift at sea like the schooner, tossing about in very choppy waters. Maybe they both were. He nodded slowly. "You're not shy about the price, that's for sure. It's a lot of money."

"I know it seems like a lot, but it's an extremely powerful

tool that could certainly help you get elected. I should add if you want an exclusive on this, or if the DNC wanted to buy it, it would be a LOT more. No one else could have access, and I would be on it full time to help you. With this arrangement, I can offer OMG to you for less money, since I hope to have other clients."

"What other clients?"

Kylie shrugged. Reinstadt was the only person she had thought about. She had never even considered he would turn her down. "I'm not sure yet. I haven't decided."

"And I'm not sure I'd be comfortable if you were running around giving this to everyone. So, who will run the searches? You?" He searched her face as if he was studying a menu board.

"I could," she said cautiously, "or I could give you a login and you could run them. It does take a lot of time to go through the reports. You could tell me what is relevant and I could find data that supports it if it's there."

"The thing I don't have is time. I have my law practice, that's now part-time since I've been running for the Senate. I don't have much of a life. There's no time for anything."

Kylie began to relax and took a sip of her coffee, not caring that it was ice cold. She could tell by his friendlier, more personal tone of voice that their meeting was going well. She wanted to pinch herself: she was sitting with Bill Reinstadt and he was talking to her like a colleague.

She was so pleased that part of her wished she could just give him the program. But Kylie knew she could not do that.

"I can imagine. You could hire me as a consultant and call me in when you need some information. For instance, when you are fundraising, your staffers might find this a really useful tool to pinpoint a select list of donors, based on their beliefs, politics, and income ... just for starters. I could quickly generate a lot of information on each one."

"How did you come up with this idea?" he asked, now looking curious.

What was she supposed to say?

I was trying to make myself feel better after my first startup flopped, and just wrote down a bunch of pie in the sky ideas? This one sounded pretty awesome, so I created a business plan and then hired a whacko hacker to build it.

She answered, "It's all about figuring out who you can trust. I wanted to build something that cuts through all the hype and brings truth to the world so I hired a programmer to make it happen," which was also true.

"So, for all intent and purpose, you did not build this? Someone else has access to it?" His tone now had a challenging edge to it.

Kylie's stomach turned. Reinstadt didn't even know Simon, and he, an objective observer, could sense there might be a danger. It wasn't just her imagination. "Yes, just this database wizard. He's like a big, overgrown kid. The truth is that now that it's built, I'm going to hire another guy to make the searches invisible to him. I don't want to totally lock him out since there will be tweaks, but you are right. It's smart to be cautious."

"But he's already got the program, right?"

Kylie's face reddened. "Yes, which is why you would want to ensure you'd be the first."

"Okay, Kylie. I'm afraid I'm out of time, but I'm going to think this over. I want some references, a resume, and your business plan. If you can send them over today, we can touch base later this week." He stood up and looked at his watch. "Sorry, but I've really gotta run."

Kylie rose too and extended her hand. His warm fingers wrapped around hers in another firm shake. "Looks like your hand's thawed out," he said, dropping her fingers and waving. As he walked out of the conference room, he turned back and asked, "What's the name of your developer, by the way?"

"Simon Whitehead."

He nodded as he rolled his lips together. Turning, he closed the door quietly behind him.

8

Misha

Kylie sensed Reinstadt saw the value in OMG and he would go for it. Her elated steps had a bounce just shy of skipping as she headed home reveling in her good luck. She replayed every minute of the meeting with Reinstadt in her head from the moment she set her eyes on him until she sailed out the door. When she reached the Boston Common, she cruised past the Park Street MBTA Station and past the ancient bare trees to the Frog Pond, where workers were transforming what was a summer swimming hole into an ice rink.

Kylie strolled along on what were originally paths set by pre-revolutionary cows but were now lined with benches occupied by homeless people, scary characters doing drugs along with young lovers snuggling against the cold. She crisscrossed her way unnoticed over the open fields leading to Charles Street and the Public Garden. All the while she felt invisible, yet buoyant and free.

Even in November, with its famous Swan Boats put away for the winter, the Garden was a lovely step back into another, more peaceful time. It was Kylie's favorite part of the city. A walk past its old, gigantic trees calmed her as if she'd taken a Valium … not that she had ever tried one. She loved the graceful golden willow vines draping over the banks of the duck pond, now gently swaying in the November wind. She crossed over the suspension bridge, designed in a slower, more elegant age, where a young saxophone player provided a jazzy soundtrack to her walk. His bare fingertips were exposed with the tips cut off his gloves so he could play. It felt like her lucky day and she dropped a dollar in the basket at his feet and was rewarded with his eyes twinkling as he played.

Crossing Arlington Street, she strolled down the tree-lined Commonwealth Mall for a few blocks admiring the handsome Victorian mansions before cutting over to Marlborough Street where she lived. She turned at the shabbiest brownstone on the block of lovely brownstones and unlocked the aged wooden door to her building. The door was the most handsome part of the building's exterior. Once she opened it, the hallway covered with gloomy faded wallpaper and worn carpet. She trotted up two flights of stairs to her tiny apartment, threw her coat on the couch and set up her laptop at the table, anxious to read the report on Misha.

He had come from Russia ten years ago to go to Northeastern for college. Based on his grades, Misha had excelled in computer programming and graduated with honors. After perusing his many work-related emails, it appeared he was now in high demand as a security and encryption expert. There was not much about his personal life except for some explicit email exchanges with women on online dating sites. Kylie read them all and had to admit, that for a Russian guy, he had a way with words that made her blush.

Curious, Kylie was able to connect to his profile on a dating site. His main photo showed a dark-haired, square-jawed guy at the beach, wearing trunks and a confident smile. She decided he was pretty cute in a Tom Cruise wannabe kind of way, but he was definitely *not* her type. His body was turned at just the right angle to show off his six-pack, and she was surprised he wasn't wearing a Speedo, not that she would have looked closely of course. He could swim commando for all she cared. His arm was loosely curved around the waist of a pretty redhead in a bikini, but by the girl's distance, she looked more like a prop than a girlfriend. Ugh. Kylie had enough of guys who treated girls like objects when she was in college. He looked much too cocky, like a small-time Euro-playboy. Lucky for her with OMG taking over her life, she didn't have time to think about her depressing lack of a love life. She suspected she was becoming as socially inept as some of the coders she had known, but evidently not Misha. But so what? She clicked off his profile. Who cared? This was business.

The most interesting piece of information on the report noted that while he had come to the USA for school, it appeared his visa expired five years ago and he was now living here illegally. Interesting. She called and set up a meeting with Misha for that afternoon at Jolt.

Recognizing Misha from his photo, she waved him over to

her table. Unlike Simon, he had a self-assured swagger. His hair was styled in a short Euro cut and he'd tied a blue and black patterned scarf at his neck, inside his black leather jacket. He sat down, sliding his tortoise-rimmed aviators into a pocket before extending his hand. She had to admit, he was cute, no doubt about it, but again luckily not her type. She was surprised his soft fingers were perspiring.

"Hi, Kylie. I hope I'm not late." His brown eyes returned her smile. "Thanks for your call. I'm interested in learning more about your project."

"Jared told me you're from Russia. You speak English well. You barely have an accent."

"I learned it in school and I've been here for a long time. Plus, I work hard at it."

Kylie liked how he met his challenges. Ready to proceed, she gave him her usual non-disclosure form before she'd even describe OMG, and he promptly signed it in an angular tiny script. She sighed, thinking this formality was ridiculous; hardly enough to stop anyone who seriously wanted to steal her project. By the time she could prove the idea was hers in an expensive lawsuit, they could have conquered the world and all would be lost. Still, she was banking on Jared, who had vouched for Misha and his reports looked safe enough. She took a chance, praying her program wouldn't be all over Russia by the end of the day.

She explained, "I've got an encryption problem. I conceived a powerful database system and had a developer build it, but now I am nervous it might get into the wrong hands. Frankly, I'm getting worried the guy who designed it could actually steal it. Plus, anytime I do a search on anyone, including him, he could easily find out by checking the log. I want to be able to work in a stealth mode. There's also some encrypted files I want access to. The program was supposed to be able to open those, but in this case, it doesn't."

Misha frowned. "Could you explain, please, more about how this program works?

"Yes, sure. Sorry. Let me start at the beginning." She described the capabilities of OMG, adding a spiel about her hopes for it to save the environment and basically save the world.

"I see. Certainly sounds worthwhile. Of course, I would need to see inside.

"Yes, of course. You can understand why this makes me nervous?"

"Yes, I can see." His eyes twinkled, but somehow to Kylie, it sounded like he was just humoring her as if he thought she was paranoid. Maybe she was, but she had enough of people not taking her seriously. *Did they all think she was stupid?*

"Look, Misha, I'm going to level with you. I know you're here illegally. I want to share this with you, but if I have any trouble, I mean any trouble at all, I'll call immigration and report you." There, she'd said it.

His brown eyes widened with surprise. "I see. You do not have to worry."

She couldn't do this alone. Even if she thought he was a bit cocky, maybe even arrogant, it didn't matter. If he was honest and could do the job? That was all that counted. With no programming skills, she was at the mercy of software developers. "Okay, good. We understand each other. What would you charge?"

"I need to see it first. Simple encryption shouldn't be too much, just hour or two once I get an understanding of your program. I have to see first how it works."

Kylie opened her laptop and gave Misha a demo.

"Looks complicated. Can I look at the code?"

Kylie switched to OMG's code view and pushed her laptop over to him. "Here."

Misha leaned into the laptop, squinting as he scrolled though it.

Kylie sipped her coffee, watching him stare intently on her screen as he scanned the code. The hum of the conversations around her faded in and out of her consciousness as she waited.

"You want me to block him altogether?"

"Maybe. What if I need him to tweak the program? And he has it on his server so he could easily steal it anyway."

"I see. Do you want me wipe files? Later if you need changes, I'll do those."

"You can do that?"

Misha nodded. "The code seems pretty clear. Have to say he looks like he's a pretty decent developer. Do you have passwords? Can you get me access to the server?"

"I can get into the server on my login, but I don't know his password. If you want to see if he has anything else on his server, I'm unable to open that."

"Not big problem. I will do work around.

"I'm not sure. it seems so extreme and he's going to be upset."

Misha shrugged. "You have to protect yourself. It's business."

"I don't know. This is pretty scary stuff. How do I know YOU won't take the thing and block me too?"

"You don't. You don't have to use me, but I'm honest. I have no need to steal this. What would I do with it?"

Kylie stared at Misha remembering how Simon said the same thing.

"Besides, you have something on me, yes?" he added when she didn't respond.

She nodded.

"How about we start by blocking him from the program. Quickly, though, I will need to destroy his files, because he can just overwrite it from a backup. Do you want me to do that?"

"Yes."

"Good. First, I'll move your program to another server to be safe. I start that right away. What is the encrypted file you want to open?"

She told him about the Lily folder. "I just have a feeling there's something in there I should know about."

Kylie was a little queasy as she told him how to get into Gerry Fox's report. She sensed something was there ... something that was going to be more than she was ready to handle.

"Can you open it?" she asked.

"I'll try."

"Okay, then you're hired." They set a price, and she wrote out a deposit check for him.

"Consider it done. Give me your number. I will be in touch," he took the check as he left.

Kylie remained at her table, resembling just another entrepreneur among the tech crowd at Jolt, getting buzzed on caffeine and code. Except she was lost in her worries, envisioning possible disasters with Misha or what Simon would do when he found out he had been locked out. She almost felt sorry for Simon, but then she remembered his lies.

She smiled grimly. He deserved it.

9

Simon

Feeling nauseous, Simon watched his feet as he power-walked back to his apartment. He tramped up the metal exterior steps and after slamming the door behind him, locked the deadbolt and chain. There was no way he was going to give Fox ... that slimy evil bastard ... access to OMG. He did consider telling Kylie, but what would he say to her...*Hello, Kylie, a murderer is threatening to shoot my balls off if I don't give him OMG?* And how would he explain how Fox even knew about the program? He had to admit there was something weird about Fox's insistence; it was almost as if Fox knew about it. And what would Fox even do with it if he got it? Simon didn't know, but it wouldn't be good.

No, he would have to figure out something else. He sank into his desk chair, not even noticing the litter on his desk of old

Starbucks cups growing various degrees of mold and a smelly overflowing ashtray. Just across the room, crusty dishes were stacked in the galley kitchen sink and garnished with mouse droppings. Besides a boxy couch and a monster TV, it was otherwise a dark and barren apartment except for his unmade bed and the towels were strewn about the bathroom. Not that he cared, but he didn't see the squalor since he was focused on what displayed on his computer monitor, or both of them. Simon touched his wireless mouse and blinked both of his dual monitors awake, brightening the room and casting an eerie blue glow on his face.

Before deleting Lily from his system, he put the file on a thumb drive, then wedged it under the innersole of an old pair of sneakers. He then opened the login page for OMG, Oddly, he was unable to get into the program. Frowning into the screen, he tried it again. He had not changed his password. *What the hell?*

He reached for the phone to call Kylie. Maybe she'd changed his login? He was pretty sure she wouldn't do that unless she was giving him a kiss-off. She had been acting weird lately, but he didn't think she'd just lock him out without a word. She probably wouldn't even know how to do it, he laughed to himself. Either way, what was the point? He laid his phone back on his desk with clammy hands. He tried to change his password but got an error; This program cannot be found.

WHAT THE FUCK? Simon opened his file manager, and the folder for OMG was there, but the only file it contained was the login screen. Had Fox gotten into his system and stolen the program? Did Fox think he was that much of a simpleton? No problem. This was totally up his alley. Simon could restore it. His stomach was jumping. He logged in to the server for the backup, but OMG was missing from there too. His forehead became damp with sweat. What was he going to tell Kylie? Now there was no reason to meet Fox. There was only reason to run.

He checked the server's log to see who had logged in and when did they do it. It showed a new IP address logging in, just a half hour before. He didn't recognize the address. He quickly ran a search and found out it belonged to Misha Kublasky. Who the hell was that? A flunky for Fox? A hacker? Simon was so screwed. If only he had OMG, he could run a report on Kublasky. Without his tools, he simply Googled the name, discovering Kublasky was an encryption expert.

Simon shut down his computer and got an electric drill from his toolbox in the closet. After blasting down into the guts of his hard drive, he threw the drill on the floor and pulled his duffel bag from his closet. He tossed in some clothes, a few toiletries, his laptop, his passport, and the sneakers with the hidden thumb drive, before locking his door and heading to the subway. At the airport, he bought a one-way ticket to San Francisco on a four p.m. flight. He didn't know what he was going to do except to get as far away from Fox as possible.

Once Simon went through airport security that afternoon, he settled in at a restaurant with a beer. He considered calling Kylie but imagined how the conversation would go. *So, hey, it's me. I just wanted to tell you someone has stolen OMG.*

Forget that. Simon drained his beer and paid his bill. Walking past a mirror in the men's room, he was startled by his white face with circles under his dark eyes. Then he lumbered down to the gate, where he would start a new life once he landed.

***

At four o'clock, Fox sat down on one of the benches by the Civil War Statue on the Boston Common. Except for a few Asian tourists shooting photos in the fading light, he was alone. The statue was on top of a hill, and with the bare trees, he had a view of the entire park. Like a bird hunting prey, Fox paced in circles around the monument, scanning the paths below for Simon. The clouds had moved in, adding a dreary gloom to the November landscape. In an hour, it would be dark and the jewel-toned Christmas lights looping around the tops of the trees below would come on. He waited fifteen minutes, surveying the practically deserted sidewalks below, before taking out his phone and texting to Simon. **Where the hell are you?**

Somewhere over Michigan, Simon heard the ding of a text coming in. It had probably been a mistake to connect to the plane's Wi-Fi. Dreading what he would find, Simon pulled his phone out from seat pocket in front of him. Fox's name flashed on his screen, canceling out the tiny bit of beer-induced calm he'd been enjoying. Simon sucked in his breath and read Fox's message and texted back. **Don't play games with me. I know you stole the program. You are not going to get away with this.**

Simon turned off his phone and slipped it back into the seat pocket. He ordered a beer from the stewardess. When it arrived, he gulped it down and selected a movie, but instead, he fell into a restless sleep for the rest of the flight to San Francisco.

***

Fox was furious. *How dare Simon play me?*

Checking his list of contacts, he found Simon's address a mere ten-minute walk from the Common. He fingered his gun in his pocket as he walked across the park, down Tremont Street and past the now dark and forlorn theaters, some seedy hotels, and on to the South End, where he turned onto Simon's Street.

He rushed past the desolate community gardens, to the apartment complex just across the street. It was in a group of shabby, three-story flats looking like they'd been built in the sixties. Compared to the old brownstones only a block away in the South End, it was relatively new but had seen better days. Fox's heavy footsteps had a hollow sound as he climbed the exterior steps to Simon's third floor unit. He pounded on the flimsy wooden door. "Simon?"

No answer. "Whitehead? Open up you fucking little rat." Met with silence, Fox removed a tiny blowtorch from his pocket. He flipped it open and fired it up. Using a torch was a trick he learned in college when his girlfriend locked him out and a supposed "no-fail" paperclip trick failed. He went out and bought the tiny torch and kept it tucked in his bag ever since. It had more than paid for itself over the years.

Fox pulled a dummy key out of a pouch and once it melted, he inserted it into the keyhole. As it cooled, it molded to the correct shape. He now easily unlocked Simon's door; piece of cake. Inside, he switched on the lights, revealing the dirty dishes and disarray on his desk. His nostrils curled in distaste from the acrid smell of stale cigarettes. *God, why couldn't people take care of their bodies?*

Then he noticed the hard drive with its fatal incision to its innards and its murder weapon, the drill still laying on the floor. He hovered his hand over the top of the computer, feeling its warmth as if it were a body that had just expired. Fox searched the apartment for anything that might have the program. There were still a few clothes in the closet, but not much else. He searched the cupboards which were practically bare except for a few dishes, a half-empty box of Pop Tarts, and some packaged macaroni dinners. The refrigerator contained a few bottles of beer, a bag of apples, and a jar of crunchy peanut butter. The kid had flown.

What had he expected?

Fox wiped off his fingerprints with a small chamois from his pocket and left, closing the door quietly behind him. He would find Whitehead, get the program, and then have him killed. He took out his phone and speed-dialed Alex, his right-hand-man, who had connections everywhere. Even on a Sunday when he was undoubtedly watching football, Alex picked up on the first ring. *Good man.* Fox explained how he was looking for Simon, who might be traveling, and could Alex use his police connections to check flights?

By the time Fox's phone rang a half hour later, he was nursing a beer and watching the Patriot's game at Salvatore's Bar on Washington Street, just off the Boston Common. Learning Simon was on a flight to San Francisco, Fox told Alex to arrange a greeting committee for Simon when he landed. Fox was explicit about Simon's fate.

***

It was dark when Simon landed at the San Francisco airport. He had planned to get a hotel room and then figure out what to do next. He swung his duffel over his shoulder and headed through baggage claim, where just outside he would get a taxi.

As he held the door for two men behind him, one of them suddenly moved in close enough for Simon to get a strong smell of his cloying cologne, mixed with pot. He encircled Simon with a bear hug that felt like a wrestling hold. Simon struggled to break away, but the man held him firm and Simon apparently wasn't going anywhere. The man now crushing him was a head taller and much stronger. Simon's face only came up to his attacker's chest and it was smashed against his black leather jacket reeking of pot.

"Hey man! Great to see you, Simon! We're really glad you made it. Welcome to San Francisco, bro!"

The second man continued, "Yeah, really good of you to come all the way to the west coast for a visit. Our buddy, Gerry Fox, said we are to take good care of you." The second man was closer to Simon's age and size. He inched close enough to point the hard nose of a gun into Simon's back ribs and whispered, "We've arranged transportation for you. I suggest you don't make any noise, just get into the car like a good little nerd. We wouldn't want a scene where you might get hurt."

Sandwiched between the two men who had clamped their arms around his shoulders, Simon was led to a silver Mercedes SUV. "Your carriage awaits," said the gun guy, bowing slightly. "Get in."

Simon obeyed. Gun Guy slid in the back seat next to Simon. "Buckle up, my little nerd boy. We wouldn't want anything to happen to you."

Terrified, Simon complied. The hugger sat in the front seat with the driver, who had on a backward Giants cap but did not turn around. When the doors were slammed shut, he drove out of the airport and turned South onto Route 101. No one spoke for an hour as they drove through the darkness. They finally turned off at the Gilroy exit.

Simon had only been to San Francisco once and frantically watched the road signs as they drove South, passing Palo Alto, Mountain View, Santa Clara, and beyond. Once past San Jose, he no longer recognized the names on the signs. His stomach churned, bubbling a new brew of acid that kept threatening to come up. Finally, the driver pulled off to the side of the road next to a field.

"We're here, bro," said Simon's seatmate. "Just to make sure you don't try anything creative, I want you to wear a little jewelry. It's not much, but just a token of our esteem." He pulled silver handcuffs from his pocket and locked them on Simon's wrists.

Hugging Guy in the front seat opened his door, got out, and stretched his long arms in the cool air and yawned. "Nice night," he said, before opening Simon's door and hauling him onto the field. "Hey, you know what kind of field this is, kid?"

Simon stumbled in some dirt and then regained his balance. "No," His throat felt so tight his voice was barely audible. He frantically looked for some way to escape.

"It's garlic, and it stinks, just like you. Did you know Gilroy is the garlic capital of the world?"

"No." Simon tried to kick his shins and bite his arm, but Hugging Guy held him at a distance with one hand, as if he were an adult restraining a child.

"I didn't think so. I suggest you settle down, cowboy. You know, our buddy in Boston tells me you owe him some information. He wants it and evidently knows what to do with it, so I suggest you play nice and give it to us, or we will leave you here to fertilize the garlic."

Simon looked him in the eye. "So, I know you aren't going to believe me, but someone hacked my computer. The program is gone. I have no way to get it." Simon thrashed, unsuccessfully trying to elbow him and butt him with his head. It was useless. He was being held by a giant.

"You were the kid who told the teacher the dog ate your homework. Am I right?" He laughed. "Yeah, you were. You totally were. I know your type." He shoved Simon for emphasis.

Before Simon could answer, the guy with the gun aimed it directly at Simon. "Would you like to rethink your answer nerd boy?'

Simon leaned over and vomited on his shoe. He wished it had gone onto the guy's face. Gagging, he held his elbows up and wiped his mouth on his jacket sleeve. "I can't because it's the honest truth. I can't give you what I don't have." His mouth reeked from his own acids.

The hugging guy smiled. "Yeah? Let's see what you've got in your bag. He pulled opened the car door and rummaged through Simon's duffel in the back seat. He opened the laptop and looked through his files. What did you do with those programs, asshole?" he called over his shoulder.

"I am telling you, my computer got hacked. It's the truth." Simon's throat was now so constricted his words only came out as a low whisper.

Hugging Guy walked from the car over to Simon. "What was that? You want to rethink that? I hear they need more fertilizer here, you piece of shit." Maybe you need a little motivation.

He punched Simon's stomach hard. Simon stumbled backward from its velocity and the pain, sobbing as he staggered.

"I don't have it." He wasn't ready to die. This was not fair. His mouth was dry, but he gathered up his saliva and shot it through the air to land on Gun Guy's face. Gun Guy looked mad as he wiped his face with his sleeve.

"Okay, I've had it. That was really bad manners. Maybe you do that in Boston, but here? Uh-uh. In California, we have manners. Didn't anyone ever tell you it's not nice to spit? You've used up your chances," said his friend.

Gun Guy raised his arm out straight and shot Simon in the chest. As Simon slumped onto the field, the condensation from his blood rose like a cloud of fog in front of the headlights. The air reeked from gun powder and added an eerie yellow glow. Gun Guy then held his hand out for the handcuff key and when he got it, he released Simon's wrists. He rolled Simon over and without noticing Simon's face with eyes round with terror, he removed the wallet from Simon's jeans and stuffed it in his jacket pocket.

"Let's go," he said, patting his pocket. "It stinks here."

10

Seedstart, Monday Morning

"Morning, Sandra," Fox announced as he passed his receptionist on the way into his office. She sat beneath his latest art acquisition, a six-foot-high Chuck Close portrait of Fox's face. It had been a commission. Close had been reluctant to take on the job, but Fox, determined to have this pricey status symbol, met his price and Close couldn't refuse. And there it was, the clear-eyed close-up of his eyes, nose, mouth, and even his whiskers, staring out at the world. His face on the painting had been broken down into one-inch squares of pixilation, best appreciated from the across the long lobby, where the image became recognizable as Fox. It was a testament to how successful and cultured he was, in case anyone needed any more proof. He only wished his white-trash parents could see him now—not that they could or would understand the art, or anything else in his life for that matter.

On the white wall behind the two white Barcelona chairs, spanned a neon sculpture of his logo, Seedstart, glowing orange across the long, white wall. The adjacent wall was orange, with an arrangement of framed covers of Money Magazine featuring Seedstart and the success stories of the companies it had funded.

"How was your weekend?" Sandra chirped.

"Splendid. You?"

"Not great. Alex has a cold again. Actually, I was going to ask if I could leave early today to take him to the doctor? I kept him home from school and my mother's with him now."

Fox held up his hand to stop her flow of words interfering with his serenity. Now he might have to do an extra morning meditation to clear her energy from the room. "Sure. Fine. No problem. In fact, with the holiday, why not just take off tomorrow since we only have a half day on Wednesday."

"Gerry, thank you. You're the best."

"You're very welcome. Can you please bring me a cup with a double shot of decaf espresso, a glass of water and some steel-cut oatmeal with fruit and nuts on the side?"

"No problem," she sprang to her feet.

God, the last thing he needed now was to get a cold from some germy little monster, transmitted through his mother.

Fox shut his office door and sat down at his agronomic chair. He rolled it up to his ten-foot long burnished aluminum desktop looking so similar to the finish on his Macbook with its giant external monitor that they blended in visually, appearing to be one piece.

Sandra brought in his coffee and breakfast on a little wooden tray. It held a folded blue and white checkered cloth napkin, a lovely flowered bowl with steaming oatmeal and its toppings, and a softly-glowing antique silver spoon. There was a small white vase holding a single white rose, just the way he liked it. She set it his desk next to his computer.

"Here you go," she dimpled.

Fox flashed her a practiced smile, holding his breath inside. He did not dare inhale until she left and he hoped she hadn't breathed on his food. He considered putting on a facemask next time he passed through the office. When she closed the door behind her, he took hand sanitizer out of his top drawer and sprayed anything she might have touched. He would have to remember to spray disinfectant in the lobby.

Next, he lined up a row of vitamins and supplements from the bottles in his desk drawer. He swallowed each capsule with a sip of water; a multivitamin, his Omega 3s for joint pain, extra vitamin B for nerves, and D for his bones. There was gingko biloba for brain function, and garlic for digestion. A man had to take care of himself. Then, he opened his email. There was the typical stuff from hotshot startup CEOs, hoping to meet in order to request funding, invitations to pitch slams, and meeting requests for the various Boards on which he served.

He sniffed. All that could wait. More important was the matter of Simon. When he'd awoken that morning, he'd found the text from Alex saying the Simon problem was resolved. Alex never failed him. It was a relief to know Simon was gone, so the young man certainly wouldn't be talking. Still, there was the small matter of the police questioning concerning his involvement with Simon.

The kid was such a mess—who would have any doubt Simon was the mastermind behind anything suspicious that might turn up? Besides, the cops did not have a single thing that could implicate him. Fox felt satisfied that killing Simon tied everything up neatly. He was certain there was no tracing of anything back to him. He felt lucky he got the Simon business out of the way so he could concentrate on the work at hand. *The sale of the virus was going to put him at the top of the food chain.*

When it came down to it, Fox, unlike Simon, was a respected member of the community. It had taken him a long time to get there, as if he was one of the Chilean miners trapped underground, clawing himself up through the dirt to the light. Poverty had been his trap, not a caved-in mine shaft, but he'd scaled that hole, one step at a time. Nobody, not a weasely little nerd, a nagging wife, or a pesky girlfriend who asked way too many questions, was going to take what he earned away from Gerry Fox.

He had laughed at Natalie's voicemail the day she died. They had fucked at Gerry's *pied a terre*, then they lunched at a quiet little bistro, where she'd bugged him again about Simon. At lunch, one of the clams on her linguine hadn't opened. Knowing better than to eat it, she slid it to the side of her plate. "It's me," she told his voicemail while calling from her office. "I'm feeling sick, and at first I thought it might be from the clams we ate at lunch. Are you okay? It could be food poisoning, but this is very strange. I'm trying not to panic, but this is so weird I think I might have been poisoned. Can you help? Gerry, where the hell are you?"

A clam? He'd heard from her colleagues how she'd collapsed in the Ladies' room. *Natalie looked hideous.* They questioned each other with worried faces. *My God. Did you see that rash? Could it be contagious?* She had no idea how she'd been the perfect Guinea pig for the lethal virus he'd been developing. He prided himself on the economy of eliminating her and testing the product at the same time.

After everyone in the building was sent home, men wearing white coveralls, masks, and gloves, came onto the floor and fumigated the offices. Steve Hahn, one of the head programmers on Natalie's team, called Gerry Fox. When Fox didn't answer, Steve left a message. "Hey, it's Steve. I thought you might want to know the test was successful. Natalie was just taken to Mass General in an ambulance."

Now that Simon was dead, there was no way he could be linked to any of that mess. Hahn certainly wouldn't implicate him since he helped build it.

There was still the matter of OMG, which was much more important than his usual venture capitalist bullshit. He typed Kylie Maynard into Google to find out what he could about her. If he had her program now, he wouldn't have to diddle around with Google, but it's all he had right then. The results were disappointing, although a little surprising.

He found some of the headlines from Kylie's college ski days and it turned out she was a serious skier; even hoping to train for the Olympics one day. She had interned at her Dad's financial firm before going for her MBA and she'd had another startup before; some kind of an app that failed just after grad school. He sniffed again, glad she'd never approached him for seed money. It was pathetic the way these desperate kids pandered to him. Most of the time, their student projects weren't realistic for the marketplace. He wondered how she'd funded it. No matter. What she'd come up with now seemed pretty useful, and he wanted to get his hands on it. It was not the kind of thing he'd want to bring to market. No, he wanted it for himself.

He researched the registration for her first business and got the address. Fox loved the peace of calmly sorting out his day and leisurely typed some items into his schedule. First, he'd deal with some of his more urgent emails, then he would see about Kylie Maynard.

The next item needing attention was an email from Emily Wickland, who had been coordinating some meetings in New York. Her expertise was PR, but she had some excellent contacts, including her supposed lover, Bill Reinstadt. She took credit for putting Gerry Fox together with Reinstadt and they made a good team.

Since the Lily virus was ready, Emily had been helpful in setting up potential buyers. As a couple, they seemed a little tepid to Fox; a little too perfect, as if they performed just for show. Since he'd met Emily in person and observed the two of them together, he'd wondered about a certain coolness between them. In her photos, she looked gorgeous. In person, she was even more dazzling. If Reinstadt did not appreciate a good woman like her, Fox certainly could. Now that Natalie was out of the way, he was just waiting for the right moment to make his move. Those legs! He could just imagine how he would like Emily to use them. That reminded him of his first order of business and he punched some numbers into his cell phone.

"This is Emily," the sultry voice answered.

"Good morning, gorgeous. It's Gerry, just checking on our meeting."

"Yes, it's all set. Maxim is extremely interested. My feeling is he'll meet our price. It will be obvious to see the value after we release the demo."

He sighed. Only a few more days and the power of Lily would be evident to all. He'd have the world at his feet. He'd sell it and disappear. No more Candice. No more demanding, entitled twins, no more pathetic startup CEOs hounding him for money, delivering their hopeful little pitches. No more cops. Those monkeys didn't know what the hell they were doing. He was certainly not a criminal; just a guy trying to make a buck and survive. It was the American way.

He planned to just vanish without even saying good-bye. He was sure nobody would really miss him and if they did, what did he care? His new mountainside house overlooking San Miguel was already furnished and waiting. Maria, his knock-out Mexican housekeeper, had taken care of it all. Now there was a woman. He couldn't wait to see her. Emily Wickland paled in comparison.

Everything seemed to be working according to plan. He'd be set and Reinstadt would have all the money he needed to literally buy his way into the Senate and then on to the White House. There were only a few details to take care of and everything would be fine.

11

Breaking News

Monday morning, Kylie sat hunched over a bowl of cereal and a cup of coffee. She was reviewing to-do list when Misha called. He had opened the Lily Folder, but he sounded worried.

By his tone, Kylie sensed it was not going to be good. "What's in there?" she asked.

"Telling you in person is better, and we should do it ... probably soon. Meet me at Jolt. Like right away?"

"Yes, sure, but can't you just tell me now?"

"Better in person."

Mystified, Kylie did not understand why he couldn't just fill her in, but the urgency in his voice had been like rocket fuel, launching her anxiety into orbit. She agreed to be there in an hour. After finishing her cereal, she jumped into the shower. While drying off, her usually silent phone rang again.

Bill Reinstadt's name flashed on the screen. Her blood pounded in her ears as she picked up, held her breath, crossed her fingers and her toes, and hoped for the best.

All she could manage to get out was a nervous, "Hello?"

"Kylie, it's Bill Reinstadt," he didn't stop there, "I discussed your platform with my advisors, and they were impressed. You are ON. When can you come to my office to meet with my campaign manager and get started?"

She broke into an elated smile. "I'm sure you want to get going on this. I could come in this afternoon if you like."

"This afternoon is good. How about 1 o'clock?"

"What plan did you want to go with?" She held her breath.

"For now, I want the exclusive. I'll draw up a contract and give you a check. You're welcome to have your lawyer look it over."

Her lawyer was her mother, so she mentally declined. "I'll read it over when I come in."

She had hardly thought of her mother for weeks except for Allison's increasingly insistent texts asking Kylie to respond about being there for Thanksgiving. Preoccupied, Kylie dismissed them, thinking she'd get back to Allison eventually. Now with Thanksgiving only three days away and Kylie suddenly feeling so excited and benevolent after Reinstadt's call, she felt fortified to take on her mother at the holiday. Still wrapped in a towel, she punched Allison's name on her speed dial. When her mother answered, Kylie's voice became singsongy. "Hey, Mom, How're you doing?"

"Fine. So, you *are* alive after all. Why do you sound so chipper?"

"Nothing special."

"We wouldn't want anything special, would we?" Her voice sharpened with her unique brand of sarcasm, which was her specialty.

Kylie wasn't going to let it ruin her mood. "What time should I be there for Thanksgiving?" She asked brightly.

"That depends on if you are coming as a guest or as a daughter. If you're coming as a daughter, it 'd be good to have you here to help with some of the cooking. So, how about coming around eleven? We'll eat around three."

"Isn't Aunt Judy going to be there?"

"Yes. Aunt Judy and Uncle Pete will be here with Andrew. He's coming home from school."

"What time are they coming?"

"Probably around two."

"Coming at three isn't an option, Kylie. I was just kidding. I'd like you to help."

"It's probably hereditary, but I'm not exactly what you'd call a cook, you know. But okay, fine, I will be there at eleven. What if I decide to bring a guest?"

"A guest?"

"Possibly. I will let you know. I assume that's okay?"

"Is this a young man?"

"I don't know, Mom. It was just a question. We'll see."

"Fine. You don't know if he's a young man? Fine. At any rate, you can demo your new app thingy to the family. I think you're going to have quite an eager audience."

Kylie clenched the phone. "About that. I know I promised, but I can't really show it now. I'm selling it as an exclusive, so I can't show it to anyone else."

There was a steely silence. "Really! You're selling it already?

That sounds intriguing. Who did you sell it to? What *is* this mysterious thing that you're doing?"

"I can't say."

"Okay, Kylie. You've lived like a hermit for months, building an application you won't explain. Now, you're selling it to someone and you can't tell me who. Is it even legal?"

"Yes, of course. I'm selling it to a lawyer."

"Really? And you can't show it to me? I'd really like to know what you're into."

"I know. I'm really sorry, but you'll just have to trust me."

"It's not a matter of trust. I want to know what my daughter's doing."

"Why? You want to make sure I'm doing something you approve? If it's not trust, it's a matter of control. Come on, Mom. Give me some credit ... and some space."

"You don't give me much choice. If I ever need any information, Kylie, I'll be sure to ask *you*. We will see you this Thursday. Until then, take all the space you like, but don't assume this subject is closed."

Kylie dressed in her usual jeans and a sweater, stuck her hair in a ponytail, and headed to the T. When she arrived at Jolt, the coffee shop was already humming. Misha waved her over to his table by the window, where he was sipping a cup of cappuccino. By the life-or-death intensity of his knitted brows and the rapid percussive circles he signaled with his hand, Kylie knew something was very wrong.

"So, what's up?" she asked, taking a seat.

Misha flipped open his laptop. "This!" he shoved it over for her to see for herself.

The document was a neatly laid out spreadsheet labeled *Lily* with a detailed introduction. The first paragraph explained the program was the plan for an airborne virus that would kill anyone breathing it within an hour. It's evidently contained in an offsite lab in Chinatown. There was a pricing schedule there as if they planned to sell it or something?

"Oh, my God," moaned Kylie. "This is worse than anything I could have imagined. What are we going to do?"

"I have no idea," said Misha, shaking his head. "It's led by Gerry Fox and was put together by Simon Whitehead."

Kylie's jaw hung slack as her face flushed with anger. Simon? How could she have trusted him? Kylie knew she should have followed her first impression. What a little weasel. Now she had to talk to him. Kylie speed dialed his number. What the hell was she going to say? No answer. She refrained from throwing her phone across the room and laid it gently back on the table. "Is there an address for the lab?"

"Yes. Here." He pulled up the address on a Google map. It's on Beech Street."

"Can you stop this thing by getting into their files and changing their code?" she asked.

"If they've already built it, it's too late. If not, I could try to mess with some of the sequencings, but I have no idea about things like that, and I could make it worse."

"What could be worse?"

"Don't know. It looks like they have a target date to release this on Black Friday."

"In four days?"

Misha nodded. "Yes. See here?" He angled the laptop and pointed to another section on the bottom where it clearly labeled: *Target Release Dates.* Boston was scheduled first, later to be followed by New York. Then maybe L.A., and Chicago, all on separate dates. There was some indication Boston was a test.

Kylie felt dizzy. She looked at her watch. There was only an hour before she had to head to Reinstadt's office. Now she was especially glad she'd contacted him. He would know just what to do. But that wasn't for an hour, and it was just enough time to take a little detour into Chinatown. No harm in checking things out. "Hmmm, I feel like getting some dim sum. What do you say we drive to Chinatown? Do you have a car here?"

"Yes, why?"

"I'm curious. We don't have to go inside. We can drive by; see what the place looks like."

"I suppose that sounds harmless. Why not? said Misha. They threw on their jackets, and he led her up Third Street past a few high-rise apartment buildings to an electric blue Porsche. As soon as they'd buckled up, Misha took off, speeding over the Longfellow Bridge into Boston and wound through the downtown streets to Chinatown. Kylie texted Simon; *Call me ASAP.*

The GPS chirped, "*You have arrived at your destination.*" Misha pulled his car into an alley. "That's it, across the street." He pointed to a shabby brick building similar to the others on Beech Street with cheap apartments on the top floors and restaurants and shops on the street level. That one had a cafe with a flashy new pink sign with fat script letters reading: Lily's Bubble Tea. The sign spanned the width of the building with festive bubbles painted behind the letters. The only people around were elderly Asians steering collapsible carts loaded with groceries.

"Lily's, of course! Now, what do we do?" Kylie wondered out loud.

"We get some bubble tea and check it out."

Inside, they were greeted by cheery pink walls and a huge whiteboard menu behind the counter with the choices in English on one side, Chinese on the other. They ordered fruit smoothies from a young Asian girl and took them to the stools at the window counter. The drinks had dark pearl-sized globules of tapioca mixed throughout and Kylie discovered the currant-sized orbs required chewing. They quietly concentrated on the new taste sensations as they watched the street, wondering what to do next. Kylie's phone rang. Simon! Finally! She pulled it from her purse, expecting to hear his familiar voice say *Hey!*

It was Jared calling. "Hi, Jared."

"Hi. Have you seen the news this morning?"

"No. Why?"

"They found Simon's body in a garlic field in Gilroy, California."

Kylie expelled the last of her breath as if someone socked her in the stomach. "What? Are you kidding me? It must be someone else!"

"No, unfortunately, it is Simon. It's all over the news. He was shot."

"Oh, my God!! What happened?" She asked, feeling horrified and yet there was something not surprising about his death. After all, she herself had felt like killing Simon, not that she did that sort of thing.

"They don't know yet."

"Okay, I'll check it out online. Thanks, Jared."

Kylie hung up. Misha watched her, his eyes round with questions. "What's going on? You look like you saw a ghost."

"Pretty much." She told him the news and felt as if the floor had dropped away. If she hadn't been sitting down, she might have passed out.

"Good grief. No! Argh!"

She Googled Simon Whitehead on her phone. Sure enough, his body had been found face-down in the dirt by a farmer a few hours ago. They figured out his identity from his boarding pass still in his pocket.

"Oh, my God. We're in way over our heads." She remembered her meeting with Reinstadt and thought if anyone could help, it would be him. "Would you mind dropping me off on State Street? I'll figure something out."

They took their drinks out and tossed them in a trash can before they got in the car. Kylie directed Misha to drop her at the corner near Reinstadt's office. When they arrived,s Misha touched her shoulder as she opened the door. "Hey, I'm sure this is very upsetting. I'm sorry about it all. It will be okay. You'll see."

***

Kylie was reading the news on Simon on her phone when Bill Reinstadt rushed into his conference room, followed by two staffers about her age. "Kylie, this is Matthew, my campaign manager, and Jessica, my assistant." Kylie rose and extended her hand.

"A pleasure," she said. "I hope you don't mind, but I wonder if I can have just a minute with Mr. Reinstadt before we all meet together?"

Reinstadt searched her face, and he picked up on her urgency. "Okay, guys, give us five."

As Matthew shut the conference room door behind them, Kylie sank into the chair and pointed to the article. "Here, please look at this."

"Yes, I saw it on the news."

"Simon was the guy who coded OMG."

"That's right. I thought his name sounded familiar. Jesus," said Reinstadt, taking the chair next to Kylie. His eyes squinted, and he searched her face as if he suspected Kylie might work for the mob.

"What's more, I had a weird feeling something was up with him, so I had him locked out of the program. I hired another guy to do it and he opened the encrypted folder. I just found out Simon was working with Gerry Fox, and they developed a deadly virus called *Lily*. Evidently, Fox plans to release it in Boston on Black Friday."

Reinstadt ran his hand through his hair over his ear. "That's very interesting. How do you know this? Do you have proof?"

"Yes. It's in a folder on both Fox's and Simon's computers. It specifically lays it out. The plan is to release it in Boston first, then a bunch of other cities. Evidently, there's some sort of an off-site lab here in Chinatown, right over a bubble tea place. You can't miss it. There's a big sign for Lily's Bubble Tea. We were there and got some."

He narrowed his eyes looking for the truth. "Do you have access to that here?"

"No. I'd have to get Misha's computer, my encryption guy."

"Can you do that now?"

Kylie nodded and picked up her phone. While she called

Misha, Reinstadt called Matthew and Jessica into the room. "Slight change of plans. Matthew, call Raymond Lane from Homeland Security. Jessica, call Stuart Anderson from the FBI. Tell them to get up here right now. We have a problem.

12

Lily

Bill led them to the FBI office only blocks away in the vast concrete landscape of Government Center to the FBI. They were greeted in the lobby by the agent on complaint duty, a tall man with angular features, who led them past the entry wall plastered with most-wanted posters. He led them down the hall to a dark conference room where fluorescent lights hung like a giant ice cube tray high over the beat-up wooden table, where a middle-aged man with piercing blue eyes was waiting. He stood up from the table and shook Bill's hand. "Good to see you, Bill. What can I do for you?"

After introductions, Kylie routinely requested Stuart's confidentiality before showing him OMG to Stuart and Bill amused smirks. She already had misgivings. Her choices had been to make up some bogus story the FBI they would see through anyway, or reveal what she was really doing to detail Misha's horrific findings. This was way too big to worry about her own consequences and now to put it mildly, she had a sinking feeling they might not be so great. She gave Misha a nod to take over.

He showed the contents of the *Lily* Folder from his computer and explained, "I was clicking around in the program and found this file. It shows here how there's a virus that will kill within hours of contact. The victims would have to touch it or ingest it. Looks like it's set to go for this Friday."

Stuart broke the stunned silence that hung like a bad smell over the room. "You're saying that you were just clicking around and you got this on someone else's computer? Am I hearing that right?"

Misha nodded, looking terrified.

Kylie interjected, "That might not be the point right now. We have a crisis and need your help, but if you want to go there, I can explain. I wasn't just snooping. I have a startup, and we designed a powerful database program meant to help people with their lives. At least that was my goal. I began to suspect this guy, Gerry Fox, might be involved in some shady activities. I paid Misha to open some encrypted files on his computer."

"Okay, let me get this right. You have a business that snoops? Unbelievable. That's even better. Why were you looking at Fox's data in the first place? That's where we're supposed to come in. You are breaking the law. You know that, right?"

"Yes, I admit that I did this, but I'm not a bad person. I might have done something not quite on the level, but it's so that some good will come of it. I promise you; it's not for personal gain. I'm trying to help!" said Kylie.

"That doesn't make it any more legal. How does this program of yours work, anyway?" asked Stuart. He appeared exasperated and was now stroking his chin.

Kylie began, "Of course you've heard of phishing, right? It's that thing when someone sends a fake email that looks just like it's from a credible organization or business. They ask you to update your profile. Once you do, they send you a link to a page to update your password that will explode in your computer like a data bomb. It works by crawling around in your computer to find a browser that needs updating. Then it inserts some code so they can capture keystrokes. It allows them to control a webcam and microphones, and even see your files. My program can do the same thing, but it can also search into financials and phone records; anything I query without phishing. It clusters the programs it needs to target and then picks up recorded keystrokes and can open any program from the user's computer. It can give direct access to everything."

Kylie caught Misha's admiring look. She appreciated it until she noticed his gaze had slipped down to her chest. She looked away, annoyed he'd be checking out her body instead of focusing on the crisis. What a jerk.

"And you thought of this all by yourself?"

"Only the idea, but not the technical part. I hired someone to build it. Unfortunately, he's the guy that turned up dead in a garlic field."

"Unbelievable. Anyway, how do you know this virus plot is real?" Stuart asked.

Kylie answered, "We don't know for sure, but my guess? It's

very real. The people involved were connected to Visiozyme. Do you remember that Natalie Saltz murder? She worked there, right? Wasn't it from some kind of deadly virus? At any rate, I certainly wouldn't want to take that chance, would you? It's headed by Gerry Fox, and we think he's a bad guy. That's why we were looking at his files in the first place. Evidently, he has a secret lab in Chinatown over a bubble tea place, called Lily's."

"When did you find out about this?" Stuart leaned into the screen his hands on his hips. His reddened face wore an expression of disbelief.

"Just about an hour ago. I brought it to Bill's office first, since I already had a meeting set with him and I trusted he would know what to do." Kylie was surprised at how quickly Reinstadt's first name rolled off her tongue but hoped she had not overstepped.

"We'll need to borrow this laptop," said Stuart, now squatting behind Misha to get a better look at eye level. His balding forehead gleamed from the window light. "You'll get it back eventually. I want you to walk me through this thing." He turned to Kylie. "By the way, you do know that hacking is illegal, right?"

She nodded. "So I've been told." How had she been so stupid? She'd arranged her own arrest. Kylie could just imagine her mother's glowering face when she called her for bail. "Look, if it makes any difference, I'm only using this to a good end. That's why I took Simon off the project since I didn't think he was trustworthy. But, if we hadn't used OMG, we'd never have known about any of this."

Stuart nodded. "Who's Simon again?"

Kylie's mouth went dry. "Simon Whitehead, the developer

who wrote the program. You know, the guy I mentioned that was found dead this morning?"

"I see. What do you say we look at your program now?"

Kylie turned to Reinstadt. "Looks like we'll need to reschedule."

"Perhaps. Let's see what happens. Thought I might hang in there with you for a while though. You might need a lawyer. I don't practice criminal law, but I can probably be of some help."

"This is your laptop, right?" Stuart asked Misha.

Misha nodded.

"You'll need you to give us access." He made a call and within moments another agent appeared who led Misha away with his laptop

The two men left Kylie, Reinstadt and Stuart, and Raymond standing around the table. Kylie could not help but wonder how many criminals had sat in the very same chairs, and how many were now behind bars. This had better go the right—she had no intention of becoming one of them.

"Have a seat. I need a statement from you and I want you to tell me everything you know about this," Stuart's request sounded like an order as his eyes penetrating Kylie glinted with suspicion.

"Sure." She gracefully sat down in the chair next to Reinstadt. Stuart turned on the recorder on his phone and laid it on the table. "I'm going to tape this if you don't mind."

"Do you want me to act as your lawyer?" Reinstadt turned to Kylie.

"I don't know. Do I need a lawyer?"

"You might. For now, I would suggest you not answer anything that might incriminate you."

"I have nothing to hide," said Kylie. "I'm just trying to help, so fine. Ask me whatever you want. I might have overstepped in the programming department, but I came here out of my own volition. It's not like I'm a criminal. If the information we have is correct, we don't have lots of time."

"Okay, let's go." Stuart pushed some buttons on his phone and spoke into it. "Stuart Anderson, agent, interviewing Kylie Maynard the FBI. William Reinhardt states he is acting as Ms. Maynard's attorney. Now, Kylie, I am going to question you, and please state are answering under your free will. Is that correct?"

"Yes."

"Please state your name, address, and phone number."

Kylie complied.

"Kylie, tell me about this database program you created and how you found this potential threat on someone else's computer."

Reinstadt turned to Kylie, bugging his eyes as if to say, BE CAREFUL. He rolled his lips together while waiting.

Kylie tried to sound matter-of-fact as if delivering her spiel at a pitch slam in grad school. "I have a product called OMG. Sometimes people have problems in their lives and the program helps them figure out what they might do after receiving information based on real data."

"Essentially, you are hacking into other people's computers. Is that correct?"

"Not exactly." She pursed her lips while searching for the right words.

"Let's stick to the issue here, Lane. You're leading Kylie." Reinstadt interrupted. "What she found is that we have an epic public health threat on our hands. Do you really want to noodle around with Miss Maynard about hacking? Let's get on with it!"

Kylie's forehead felt cold with sweat. She shot Reinstadt a grateful look, but his eyes were downcast studying the table.

Raymond continued, "Okay, Kylie, what did you discover?"

Kylie's phone rang in her purse. She quickly fished it out of her bag saw it was her mother calling. Ugh. Allison had a world-class talent for picking the worst moments to call. Kylie set the phone on vibrate and slid it back into her purse where it belonged.

"Sorry, that was my mother. So, a few days ago, I began to worry my developer might be misusing a program he designed for me, and I investigated him with my program, OMG. I discovered he was working with Gerry Fox, who may have had something to do with the murder of Natalie Saltz, his boss at Visiozyme. Then, I ran a report on Fox. They both had an encrypted folder titled, *Lily,* on their computers. Generally, OMG could open them, but not these two. My developer, Simon, had made them inaccessible ... which I found very weird."

Stuart stared at Kylie open-mouthed.

Reinstadt drummed his fingers on the table.

"So, I wanted to find out what he was hiding and I hired Misha to open the files and to block Simon from the program. As I'd mentioned, Simon wound up dead soon afterward. We didn't have anything to do with that, but my guess would be that his murder had something to do with what he was working on. We didn't know what it was until Misha just opened the encrypted *Lily* files this morning. The file contains a plan for the release of a deadly virus on Black Friday. I told Bill as soon as I could, figuring he'd know how to handle it. He called you guys." She cringed inside at how easily she'd called the man sitting next to her ... Bill. Kylie hoped she hadn't overstepped.

"You mentioned there was a lab, right?"

Just then, an agent blew into the room followed by Misha, whose white face appeared squeezed tight with worry.

"That's right, the agent said, out of breath. "We have an address, and we need to move on it NOW. I've already got a team, and we are going to Chinatown. Kylie and Misha, I'm sorry to say that I am going to place you under arrest for hacking."

Kiley clenched her clammy fists on her lap and looked at Misha. His jaw had tightened as if he had just realized that the thin line they'd been walking between crime fighting and getting locked up themselves had been crossed.

"Wait a minute," Bill interjected. These two came to me as good citizens because they were trying to stop a crime. You can't keep them here like prisoners. They've already helped you enormously. How about if I take responsibility and keep them in my custody? You can assign someone for protective custody if you want, but I can vouch for them."

Kylie shot Bill a grateful look in the brief moment while Stuart thought it over. Misha's face was white with terror if he was already picturing himself being deported.

Stuart was quiet for a moment, thinking it over. "I'll tell you what. I am going to let you out as cooperating witnesses. That means you will be testifying and reporting EVERYTHING you know back to us. You will be informants and will be working with us. The charges have not gone away, but let's see what you can do? Is that clear?"

"Yes of course," Kylie rushed.

Stuart narrowed his eyes at Kylie. "Don't think that this is a pass. We are starting an investigation and need to know your absolute whereabouts until this is resolved. Do you understand me?"

"Of course," she said humbled. "Anything."

Stuart looked at Misha. "I need your statement too. We will keep your laptop for now."

"No problem," said Misha, staring at the table.

Stuart turned the recorder back on and taped Misha's statement. When he was done, he switched it off. "What's the status of your citizenship?" he asked.

Misha's voice was constricted. "I came as a student, but my visa expired. I have citizenship papers but I haven't filled them out. I guess I was afraid I would be deported."

"Right. That is possible, you know. We will look into some deferred action until this is resolved. In the meantime, I suggest you start the process." Stuart turned to Reinstadt. "I think we're done here. Keep your eye on these two. Meanwhile, we will be checking them out." Stuart stood up. "Now if you'll excuse me, we have a case to solve. If you think of anything we have overlooked, call me." He looked at Kylie and Misha. "I want you both to check in with me every two hours. Clear?"

"Clear," they said in unison. Kylie asked, "Is there anything I can do?"

"No, you've done quite enough already," answered Stuart.

"But we will want to talk to you some more about your program. "Okay, kids. Stay close, and keep in touch. I mean it."

"Sure. Whatever you need." Kylie felt weak-kneed and drained.

When Stuart was gone, Reinstadt turned towards Kylie. "For all intensive purposes, I feel responsible for you two. Unfortunately, I'm afraid our meeting about OMG has to be after this all blows over. This Lily virus is our top priority right now. You can call my office and make an appointment after we get through this."

"Absolutely." she agreed, relieved to have him there and that OMG was not off the table. "What now? Should we come to your office?" Kylie secretly loved the idea of spending time in Reinstadt's orbit.

"I don't know. I'm thinking. Just follow me." He led them out of the FBI onto the plaza.

"About that. I know that you are a responsible citizen and I assume, giving your nosiness and need to vet people, that Misha is as well. How would you feel about just hanging out in the lobby of my office and staying out of trouble?"

"Not great," said Kylie. "Look. I promise to let you know our whereabouts. We haven't done anything wrong. We're just trying to help."

"I know. I know. Look, how about this? How about you text me every hour or so, just to let me know that you're okay?"

Kylie wanted to throw her arms around his neck. "That would be great! I will, I promise. No problem."

Reinstadt gave Kylie his mobile number. "Okay, then get out of here."

Kylie left with Misha trailing after her. "Now what?"

"I have no idea. Sorry about them keeping your laptop, but I'm sure that you'll get it back."

"Not such a big problem. At least I have a desktop computer at home."

Misha was quiet as they walked across Government Center to the parking lot. "Do you want a ride somewhere?" he finally asked.

Being with Misha sounded better than sitting around waiting for news. "Yes, I suppose. I could take the T and go home, but for sure I'm going to just be a wreck. I should be doing something to keep my mind off all of this."

"Yeah, I know what you mean. Maybe we could go back to Chinatown. It would be really cool to watch what's happening, yes?" Misha asked as they rode the elevator to the tier where he'd parked.

She rolled her eyes and articulated her words slowly and with pained patience as if he were a child. "No. That's a really a bad idea. Stuart was clear. We're supposed to stay out of trouble. Plus, they've got it under control. We'd be in the way or Stuart would lock us up. We could even get hurt," she answered, getting into his car. When her phone buzzed again, she pulled it from her purse to see it was an encore from her mother. She dropped her phone back inside her purse.

"Your mother again?"

"Yes." Kylie decided to ignore the phone. Suddenly she felt overwhelmed and frightened by what was happening. Misha seemed nice enough and he was a good encryption guy, but he appeared to have no common sense. She certainly wouldn't feel any safer being with him. She should go home and text Reinstadt and Stuart.

She sighed, "I think I should just go back to my place."

She gave him her address as he paid for parking. He gave her a mischievous grin. "Look in my glove compartment." He reached over and popped it open as he turned onto the street.

Kylie looked inside and saw the gray metal of a revolver handle neatly tucked over his owner's manual. There was also a small packet of tissues, festooned with an array of various colored packages of condoms. *This guy was unbelievable.*

"Which thing was it you wanted to show me?" she asked sarcastically, as the car headed down Cambridge Street.

"The gun, of course. It will make us safe if we go down there."

Was he delusional? "What planet are you on, Misha? NO. I don't think so. I'm an entrepreneur, not a cops-and-robbers person. This could be dangerous and we should stay out of it. I think you must have watched too many movies." She decided then to keep her eye on him to make sure the clown didn't erupt into some macho gunman.

It was just a short drive and soon they reached Marlborough Street. "That's it over there," she pointed to a building looking dark and unloved compared to the mansions around it.

"Why do you keep a gun?" she pointed to his glove box as he double-parked.

"Can't really say."

"Great. You're here illegally and you have a gun. Right then. Great combination. Can you say why you keep condoms in there?"

"Hah, hah. You are so funny. You know, I could get lucky sometime. Actually, it is good to be prepared." He angled his smile at her and dimpled one of his cheeks into a lopsided grin.

Kylie unbuckled her seatbelt. "Thanks for the advice. Listen, stay close to your phone. Where will you be in case anything comes up?"

"I am in Brookline. Not far, so call me. By the way, nice job explaining everything back there. Guess you are more than a pretty face, yes?" he peered over the tops of his aviator shades.

"Yes. I am, as a matter of fact. I have a body too, as you were evidently checking out. Hey, thanks for the ride." Kylie shook her head as she climbed out of the car.

"Could not help it. What can I say? You're cute."

"This really isn't the time, Misha." She shut his door a bit harder than necessary.

"Easy with that."

She let herself into her building. When she reached her landing, Kylie was horrified to find her door ajar. She was even more shocked to see a middle-aged man with a ponytail sitting on her couch, pointing a .22 at her. Stepping inside, the room reeked from his musky cologne.

"Hi, Kylie," he said, quietly. "I'm Gerry Fox. I understand you know all about me."

13

A Little Trip

Every hair on Kylie's body stood up seeing Fox in her space. "What do you want?"

"Don't be coy. Your buddy Simon gave me a demonstration of the program he wrote for you, and now I'd like to take it for a spin. Very impressive, Kylie. I did ask Simom very nicely to give it to me, but no. I couldn't get any cooperation from him." He let out a loud sigh sounding heavy with exhaustion. "I'm tired of playing nice with you whiz kids."

To make his point, he angled the gun from his lap to point at her heart. His gravelly voice stayed calm as if he were trying to sound as friendly as if they had been hanging out for years. The corners of his mouth naturally fell into a nasty scowl, so frightful, Kylie had to look away. She remembered an expression she once heard; A man of fifty is responsible for his face.

From Fox's thinning oily hair pulled into a ponytail so he'd blend into the tech world, to the deep bags under his eyes, Gerry Fox had an evil energy. His looks alone revolted her, plus he reeked from too much cologne mixed with garlic. She felt pretty sure the only reason he sat on the board of a major biotech company was due to his wealth, or he must be a hell of an actor. Then Kylie remembered Natalie Saltz who liked him ... why?

"You can kill me, but then you'll still never get it." She did her best to sound brave and reasonable, but even Kylie heard the trembling in her voice. "That'll give you three murders."

"True, but you're going to give it to me before I kill you," he said patiently as if he was explaining his point to an imbecile. He patted the couch next to him. "You're a nice kid, Kylie." He pointed to her framed diplomas on the wall. "And a Harvard MBA. You're a smart girl, so I think you can figure out it might be a very good idea for you to sit down over here next to me and demo this thing you had Simon design. What do you call it? OMG?"

"Yes," she whispered but did not move.

His friendly calm demeanor disappeared and became a growl. "Take a sea!."

Petrified, she stared at the spot on the couch where she was being ordered to sit and weighed her options. Her eyes darted as she considered making a run for it. There were two possibilities. Her front door and down the steps was one way out. There was also the fire escape, but the access to that was in her bedroom. Fox could shoot her in the back either way.

Kylie obeyed. She sat on the couch as far from him as possible, silently gagging on the stench of his cologne. Did he think the cloying, heavy smell would attract females? Kylie found him to be vile and his sickening cologne was the perfect olfactory warning of his evil.

"I can demo this program," she kept staring at the door, "unfortunately, you can't have it. That's actually your own fault. Simon was the only one who knew how to give access to anyone. Anyhow, he's gone. Tsk. Pity for you."

"You're trying my patience, Kylie. Don't insult my intelligence. I'm sure you could give me a simple log in. Now open your laptop."

Kylie slowly opened it, buying time to conjure up some distant memories of karate moves from long ago. Her muscle memory didn't fail her. Suddenly, she twisted her torso and power-elbowed him in his chin. Stunned from the impact, he lurched back into the couch. Still holding her laptop, she raised her arms and with her full force, slammed a rounded corner of her MacBook into his head. Fox's dazed look gave her the second she needed to get away. But as she rose, Fox reached out and clenched her thigh with a vise-like grip. Still, he didn't have her upper body. She swiftly twisted around, using the momentum to thrust her other knee into his jaw. Stunned, he loosened his grip on the gun and it slipped to the floor with a thud. Kylie kicked it under her couch and headed for the door. Clutching her laptop, she leaped down the stairs, taking two at a time. Fox's heavy feet pounded the stairs just a flight behind her. When Kylie reached the ground floor winded, she sprinted down the hallway towards the door. His steps were getting closer as she was unlocked the deadbolts. Suddenly, Fox landed behind her, panting. She felt his gun in her back and smelled the sickening smell of his cologne.

She felt his hot breath in her ear. "You shouldn't have done that. Just when we were getting along so well, too. Now I'm going to have to take you and your precious laptop with me. We're going to walk, and you are going to take my arm, like you like me. I will have my little friend, Angie here, just to make sure you do." He took her laptop and tucked it under his arm, and he wiggled Angie up and down on her back for emphasis.

"She doesn't like to get upset, so let's play nice, okay?"

"Let me go. You can keep my frigging laptop. It's all yours."

"Walk," he said. He held her arm tight as they headed to his black BMW sedan, parked around the corner at an expired meter. As he opened the passenger door and pushed her into the car, she noticed a trickle of blood dripping down his forehead. Kylie heard her cell phone vibrate in her purse.

"Give me that phone," he said.

She handed it to him, and they both saw Bill Reinstadt's name as the incoming caller. He eyed her with one eyebrow raised. "My, my. Reinstadt? What are you into, Kylie?"

"Nothing that concerns you."

"Well, just to be sure, you won't be needing this." He threw her phone out the window where it landed in the snow next to a tree. Kylie felt sick with fear and hopelessness. So much for texting Reinstadt. Now most likely the FBI would be after her too.

Fox headed the car towards the entrance of eastbound Storrow Drive. "Nice day for a little trip, don't you think? We finally got some sunshine. Too bad it's so cold. I can't remember November ever being this cold." he chatted, speeding the BMW East with a view of the icy Charles River to their left and the backs of fancy Beacon Hill brownstones to the right.

"Where are you taking me?" Kylie squeezed out the words, despite her throat choking them like a vise. "You know that someone will find me. Count on it."

Fox smirked as he silently turned off onto the ramp for the Tobin Bridge. He sped past Chelsea and Revere and on past all the strip malls on Route One. Then he cut over to Route 95 at the Golden Banana.

"Ever been?" he asked, pointing to it. "Great strip club. A girl like you could do well there."

Kylie didn't answer but lowered her head and cried into her woolen scarf with silent tears. Finally, Fox exited at Newburyport and sped through the town of grand houses that had once belonged to sea captions, and onward towards the beach. Shortly, they reached the long causeway out to Plum Island. Kylie had loved going there with her friends to swim in the summer, but on a raw November day, the wide expanses of brown reeds in the marshes and sky that had turned grey with clouds looked ominous and bleak as a bad omen. Once they neared the ocean, Fox slowed on a side street and turned into the driveway at a modern beach house with multiple decks that overlooked the Atlantic.

"Sit tight and don't try anything," he said, stepping out of the car. While he came around to get her, Kylie dried her eyes on her sleeve. Fox opened her door, grabbed her arm, and pulled her from the car with one hand. With the other, he held the gun. As Kylie emerged, she inhaled the pungent smell of the fishy salt air.

Frantic, Kylie looked around for a way to escape. At low tide, the empty beach with powerful gray waves slamming the shore was one option, but she would be visible and an easy target. The other choice and was the deserted street of desolate-looking weathered houses. With his gun nosed into Kylie's side, he pulled her up the icy steps, through the front porch, and unlocked the door. "Welcome home," he smirked.

The air inside smelled musty and was practically as cold as the outside, just not as windy.

"I have to use the bathroom," Kylie announced, shaking inside.

"Sure thing. I wouldn't want you to be uncomfortable. It's down the hall to the left. Do not even think about trying anything."

The bathroom had no windows. Kylie checked the medicine cabinet, careful not to make a sound. She was hoping for a razor, imagining that she could give him a good gash, but it only contained a huge assortment of vitamins and supplements. She shook her head in disbelief. Evidently, Fox was a health nut. As she came out of the bathroom, oh so quietly, she heard him on the phone. "Yeah, NOW," he said, hanging up.

She imagined Fox's reinforcement appearing at any moment for her. Apparently, Fox hadn't heard her come out of the bathroom. She flattened herself against the wall and scoped out into the living room for something to hit him with from behind while he was still on the couch fiddling with his phone. Kylie only had a moment where surprise would be on her side, and she took it. Suddenly, she charged into the room, yanked a wrought iron lamp from the table, and with all her strength, smashed it on his head from behind. She fled, taking only a second to look at him and to see blood streaming down his dazed face, this time in full force.

Kylie leaped down the icy steps, skidding as she landed on some ice. Regaining her balance, she crunched through the snow in the yard to the gravel driveway, hoping to hide behind the house next door. Fox's house was oddly quiet. In fact, the only sound was the thunderous crashing of the waves, rhythmically hitting the beach. Her heart beat wildly as the cold air stung her nostrils. After a few moments of watching the beach house, Kylie realized that Fox wasn't going to emerge. She sprinted as fast as she could down his street, dashing past a row of cottages until the street ended at the main beach. There she turned towards town, running along the salt marsh on the causeway, the cruel wind biting at her cheeks. All the while, she prayed Fox didn't come for her, and the thought made her press on. The quarter mile to the bait and tackle store on the causeway with the whipping wind felt like a ski run. Breathless and hopeful, she rushed to its door and yanked it open. A surprised clerk in a flannel shirt looked up.

"Please help me," Kylie panted. "Please. Do you have a place where I can hide? Can you call the police?" Then she noticed three rolls of duct tape and a deep-sea fishing reel loaded with heavy fishing line sitting on the counter. Perhaps this was an order that Fox had been calling in, and it was meant for her.

"Well, now," he said. "I'll take care of you, honey. You're not from around here, are ya? You get in a tumble with one of our local boys? Seen ya coming from the direction of Gerry's place. No one up there but him this time of year."

He reached for his phone just as Kylie, envisioning herself bound to a chair and gagged with the tape, turned and fled.

The road that ran along the marshes was wide open, and anyone would be able to see her running back towards Newburyport. Frantic, her heart hammered as she ran down to the salt marsh where she could hide among the tall reeds. In the summer, the muck beneath her feet would have swallowed her shoes, but it was now frozen and allowed her to walk it without sinking. Cautiously, she peeked her head above the cattails when she heard a car on the road only twenty yards away, and saw the bearded clerk, slowly driving a white pickup truck towards the beach. She crouched until she was sure that the only sound was the howling wind and the distant pounding surf. But after waiting five minutes that felt like an hour, Kylie saw the truck drive towards town, and then back again towards Fox's beach house. She squatted lower into the cattails, praying that he didn't see her. When it appeared that he had made his last pass over the causeway and the road had been empty for some time, she continued her trek towards Newburyport, her thigh muscles burning.

The ice on the inlet under the bridge looked solid. She looked around, and not seeing anyone, Kylie quickly crossed the fifteen feet of ice, leaping lightly onto her toes, just as she heard it starting to crack beneath her feet. She had learned balance from skiing, and her muscles recalled it, as she centered herself on the bumpy ice and then climbed the frozen bank to the other side. She headed towards the tiny Newburyport Airport that she remembered, just down the road. When the marsh gave way to an open field, she nimbly hoisted herself up from its banks and saw a helicopter parked near a row of tiny ultralight planes, that looked more like toys. She remembered going there for an ultralight ride years ago, with her friends. Grateful to see the light from its window, a beacon welcoming her from its squat little office, she sprinted across the field to the door of the tiny airport.

Inside, a man in a fleece jacket and wire-rims looked up, startled. "Yes? Can I help you?"

"Are you a pilot?" she asked, searching his face and trying to sound casual and not to sound breathless. Not knowing if he was in with Fox, Kylie was not going to tell him anything. All she wanted to do was get out of there.

"Yes." He studied her as if she'd descended from outer space.

"I lost my phone and am having a bit of an emergency. Can you fly me to Boston?"

He narrowed his eyes. "I suppose so. Yes, if you give me a few minutes. We can land at the airport if that works."

"That works. How much?"

"A couple of hundred dollars."

"Can you do it now?"

"Yes. Just let me get permission to land."

"Okay. Let's go." She pulled out her wallet and handed him her credit card, thinking that felt so normal during all the chaos.

He looked at the card. "Sure, Kylie. Just give me a minute to get my stuff together. I'm Mark, by the way." He ran her card and with excruciating slowness, made a stack of some papers and tucked them into a desk drawer. Unable to watch what felt like a slow-motion movie, Kylie hugged herself and paced by the window to keep herself from screaming at him to hurry up. All the while she scanned the horizon, looking for the dreaded white pickup truck. Was Mark in with them? He was slow enough that it felt like he was stalling. She considered that she might need to run, but finally, he made a phone call, he got the approval and hung up. Only when she heard the jingle of keys, and she turned to watch him grab his coat off the hook by the door.

"Okay! Ready?" he said.

Kylie nodded vigorously.

"Let's go, then."

She followed him out of the door to the helicopter, grateful that the door he opened for her was not facing the road. She climbed the steps on the wooden platform, and Mark jumped in, closed the door, and took the pilot's seat next to her. The helicopter whirred loudly, and he shouted, "Sorry, but you have to put these seat belts on," he said. He then crisscrossed her securely with the belts and snapped them in. Then finally, feeling like salvation, and as if by magic, they lifted in the air. As the helicopter headed South, Kylie saw the weathered beach houses below. A white pickup truck parked behind Fox's BMW.

Only when they were well on their way, flying over Ipswich, then the North Shore, did Kylie sat back in her seat and was able to breathe normally. She shut her eyes to keep tears from falling. Mark looked over at her.

"Ever had a copter ride before?"

She shook her head no."

"You okay?"

"Yes, I'll be fine. I just had a rough morning. How long will it take?"

"We should be on the ground in ten minutes."

Kylie wished she could enjoy the sensational view of the

coast, but inside, she was shaking from the morning's events and was still numb with cold. When they landed on the runway, she thanked Mark and speed-walked through the terminal to the taxi stand on the street. She directed the driver to near the corner where Fox had thrown her phone out the window on Berkley Street.

When they arrived, she paid the driver and hopped out. Slowly, she circled around the tree. At first, she didn't see it, but then her heart leaped as she spotted her iPhone, still in its black rubber case leaning up next to the trunk. A woman with a poodle paused by the tree, allowing her dog to sniff around it. Seeing that the dog had raised his back leg and was about to mark her phone to make it his own, Kylie snatched it up and shook off the snow. The woman gave her a strange look. "Come on, Ollie," she said.

When the phone lit up, Kylie cried with relief. She dialed Misha's number. "Hey, this is Kylie. Where are you?"

"Home. Everything okay?"

"No. Not really. Listen, it looks like I need your help after all. First, can you please change my password on OMG? Fox has my laptop. I'm going over to the Apple Store now to replace it. Can you meet me there? I can't go back to my apartment. When you dropped me off, Fox was sitting there on my couch with a gun. You won't believe what I've just been through. I'll tell you about it when I see you. I'm not sure where I should go or what I should do. I guess I'm feeling pretty shaky. I don't think I should go home, that's for sure."

"Give me ten minutes. I'll change password now. I'll meet you there as soon as I can."

Next, she texted Reinstadt. Sorry for the delay. *Fox*

kidnapped me and threw out my phone. I just found it. He has my
laptop. I am going to the Apple store now.

As she walked, Kylie checked her messages. One was from her mother, asking her to make a pie for Thanksgiving. She groaned. The others were from Bill Reinstadt with various versions of, "Hi Kylie. Where are you? Please call me immediately."

14

The Return

Reinstadt answered his cell phone on the first ring. "My God, Kylie. Are you okay?"

"Yes, I'm okay," she said, although she was unsettled and panting from her rapid trek to the Apple Store, never mind being kidnapped and escaping. But she was confused by his urgent tone. Did he somehow know about her morning?

"For all intensive purposes, we should have given you some protection right off the bat. I never should have let you go on your own. I was so worried when I didn't hear from you. You were supposed to text me every hour, remember? Are you sure that you're all right?"

"Really, I'm just fine," she said, realizing that he probably didn't know anything about her morning's activities or her whereabouts. He was probably just concerned or worried about her. Relieved, she told him the whole story.

"You poor kid. Good grief. I am so sorry. Where are you now?"

"On Boylston Street. I'm on my way to buy a new laptop."

"Listen, I'm going to call Stuart. I'll tell him where you are and have him send someone to keep you safe."

"Stuart's going to be really mad at me. He might even lock me up. I've already called Misha. He's on his way to pick me up. Can you just tell Stuart that I'm okay? I don't need a babysitter."

Reinstadt paused. "How well do you know Misha?"

"Not well. I just hired him to do some encryption work. I didn't have time to find out too much about him. Anyway, I have to see him to talk about the program. Why do you ask? Is there something that I should know?"

"Okay. Listen carefully. Meet him at the store and do what you need, but I then want you to wait outside and someone will meet you there. I'm sorry, but you need to be under protective custody. Misha could be perfectly fine, but at this point, we don't know anything for sure."

"Okay, but how will I know who this agent is? Those guys don't wear uniforms, right?"

"Right. Listen, he'll use a code word. He'll ask you if your name is Lily. How does that sound?"

"Fine."

"Okay, I will meet you over at the Bureau. I don't think you can go home. Call me when you're on your way."

Kylie agreed and jogged the last block to the Apple Store. Normally, a visit there dazzled her with the latest and greatest computers and phones, beckoning from the rows of long, wooden, display tables where they cast their spell. Going there in the middle of this crisis felt bizarre, and there was no time to gawk at new technology or to be fussy. Kylie promptly selected a laptop exactly like the one she'd left at the beach house. She was paying for it when Misha swaggered to her side, wearing his leather jacket and aviator shades.

"You okay?" he asked, searching her face.

"I think so. I'm just shook up. It was scary, but I guess I'm fine. I'm not so sure about Fox. I didn't stick around long enough to find out, but I did hit his head pretty hard with a lamp. He was bleeding a lot. Did you change my password?"

Misha shook his head in disbelief. "Unbelievable. As far as the program goes, I assume that you will be working on cloud backup, right? I wouldn't install anything on your computer at this point. Are you sure that you're okay?"

"Yeah, I'm all right. I need full access to the cloud version though."

"No problem. Here. This is for you." He handed her a folded envelope from his pocket. Kylie opened it and found a piece of paper with a thumb drive inside. It's your program," he said.

"Thanks, Misha. You've been great." She had her life back: her phone, a new computer, and her program. Her heart expanded a bit with gratitude. Maybe he wasn't as full of himself as she'd thought.

He bowed slightly. "No problem. Don't lose it."

"You do have a backup, right?"

"Of course."

Kylie angled her head towards him. "Misha, I have a

question. Seriously, why do you keep a gun in your glove compartment?"

"Again, no problem. It makes me feel safe."

"But why don't you feel safe?"

He gave her a wry smile. "Do you?"

"I see your point, but I never got a gun. Were you into something before where you needed one?"

"No. Look, it's no big deal. I can't really discuss it."

Kylie bit her lip. "Okay. Hey, I just wish I knew more about you. Learning about people is how you trust them."

"Trust is a funny thing," he said. "You either trust someone or you don't."

"You can be wrong about someone. I've trusted lots of people and I was wrong about them. Look, I trusted Simon, and look what happened."

"Maybe some time I'll talk about it, but it has nothing to do with what we're doing. You're in good hands with me."

"That's okay for now. I can't make you tell me. Listen, I'm not sure what I'm doing next, but I may need you. Will you be around?" she asked.

"Of course."

He walked Kylie outside. "You need a ride anywhere?"

"No, I think I'll just walk, thanks. I need to calm down. I might call you later, depending on what happens, okay? Say, can I ask you another question?"

"What?"

"What's up with you're being here illegally?"

"My student papers ran out and I just forgot to file. I've got the paperwork for citizenship, so not to worry. I was just worried that they'd arrest me for being illegal if I brought it into immigration. Trust me, I'm not a Russian spy if that's what you're thinking."

"I didn't think you were. Look, you better text Reinstadt and tell him where you are, just to make him happy. Kiley gave him the number and waved goodbye.

Not seeing anyone waiting for her, Kylie started walking in the direction of her apartment. Curious where Misha was headed, she looked back and watched him cross the street before getting swallowed into the crowds near the Prudential Center. Kylie stopped in front of a furniture store to wait for her contact. With nothing to do but wait, Kylie called her mother.

"Finally," Allison answered with exasperation. "Kylie, I've been trying to reach you for days, and you now you've caught me in the middle of some work. Listen, can you make an apple pie for Thanksgiving? It would help with the prep in the kitchen if you did it at home."

Her question seemed absurd after Kylie's morning adventures. She paused, not knowing how to respond.

"Kylie, is this a problem?"

"Maybe. Honestly, there's a lot going on and I'm not even sure if I'm going to make it at all. I'm just really busy."

"Just count on my daughter," she said. "This is *not* an option, Kylie. I expect you to be there, pie in hand at eleven a.m. on Thursday. You're part of this family and showing up is what you do. Don't think you can get out of this by laying one of your Gibran quotes on me."

"Fine. I'll try." "UGH," Kylie groaned after her mother hung up.

Her phone rang while she was still holding it. Startled, she answered right away. "Is this Lily?" asked a woman.

"Yes." Kylie scanned the sidewalk. She only saw a mother with a stroller, some students, and a dog walker with three poodles wearing matching puffer coats, each in a different color.

"Just head up the block towards Fairfield Street. You'll see me at the next corner by the light, talking on my phone. Stay on your phone."

As she headed towards the corner, Kylie noticed a pretty blonde woman in a black parka and jeans, holding a phone to her ear, waving as she approached.

"Kylie, I'm Janice. We're going to be hanging out for a while. My orders are to bring you in for a statement, and then you'll stay with me in protective custody. You're not under arrest of course. Are you okay with that?"

Janice looked her age or only a few years older, but she exuded confidence and a sense of calm as if everything was fine. Kylie was relieved. "Yes, but can I pick up some things at my place?"

"Sure. We'll stop by there on the way. Ordinarily, I wouldn't let you go in there, but there are some agents there now, so it should be safe. I parked up the block and we can drive. By the way, where is your buddy, Misha?"

"I don't know. I'm pretty sure that he went home. Why are there agents there?"

"As I recall, you got kidnapped from there this morning, remember?"

"Yes."

"You were supposed to be with Bill Reinstadt. What happened?"

"It's a long story."

"No more funny business, okay?" said Janice, leading her to her unmarked Ford on Boylston Street. She drove the few blocks to Kylie's apartment and parked in the rear alley. The back of the fancy brownstones looked more like tenements with fire escapes, unrelated to the elegant facades that faced the street. They walked the alley to the street where Janice surveyed for possible danger before deeming it clear. Just hours before, Fox had forced Kylie into his BMW at the same corner.

As they turned onto Kylie's street, Janice picked up the pace to her building. Kylie unlocked the door and they climbed two flights of stairs to the top floor, where Kylie could see that her door was ajar. From the hallway, they heard male voices coming from the inside. With her gun ready, Janice swung the door open with her foot, as she pushed Kylie behind her. Janice went inside to check it out and had a strange expression on her face when she beckoned Kylie into her apartment. It had been ransacked. Two agents were gingerly examining every item. They had roped off her living room as a crime scene with yellow tape as if it were for a prize fight.

Kylie's heart fell to her feet. She gasped, "Oh, my God." The contents of her bedroom drawers were strewn across the living room floor. The couch cushions were slashed, their innards were bleeding stuffing out of the gashes. Food from her small freezer had been dumped onto the floor and was starting to defrost on the linoleum.

Janice steadied Kylie with a firm hand on her forearm. "I'm sorry, hon. Wow. It's a disaster. Some Boston cops went up to your place after someone called, saying that they'd seen some guy force you down the sidewalk. When they called it in, the found out about the kidnapping and called the Bureau. This must have happened just after you left with Fox. Someone must have been watching your place. Why don't you pick some things to stay away for a few days?" Janice turned to one of the officers. "Okay with you, Brett?"

"Yeah. Just show me what you're taking before you leave," he said to Kylie.

"You're FBI?"

"Yes. We're working with the Boston Police."

"Fox was with me, so he couldn't have done this. Evidently, there were other people in on this."

"For sure," said Janice. "Don't worry, hon. We'll find them."

In her bedroom, her duffel bag which ordinarily was stored under her bed lay in the middle of the floor and unzipped with its innards exposed, as if somehow violated. She tossed in some underwear and a couple of changes of clothes that she retrieved from where they'd been scattered around the apartment. In the bathroom, the contents of her medicine cabinet had been expelled and were littering the counter and the sink. She picked her toothbrush, toothpaste, and a hairbrush out from the mess. Kylie glanced in the mirror and was shocked to see the reflection of her face, white and stricken. Her eyes were round dark orbs, and somehow, she'd sprouted tiny frown lines around her mouth that reminded her of her mother.

"Don't worry about shampoo and that kind of stuff," said Janice who had followed her into the bathroom. "We're going to a safe house that has everything you need, and if not, we can buy you stuff. Are you ready?"

"Just one more thing I want to check." Kylie went into her living room where her file folders were strewn across the floor. She thumbed through them, frantically searching for the "P" file, where she stored her passport, just in case she needed it. It was gone.

"They took my passport," she groaned.

"Oh, shit. Look, don't worry, Hon. We will report that right away. Let's get you down to the bureau, okay? It's not like you're going to leaving the country anyway, right?"

"Right," she said.

15

It Ain't the Ritz

Janice led Kylie through her bedroom window to the wrought iron fire escape. The steps had not been shoveled since it snowed as if fires would never happen in the cold. Janice apologized over her shoulder as they gingerly maneuvered the slippery staircase, "Sorry, but we need to go this way as a precaution. We don't know if you're being watched, so I didn't want to go out the front."

"No problem," Kylie said to Janice's back. "But this is a fine time to think of that. If you remember, we already went *in* the front." Kylie suddenly wasn't feeling so safe in Janice's custody, since her judgment wasn't very rational, but she obediently followed her across to the alley to her car since she had no alternatives.

"Nothing's happened to you with me, right?"

"So far. It hasn't even been an hour though."

"Hop in," Janice said, unlocking Kylie's door.

Kylie brushed the snow off her shoes. "Wow," she said, admiring the computer equipment mounted on the dashboard before throwing her bags in the back. Once they both were buckled in, Janice tore down the alley to Berkley Street that fed directly into Storrow Drive, where only hours before, Kylie been driven past the same view as a captive.

Janice was quiet for a while and then admitted, "You're right, Kylie. That was a dumb thing for me to do. I promise, no more mistakes."

"Thanks. I will hold you to that."

Within minutes, they were back at Government Center. Janice lurched the car into a parking spot on the Street, and they rushed to the Bureau.

Stuart met them in the same conference room, and Kylie told him everything that had transpired since earlier that morning.

"I should have locked you up. But never mind that now. We will revisit it later. What can you tell us about Fox's beach house?"

Kylie described the house and the street, wishing she had OMG set up on her new computer. She remembered the envelope Misha had given her. "Do you want to try OMG? She asked him. "It might help."

"Thanks, but at this point, we can already look up this kind of stuff. What do you remember about the guy at the bait and tackle place?"

"I was just there for a couple of seconds, so not much. He was bald. Kind of a burly guy. I think he was wearing a plaid shirt and had a reddish scraggly beard. He might have been in his forties, or maybe his fifties. I can't say for sure, but I do know that he drives a funky white pickup truck."

"What kind of a truck was it?"

"I don't know. A big one. It was kind of rusty. Maybe a Ford or a Chevy?"

Stuart punched a number into his phone. "Terry, we need some backup in Newburyport. Can you put some people on this? I'll meet with you in five for a briefing."

He turned to Kylie and shook a stern finger at her. "I want you to stay out of trouble. Do you think you can possibly do that?"

"Hey, this wasn't my fault, but yes, I'll try my best. What's happening with Fox's lab? Did they find anything?"

"We'll let you know," he said. "Okay, Janice, take her, and I do NOT want her going anywhere alone else until we clear this up. Understood?"

"Yes, sir." Janice nodded. She smiled at Kylie, but even her friendly grin couldn't distract Kylie from the fact that she was undeniably in danger.

"This is just protective custody, right?" she asked, aware that she was practically a prisoner.

"Exactly," said Janice. "Let's consider this more like hanging out together, okay?"

Kylie gave her an incredulous look. "Nothing personal, since you seem pretty cool, but it's not exactly like we're friends."

"Here's the poop. Ever heard the expression, fake it until you make it?" asked Janice. "Honey, you might not think I'm your friend, but when it comes down to it, I might be the best friend that you have right now."

"Right. We'll be fake friends then."

Janice extended her hand to Kylie who shook it. "Nice to meet you, fake friend. Now let's get you into the car."

Once buckled in, Janice wound the car around some streets to make sure that no one was following them before taking to ramp onto Route 93. Kylie relaxed a little into her seat as they crossed from Boston into Somerville and neared the exit for Kendall Square.

"Do you think we can stop for a sandwich or something? I'm starving," asked Kylie, longing for the familiarity of Jolt, a good cup of some strong coffee and panini. The thought made her mouth water.

"No can do. We'll be at the safe house soon, and there should be a little food there. I'll make you something."

Kylie's voice dripped with sarcasm, "Thanks, Mom."

Janice chuckled. "You're pretty independent, aren't you? Think of me as more like a friendly babysitter with a gun. Look, Kylie, I know this is hard for you, but it's pretty obvious that you're in danger. I'm watching you for your own good. You do understand that, right?" She fixed her bright blue eyes on Kylie. "What will help us the most is letting us do our jobs. Understood?"

"I do. I just think that I can do something and I shouldn't be cooped up. You realize that if I hadn't run OMG and found out about Fox and this Lily virus, then you'd never have known until it was too late. If I hadn't gone back to my apartment, you'd never have known about Fox's beach house or how crazy he is. Think of me as an asset."

Janice thought about this for a moment. "True, and we're grateful, but since you did find this out, and especially now, you need protection. You are done. End of story. Got it?"

"Yes, I've got it," Kylie said glumly. "How long have you been doing this, anyway?"

"I've been in the field for about a year now."

A year? Kylie wondered if that was supposed to make her feel safe, which it didn't. She was now positive that she'd do just as well on her own. "So, you're a rookie. What made you decide to join the FBI?"

Janice answered, keeping her eyes on the road. "My dad was a teacher and he was killed by a bomb that some psycho threw at his school about five years ago. I could have become a cop, but the FBI seemed more far-reaching and was a place where maybe I could do some good and prevent terrible things from happening. I know it's not going to bring my dad back, but I feel good about what I'm doing."

"Wow. That's tough about your dad," said Kylie, looking at Janice with new appreciation. They might be close in age, but Kylie suddenly felt younger since Janice had actually experienced suffering and pain. Other than losing Simon, Kylie had never even known anyone who'd died. Her life had been pretty soft and now by comparison, she felt like an inexperienced child. Even with Janice's new mystique, Kylie wasn't so sure that she could keep her safe.

Janice cut over two lanes to exit in Medford. She drove through the town and then veered off towards Arlington. She turned onto a tree-lined side street with older duplex houses and turned into a driveway of a tiny house about halfway down the block. She parked the car.

"Okay, kiddo. We're here."

Janice led Kylie into the back door which opened to a mud room. The floor was imitation marble linoleum tiles, yellowed from age and some grimy-looking white walls that probably hadn't been painted in twenty years. Janice dead-bolted the lock and threw her parka on a hook, revealing a gun in a holster around her waist. She was slim like Kylie, but Janice had a sturdier build as if she'd been a serious athlete or a cheerleader.

"Put your coat over there." Janice pointed to a hook. "Bring your stuff. I'll show you your room and you can make yourself at home." She led Kylie through a sunny yellow, but 1960's style kitchen to a long hallway with worn plank floors and old etched-glass ceiling light fixtures. At the end of the hall, Janice stopped outside a bedroom with the door open. "It's small, but it works. I'll get you some towels and put them in the bathroom, which is across the hall. Sorry it's so bare bones."

She left Kylie alone. The room reminded her of a monastery. Its stark white walls backdropped a cot and a dresser with its veneer peeling like tongues. All it needed was was a large wooden cross on the wall to complete the effect. She opened the rickety blinds and gazed out at a postage-stamp backyard edged with a rusty chain link fence. The place gave Kylie the creeps. It looked like the perfect place for a shoot-out or a murder. Anxious to access OMG, she gingerly sat on the faded chenille bedspread that covered the lumpy-looking rollaway.

As she removed her laptop box from the bag, Janice hollered from the kitchen. "I found some eggs in the fridge. Is a cheese omelet okay?"

"Sure. That sounds great." Kylie yelled back, admiring the beautiful Apple packaging. The clean white box, pristine and well-constructed, gave her a certain comfort in her shabby surroundings. She unpacked the laptop and carefully went through the setup.

"What's your internet password?" she yelled into the kitchen.

"Aftermath," Janice said and spelled it out.

Kylie was about to install OMG when Janice called her into the kitchen for lunch.

"This looks great," said Kylie, sitting down at the old Formica table, her appetite suddenly raging. Janice had set out worn plastic plates with omelets and buttered white bread toast cut into triangles. Kylie hadn't had white bread since she was in third grade when her mother decided that they would only eat whole grains.

"Do you drink coffee?" Janice filled her cup and held up a mismatched empty one for Kylie.

"Definitely. Just black is fine, thanks." She took a bite of toast while Janice set her coffee on the table and sat down across from Kylie.

"So, what now?" asked Kylie. She cut a bite of her omelet and popped it into her mouth. It was perfect, with cheddar cheese oozing out from the middle. It was possibly the best she'd ever tasted.

"I'm not sure. They're trying to solve this thing, so hopefully, you won't need to stay here too long."

"No matter what you say, I feel like I'm locked up."

"Look, like I told you, you're not locked up. In fact, you don't even have to be here. Staying here is for your protection and if you chose to go out, you can, but we can't make sure that you are safe. Maybe you should think of it as a little vacation. It ain't the Ritz honey, but hey…"

Janice's phone beeped with a text, and she pulled it out of her pant pocket. Two lines over her nose deepened into a "W", and she pursed her lips as she rapidly typed a response with both thumbs. When she set the phone down, she stared at Kylie.

"They found Fox dead at his beach house. He was shot."

16

Circling Back

Stunned, Kylie sunk back into her chair. She remembered the man at the bait and tackle shop. Was it him? Based on how he'd come after her in his truck, he was definitely involved somehow. He could be Fox's killer, but Kylie had the impression that he worked for Fox, so it seemed more likely that it would have been someone else. Since Fox was killed shortly after her apartment had been ransacked, it now looked like there were several people involved. But who? Would whoever it was come after her too? And why would they release a deadly virus? None of it made sense. Her stomach churned. Her omelet, that only a moment ago had seemed so appealing, now it looked like a slab of congealed yellow rubber. She couldn't eat it.

"Did they find my laptop?" she asked. "I had to leave it at the beach house when I escaped."

"I'll ask." Janice texted again.

"Actually," said Kylie, opening an app on her phone. "Come to think of it, I can find out where it is myself with an app."

The app displayed red concentric circles radiating around the red dot in the center. Kylie was confused. She'd left her laptop at Fox's beach house in Plum Island about fifty miles away, but it clearly beaconed its location to be just five miles from where they were, in Kendall Square. She leaned in closer to make sure.

"What's the matter?" asked Janice.

"I think something's wrong with my app. It's saying that my laptop's in Kendall Square."

"Oh, shit. We can't discount that someone took it there. It was most likely Fox's killer. Let me see." Janice held her hand out for the phone.

Kylie plopped it into her palm. Janice enlarged the image and pointed. "Look, it's here on Main Street."

Kylie looked again. A shock ran through her when she realized where the red circles were radiating from. "Oh, no. It's at Visiozyme! Fox was a board member there, and it's where Simon, a kid who was mixed up in all of this, used to work. Kylie bolted upright. "Duh! It's a biotech company. Who else could so easily design a biological weapon? I have no idea why they'd do that, but if they did, and if they have my laptop, they can also find my phone and our location too."

"Kylie, listen carefully. You have to turn off the app on your laptop immediately, and your phone too. Then we're going to get rid of your phone," commanded Janice. "Let's just hope that whoever has your laptop hasn't already figured this out and is on the way over here." She pushed her chair back and went to the living room window and stood to the edge of the translucent white drapes where she could get a good view of the street. Kylie joined her on the other side but only saw the cars of a few neighbors parked in a couple of driveways. Otherwise, the street lined with tiny bungalows looked quiet, devoid of people and cars. Janice speed-dialed a number while Kylie turned off her app.

"Stuart, there's a problem. Kylie located her laptop at Visiozyme through some app, and she's afraid they're going to be able to locate her."

Janice clenched the phone to her ear and paced back into the kitchen as she listened.

"Yes, I do," she said, finally, then added, "Yes. Right now." Janice hung up and quickly set the plates in the sink, not bothering to rinse them. "Okay, get your things, and hurry! We're going to another safe house."

Kylie sprinted to her room and threw everything into her bag, leaving the packaging for her laptop on the chenille spread. Her hands felt clammy as she rushed towards the back door. Janice was already waiting in her parka, and tossed Kylie her jacket. Within minutes, they were buckled in the Ford. Janice jerked the car into reverse and then sped down the empty back streets before reaching Arlington Center, which looked as calm as any normal Monday mid-afternoon. Kylie knew the town. It was just a couple of miles from where she'd grown up. She'd always loved its vibrant main drag with a plethora of restaurants and mom and pop stores, but it now looked oddly foreign. She considered that to anyone who might notice them, she and Janice must appear like just two friends driving down the street, possibly going for coffee...certainly not like two terrified women running from a possible killer. She vowed never to assume things were as they appeared at first. If she couldn't trust her eyes anymore, was there anything that she could trust?

Janice headed across Mass. Ave. onto Pleasant Street. Suddenly she did a crazy swing of the steering wheel, swerving the car onto a side street, laying a small patch on the pavement. She sped up a hill. So much for looking like two friends leisurely going for coffee.

"What the hell was that?" asked Kylie who braced herself against the car door.

Janice watched her rearview mirror. "Duck down! Someone's following us." She turned right at the top of the hill and floored the gas pedal. "Hold on."

Kylie slid down in her seat, but inched up enough so that she could see out the window as they flew by the old stately homes surrounded by graceful trees. Janice swerved to take a sudden right, heading back down the hill to Pleasant Street.

"I don't see them," Janice reported, taking another look in the side mirror. "We might have lost them." They were soon on Route 2, heading away from the city. Kylie sat up in her seat, her heart still beating hard. Janice glanced nervously at her rearview mirror as she sped up the highway, approaching Lexington. "Change of plans. Better hold on." Janice veered into the right lane and exited a minute later to a long ramp, backed up with cars waiting for the light at the top. She swerved onto the shoulder, the gravel crackling against the car as she circumvented the line of cars. People honked and gestured with their middle fingers.

"Sorry about that, but they're back. I hate this friggin' light, but I don't want to turn on a siren," Janice explained. "It's the downside of using an unmarked car."

Kylie had exited on that ramp hundreds of times —it was only blocks from her parents' house. Now she shrunk back down into her seat, bracing herself with her hands on her legs and her head down as if she were prepping for an airplane crash. She meditated on her knees, praying that her parents hadn't seen her face. It would be just her luck if they were n the line of cars coming home from somewhere and she and Janice had passed them in the lineup. She expected her mother to call her any second.

At the very top of the ramp, Janice cut in front of the other cars all the way from the shoulder and turned left onto the overpass where she could see the traffic below. "Sorry about this, but give me your phone," she said, holding out her hand.

"Ugh. Not again. Do you have to? The app is on my laptop you know. This is kind of ridiculous." Kylie groaned.

"Unfortunately, yes. The phone has more tracking capabilities that make you findable, and we have to assume that they have the technology." Janice rolled down her window.

"I already turned the app off. Isn't that enough?"

"Possibly, but we don't know what they have. Let's just be sure, okay?"

Kylie handed Janice her phone, and for the second time that day, she grimaced as she watched her phone fly out of a car into the snow onto the side of the road; this time to surely meet its death.

"Good girl," said Janice, scanning the highway below. "That son of a bitch *is* following us. He just got off at the exit. Hold on tight!"

Janice floored the car and sped over the bridge, skidding down the ramp onto Route 2, heading back towards town. Janice punched a key on her phone, that was mounted on the dashboard. "Hey, it's Janice. We are heading East on Route 2 from Lexington, and we're being followed. A slight change in plans. I'm taking her to location three. Can we get some backup there?" Her voice sounded calm as if it were just, ho-hum, yawn, just another typical day at work. It had no correlation to Kylie's anxiety, which was off the charts. Open-mouthed, Kylie regarded Janice as if she were from Mars.

"You got it," a woman answered."

Janice sped towards the end of Route 2 and stopped at a light to turn onto Fresh Pond and glanced over at Kylie. "I think we're okay, but probably not for long."

Just then, an SUV came up inches from Janice's rear bumper.

"Get down!" Janice screamed. She checked her side mirror and veered around the cars waiting at the light onto Fresh Pond. The SUV followed by attempting to drive onto the median strip, but without much luck. It was struck broadside on the driver side by a Toyota that couldn't stop in time. The crash made a terrible explosive sound.

"I need to get you out of here," said Janice. She called in the accident as she sped up towards the MBTA station.

Kylie put her hand over the African drum circle beating inside her chest. She could hardly breathe.

"You okay?" asked Janice, checking her out when she stopped at a light.

"No," said Kylie, needing some air. A headache rooted in her forehead and began shooting branches into her temples. She silently unbuckled her seat belt before the light changed. "Janice, nothing personal, but I honestly don't think I'm any safer with you than on my own. Thanks for everything, though. I mean, really. You're a hell of a driver. Plus, you make an excellent omelet." Before Janice could stop her, Kylie grabbed her bag, opened the door, and hopped out. "Hope to see you again sometime. Really, I do mean that. You're the best fake friend that I've ever had."

Janice didn't look amused. She looked as if she was considering reaching for her gun, but instead, tried reason. "Kylie, don't do this. You're making a big mistake. On your own, you're totally unprotected. Helpless, really. Look what happened to you this morning. You saw how we were being followed. Do you think that they're just going to forget about you?"

"It doesn't matter if they can't find me. And trust me, they are *not* going to find me. I'll check in, I promise. They think I'm with you, and we have this chase thing going on so whoever it is will be looking for your car, not me lost in Boston somewhere on my own. I think it's best for me just to disappear. Don't *worry*. I survived this morning, didn't I? I'll be fine."

Janice's blue eyes pleaded, "Kylie, wait. Listen to me. You're in danger. You're being pretty naïve if you think you can fight this by yourself. I can keep you safe." She checked the rearview mirror as she talked. "They could exit and pull up behind us any second."

"I'll take my chances. Look, the person I trust most is myself and I know that I'll be fine. I should go now."

"Where're you headed?" the faint lines on Janice's forehead arched.

Kylie shrugged. "I'm not sure."

"As soon as you get there, promise me that you'll call Stuart." Janice shook her head with exasperation. "Alright, go. But hurry up and disappear. You're out in the open here. I don't like this at all."

Kylie closed the door and shouted over her shoulder as she fled. "You've got it—I promise that I'll check in." She ran towards Alewife Station where she could pick up the Red Line into town. On top of already feeling traumatized by everything that had gone on what she was sure was the worst day of her life, Janice had frightened her even more. Although she tried not to turn all the way around, she shot nervous looks over her shoulder, just to make sure it was clear. She trotted to the station where she ducked into the first door she could find.

In two hours, the nearly-empty MBTA station would be full of rush hour traffic, but now, Kylie thought the glass, structure looked like an abandoned space station. Slowly, her stomach muscles unclenched and her breathing returned to normal, but she still felt shaky. She eyed some food vendors for her first order of business. She hoped food would help her headache and her growling stomach. She bought a bagel sandwich at Dunkin Donuts, planning to eat it on the train, but devoured it on the platform as she nervously watched for trouble until her train arrived moments later.

She texted her whereabouts to Stuart on the ride to Downtown Crossing where she climbed the steep steps to Washington Street. *On my way into Boston on the Red Line.* She headed past the shops to a Staples a short walk from

Reinstadt's office, and where she'd take care of her first order of business. With a new disposable phone in her bag, she marched up State Street to his building. The battleship grey sky was already slipping into an early November sunset as she entered the marble and gilt lobby. She rode the elevator to 15th floor.

"May I help you?" asked Reinstadt's receptionist. She was a plump woman in her mid-thirties, with an apparent case of amnesia who didn't appear to recall Kylie from that morning.

"I'm Kylie Maynard. I need to talk to Bill Reinstadt for a minute. Is he in?"

She squinted at Kylie's two-toned hair and duffel bag. "What's this about?"

"He'll know. Is he here?"

She lowered her eyes. "I'm not sure. Why don't you have a seat and I'll check."

Kylie dutifully sat on one of the upholstered chairs at the other end of the room and watched the receptionist sigh as if her workload was insurmountable, and Kylie had put her out. Then she resumed her work on her computer. She texted Stuart: *In Reinstadt's waiting room.* After five maddening minutes that Kylie spent staring hard enough to burn holes in the receptionist's mousepad, she cursed silently. She headed up to her desk. *Idiot.*

"Excuse me, but this is time sensitive." Kylie leaned her hands on the desk. "In fact, I probably should have told you, but it's an emergency."

"As I said, I'm not sure that he's here."

Kylie gave her a pained smile. "Would you please check?"

"I will, as soon as you go sit down." She pointed a long red fingernail to the other side of the room.

Kylie crossed her arms around her waist and glared at her. "I won't sit down until you call him." She heard the rising irritation in her words. After years of watching her mother, an expert role model for being commanding, the lessons kicked in. Kylie figured that after the day she'd had, she deserved respect, if not a little kindness. If the receptionist didn't do something any minute, she might lose it and start yelling. She'd hardly be to blame. She eyed the door which led to the offices and considered storming it, but the receptionist shook her head with exasperation and picked up the phone.

"I have a Kylie Maynard here to see you," she said. "Okay, sure. I'll tell her." She hung up and beamed pleasantly if Kylie had suddenly transformed into Julia Roberts. "You can go in the conference room now." She pointed the red fingertip again and then returned her gaze to her computer screen. Kylie looked over her shoulder as she walked past, getting a glimpse of the spike-heeled shoes that the receptionist was purchasing on some website.

Kylie pulled out a chair and sat at the conference table. She removed her new phone from her bag, but before she had time to play with it, Reinstadt hurried in the room like a wind gust and sat down next to her. She was close enough to feel his special brand of magical Reinstadt energy vibrating off of him. "Good God, Kylie, what happened? Are you all right?"

"Yes, I'm fine." Suddenly the sun had come out. "Did you hear about everything else that's gone on today?"

"Illuminate me."

Kylie recanted everything that had happened since that

morning. He slowly shook his head from side to side and finally responded, "I did hear that. Stuart's been keeping me apprised. What I don't understand, however, is why you left Janice. You're lucky that you're not in custody. She was assigned to keep you safe." His eyes narrowed into slits as Reinstadt swiveled his chair to look at her.

"I know, but I didn't *feel* safe with her. She's only a little bit older than me and she hasn't been an agent very long, so what's the point? Just because she carries a gun doesn't mean that I'm going to be safer with her. I think I can do more good if I'm on my own. I'll be fine. Look at everything that already happened, and I lived through it. I'm sure that the worst is over. You know that Fox is dead, right?"

"Kylie, you have illusions of grandeur. And, you rationalize everything. I realize we don't know the full extent of this yet, but it's not your job. You're a civilian and you should be protected. Janice is a trained agent."

Oh, that reminds me. She texted Stuart: *I'm In Reinstadt's office.* Then Kylie shrugged and changed the subject. "Has the FBI found out any more about the Lily virus?"

"They sent a team down to Chinatown this morning and found the lab. It was the whole deal; microscopes, centrifuges, lots of beakers and test tubes, and an empty tabletop refrigerator with the door swung wide open. Everything was wiped clean. If there's a virus, it's now out there somewhere, and we don't know where, who has it, or why anyone would want to do this."

"Oh, my God," said Kylie.

Reinstadt laughed ironically, "That's what I was thinking. Do you have access to your program?"

Kylie pulled the thumb drive from her purse. "Tadah!" But her voice held the fear of what she might find, instead of triumph.

17

Taiwan to Boston

Long before prostitution became illegal in Taiwan, Lily's mother Jiang, worked as a bargirl, a job Jiang's father had found for her. For months, he sent messages from the island where they lived to a connection in Taipei and it was arranged. Jiang's mother waved goodbye at their doorway and he took Jiang on into town where they would catch a boat. When they docked in Taipei, he left her with the manager at the bar. In this new and frightening world, Jiang was expected to provide "comfort" services to American soldiers along with their drinks. She took one look at the dark, shabby bar and pleaded with her father to take her home...but he told her that it was time to help support her family and that was that.

Jiang had no knowledge of how to act or what to do. The manager, a woman as old as her mother, taught her how to dress, how to eat politely, and how to smile at the customers when she sat on their laps. She taught Jiang what to say to get men to pay for her. After two weeks of training, Jiang was put to work. Each week, the manager would deduct rent from her pay for the rooming house where Jiang shared a bed with two other girls. Jiang always sent the rest of the money home.

It wasn't long before Jiang's belly became swollen with a child. It was unseemly for her to be a bargirl in her maternity clothes and the manager sent her home in shame. When Jiang's baby girl was born, she named her Lily. Her father beat Jiang for this failure and as soon as her wounds healed, he sent men to her room so that Jiang could still support the family.

By the time Lily was ten, she'd received very little schooling, although Jiang made sure that she learned to learn to read and write, sending her to the only neighbor she knew with those skills. During the day, Lily helped with the cleaning, cooking, and her lessons. In her spare time, she'd watch what her Jiang did with the men through a keyhole. Occasionally, Lily saw the men beat her mother and she wept for both her mother's pain and humiliation as well her own helplessness. She vowed that one day, she'd be powerful. She knew that she'd never let men beat her. She would kill them first.

Even at ten, she'd seen how men looked at her perfect almond eyes, creamy skin offset by her sheet of black hair. Her body was slender and beautiful as a budding flower. She'd glare back at any man who stared at her just a moment too long. She didn't want her mother's life.

The best thing in her world was the stray cat that came slinking around for food. There wasn't much left over, but she always saved something in her bowl for him. The grey cat sat by the door to their house, watching for her with golden eyes. When Lily appeared, he would pace impatiently until she set the dish before him and he'd devour its contents. Then, she would sit on the stoop and hold him as he gave himself a bath with his pink paws. She had never loved anything like that cat, who rubbed against her and purred when she caressed his belly. Still, the cat remained unnamed, since Jiang wouldn't allow Lily to bring him inside.

When Lily was fifteen, Jiang said that was time for Lily to go to work too. She took Lily on the boat to Taipei, as her father had once taken her. She searched the streets for the bar where she'd worked, but it had been torn down and replaced by a parking garage. They walked the streets where big buildings had sprouted in her absence, while Jiang tried to figure out what to do. She knew that Lily was hungry. She stopped at a plaza outside of a large office building where she'd noticed some people sitting on the concrete eating their lunches. She pulled a container of spiced chicken and rice from her bag and then handed Lily some chopsticks.

While they were eating, a woman about Jiang's age sat down nearby. As Jiang talked to Lily, the woman kept looking over at them. Finally, she called out, "Is your name Jiang?"

Jiang squinted at her. "Li Min?"

Suddenly Jiang and Li Min hugged and screamed. Lily was shocked to see her mother behave like this. Had her mother had friends? When the two women finally calmed down, Jiang introduced Li Min to Lily as one of the girls she'd shared a room with when she'd worked in Taipei.

Li Min told Jiang about how the bar had been closed when the government changed its laws, making prostitution illegal.

The girls were let go and had to find other work. Li Min been lucky and had married Wang Wei, a karate master at a martial arts studio.

Jiang told her how she'd brought Lily over on the boat to find work. Li Min was quiet for a moment. "Do you know how to clean and cook?" she asked Lily.

Lily nodded solemnly. Of course. That had been her job while her mother worked.

"I will take you to the home where you can live with us and clean and cook until you find work," Li Min told Lily.

"What do you pay her?" interjected Jiang.

"We can only give her a place to live."

"No," said Jiang.

"It's the best I can do, but perhaps my husband, Wang Wei will teach her karate."

It was agreed. Lily and Jiang met Li Min later that day at the address that Li Min had scribbled on a piece of paper.

* * *

At five 0'clock, Lily and Jiang strolled down the lantern-lined crowded street in an older section of Taipei to Li Min's House. The packed narrow streets were with colorful storefronts with open-air stalls. Each house was painted in a different pastel color and on top, had a living space with an open porch. They had iron bars to keep out burglars, giving the impression of jail cells. Finally, they found the sign for Dragon Martial Arts. It was on the street level of a red house and they could see the open-air dojo. Inside, children wearing white gis with assorted belt colors were performing katas in unison with their teacher.

Jiang rang the buzzer on for the door that led to the steps that would take them upstairs. After a short wait, they heard someone coming down the steps and Li Min swung the door open and invited them inside.

Upstairs, the main room looked grand to Lily. It had two black leather couches and a large TV on the wall. She gaped at this since few people in her village owned a TV. Next to it was a floor to ceiling aquarium, filled with golden koi, as big as cats. Lily gasped. It was the finest home that she'd ever seen. The main room was bigger than the entire dark apartment where she'd lived with her mother.

"You like?" asked Li Min.

Not trusting her voice, Lily just nodded.

"Good. I will show you where you sleep."

Lily and Jiang followed her down a long white hallway to a room, hardly bigger than a closet, and just big enough to hold a cot. Still, it looked so clean and it had a real door, not just a hanging curtain-like she'd had at home. What else did she need? Jiang beamed at Li Min. It was agreed. Lily hugged her mother goodbye.

"Time for you to cook dinner," said Li Min when Lily was gone. "I will show you to the kitchen."

* * *

Every dawn, Lily prepared breakfast before cleaning the dojo. She loved the spotless, open space of the dojo with its wooden floor and mirrored wall in the front. It was empty in the morning, but later in the day, it would be filled with students practicing their drills and routines. The side walls had two framed prints: one of a ferocious dragon and one of a crane. The sparring room in the back had hooks that held facemasks and padding. This more private room was dark with no windows. It was only for the more serious students and had a certain mystery of earned privilege. She wondered if she would ever be good enough to use that room.

After cleaning the dojo and before she was free to take lessons, Lily had to prepare meals and clean Li Min's house. It was hard schedule for a young girl, but she looked forward to her karate class at the end of each day where she joined the class. Sometimes after dinner, she'd get some private help with Wang Wei.

As a white belt beginner, Lily didn't even know how to make a fist. In her first class, Wang Wei patiently unclenched her slender fingers and reorganized them, placing her thumb on the outside. He explained she was less likely to break it this way when she threw a punch. Lily quickly learned her blocks and punches through his repetitive drills, taking inspiration from the energy in the class as they would loudly kiai in military unison. She was also inspired by the image of the dragon on the wall. Remembering how her mother was treated, she tried to absorb its fierceness, mentally defeating her mother's attackers with every punch she threw into the air. She learned her katas and within a year, she'd tested out of three belts. Lily's technique was impeccable and by the time she was eighteen, she'd earned her black belt. Wang Wei was as proud of her as a daughter and encouraged her to become a master.

One night, Li Min sent her to the market to get extra food for dinner since they were to have company. It was nightfall, but even though her neighborhood was sometimes tough, Lily was not afraid of the dark. She could take care of herself. She cut behind the houses to the alley where she would save time. As she walked, she heard the loud screams of a woman begging someone to leave her alone. There were violent crashes. Lily ran towards the sounds and as she turned into someone's yard, she saw a young, hoodlum, attempting to rape one of Lily's neighbors at knifepoint.

Without thinking, Lily kicked the knife from his hand, punched his solar plexus, and kneed his groin. He moaned with pain, crashing into a row of trash cans as he doubled over. In another swift kick to his knees, she took him down to the ground. Lily told the woman to remove her pantyhose. She obliged while Lily rolled the man over onto his stomach. Lily tied the pantyhose like handcuffs around his wrists while the woman called the police.

When a squad car arrived, the police took the man away. Moments later a second car arrived to take the women to the station to make a statement where a reporter interviewed Lily. The next morning, there was a big photo of her in the paper with an article about how she'd saved her neighbor.

The following day, Wang Wei went downstairs to the dojo to do paperwork in his office. Lily was cleaning the studio bathroom when she heard a visitor jingle the door and walk across the dojo with heavy footsteps. She was surprised since people always removed their shoes before entering and moved silently across the wooden floor. An hour later Wang Wei yelled for Lily with an unusual request. *Could she come to his office to talk?*

Afraid that something was wrong, Lily sped down the hallway to his office. She was surprised to see an American, sitting with Wang Wei in one of the two chairs in front of the black lacquer desk. Wang Wei told Lily to sit down, and he introduced Gerry Fox to her as she took the other chair. Wang Wei, who spoke English moderately well, explained that Mr. Fox was in Taipei on business and he wanted a bodyguard at home. Mr. Fox had seen the article in the paper and was impressed. If Lily was interested in the job, he would take her back to the states, where he promised to educate her and teach her English in exchange for her work.

Lily took in the man's greying ponytail and scowl. He didn't look like a nice man, but she could take care of herself. America! She would go to school and could become an American. She smiled bowed as much as she could in her chair. Yes. She would go.

18

Steve Hahn

Meeting women had been Steve Hahn's main, but very elusive life challenge. Given the mostly male climate where he worked at Visiozyme, plus his crazy hours, he found it nearly impossible to have a social life. The only thing left was online dating, which proved fruitless. Realizing that his romantic future was hopeless, he'd given that up too. But now, a month later, he wrapped his arms around Lily from behind as she selected a bottle from her temperature controlled wine vault. He held her as close as a teddy bear while burying his face in her shiny black mane, inhaling her spicy scent. He inched his hands up and felt her breasts, warm under her cashmere sweater. The novelty of holding her was heady; not something that Lily had allowed. The move felt empowering and daring.

But he didn't care anymore about her rules. He had needs too. It was time that he laid down some rules of his own.

Lily froze, gently extricating herself as she slowly turned around. Her red dagger nails were wrapped around the bottle of white wine that she'd chosen. She nodded towards the table in the kitchen as if she wished he'd stop touching her and just get on with it.

"There's sushi waiting. Here, open this." She said coldly, handing Hahn the bottle.

"Anything for you milady." he took it to a counter where Lily had already laid out a corkscrew. Even though he'd been living there for a month, he still didn't know where anything was. He fumbled around with it, finally succeeding in removing the cork, and poured wine into the two elegant stemware glasses that Lily had set out. Unlike his own wine glasses that he'd bought at Target, the crystal was top notch, like every detail in her house. He handed her a glass and raised his in a toast. "To a new phase.

She eyed him with suspicion and clinked his glass before taking a swallow.

Since the first night that he'd been with Lily, everything in his life had become weird and wild, starting with food. The cupboards were filled with exotic Asian ingredients; not that Lily ever cooked. It had been one Asian take-out meal after another. He'd grown tired of eating cold leftovers out of little white boxes for breakfast and began stopping at Starbucks for a coffee and muffin on the way to work. Lunch was easier since Visiozyme's lunchroom offered him some sense of normalcy. Hamburgers and fries in the lunchroom were about the only thing that tied him to his prior life. Hamburgers and work.

He had never dreamt that his life could be so crazy. It had started with Fox nosing around, wanting to build a nasty virus. Hahn had no taste for killing people. He was just a project manager and programmer. But Fox had pressured him, promising him a management position with a hefty check if he cooperated, for starters, the delivery of a pink slip if he refused. Hahn was sure this virus thing would never be deployed, so what the hell. The cash was going to make a healthy down-payment on a sweet little condo he'd been eyeing in Cambridge.

Only a few days later, Lily, the smoking-hot Chinese wife of the CEO, bumped into him in the lobby on her way to a shareholder's meeting, spilling his coffee all over his new ski jacket. The next day, a replacement jacket, more tasteful and expensive, arrived in his office. There was a card.

Sorry about your jacket. I hope this makes it up to you.
I'm going through a divorce and am very lonely. Come to dinner tonight?
Lily

She'd included her address on the bottom. Of course. She could spill anything she liked on him. Who was Steve to deny her a little company? This was like a pot of sunshine lighting up his office.

He was in a good mood all day, even being civil to his office mate Simon, the nerdy twerp who was helping him with some code. Well, why not? Why shouldn't he have a date? He was a nice enough looking guy. He imagined the series of romantic dinners, ski trips to Vermont, and of course, lots of hot sex that would ensue. In anticipation of the date, he stopped home after work and changed from his usual blue jeans and polo shirt into a cotton button-down shirt and sweater with khakis. Then he stopped at the corner wine shop and picked up a bottle of Cabernet before driving his Jeep out to Newton, singing oldies with the radio.

When Steve found the large Tudor house, he parked in front and checked himself in the mirror in the pull-down visor. He combed his brown hair out of his chestnut-colored eyes that seemed to be sparkling. He ambled up the walk and rang the doorbell. It wasn't in the usual place on the door frame but had been installed as one of the eyes of the carved relief wooden dragons on Lily's front door. It glowed bright red until he pressed it, then it turned black. As an added bonus, the dragon emitted steam from its mouth in short panting bursts as he waited. Lily answered the door, wearing knee-high stiletto boots, a spiked leather neckband, and nothing else except for the huge orange, long-haired cat that was snuggled against her body. Lily's hair hung like a glossy black cloak around her shoulders. She kissed the cats head. "Hello," she said, cocking her head and giving him an "I dare you" stare with her almond-shaped black eyes.

"Hi," he answered, hardly finding his voice. She was gorgeous. Lily was probably in her mid to late thirties, but from what he could see around the edges of her hair and the cat that she used to almost cover herself, she had the body of a twenty-year-old nymph.

She took his hand and pulled him inside. Her long hair shifted like a sheet of black satin when she moved. She put the wine on a table by the door. "For later," she said.

"This is *Wang Li*." She held out the cat to say hello to him, exposing her body from where he had been shielding her. The cat's green eyes glowed with secrets. "*Wang Li* means beautiful," she added, rubbing the cat's belly. Hahn was more interested in Lily's pink nipples that peeked out than the cat.

"You like her?" she asked, kissing her orange fur. "I got her when I came to this country. She brings me luck. Follow me now."

The house was surprisingly modern inside as if it had been recently renovated. She led him down a hallway with slick white walls and a white marble floor and up a white spiral staircase. At the top was a room that must have been built over the garage. It was painted blood red and lit by flickering candles, held by golden wall sconces. The floor was carpeted in a fiery-red shag. Hanging metal gadgets filled the space and reminded him of a cross between a gym and a bordello.

"You won't be needing your clothes," she said. "Leave them over there. I don't like clutter." She pointed to a closet.

"Okay dokey," he said. Things were definitely looking up. He slowly stripped and hung his things on the hooks inside.

"You like my new room?" She set *Wang Li* on the floor. The cat hopped up on the window sill, but instead of turning to watch the birds out the window, she sat expectantly as if a show were about to begin, flattening her ears in anticipation.

"I guess." Once Steve looked around and took a good look at the equipment, he wondered if it was too late for him to leave. This wasn't at all the evening that he'd imagined. Lily saw his gaze and locked the door.

"I built this when my husband left. He was so weak. I couldn't wait to get rid of him. I don't like weak men. He disgusted me. You know him, right? He's the CEO of your company, so you should."

"Yes. I met him once or twice. Seemed like a nice guy."

She removed a whip from the wall and appraised him, poking at his biceps and then his abs. "Not bad. You are not a bad looking man. You have a good body. Strong. I have two rules. Number one, no kissing. Number two, you do what I say. You agree?"

Steve gulped. "What if I don't agree? This isn't exactly what I had in mind."

"What? You thought I would be a sweet little girlfriend like they have here in America? No power? Men are crazy. I am strong. I think you might like this after all."

She pointed at Steve's fully erect penis. Embarrassed, he covered himself with his hands as if he was Adam, running from the serpent in the Garden of Eden. Lily walked over and removed his grip. "Here. Allow me." She stroked him and despite himself, Steve let out a groan. He reached out his hand to touch her breast and she slapped his face. "Do not be so fresh. You may not touch me unless I say so."

Steve moaned and rubbed his stinging cheek.

"Trust me. You need this attitude adjustment." Lily led him to the hanging handcuffs a few feet away and cuffed his wrists. She paced behind him for a few moments and then gave him a painful lash with the whip. "This is to teach you manners."

Steve winced and bit his lip. He wouldn't give her the satisfaction of knowing how much it hurt him.

Lily stood in front of him and traced a line down her abdomen with her red fingernail and then slipped it between her legs. She began to delicately rub herself. "I don't need a man for sex. I can do it better anyway. You just watch." As she became more excited, she reached out and stroked him. Steve was shocked when they both came at the same time since he hadn't even touched her.

Lily unlocked his handcuffs. "Go clean yourself. There's a bathroom around the corner." She sounded disgusted with him. *Wang Li* stared at Steve as if waiting for him to move.

Steve retrieved his clothes from the closet on his way. In the bathroom, he felt dizzy and disoriented from what had just happened. He was happy to see that there was a lock on the door and a large, glass-enclosed shower. He wanted to be alone to process what had occurred. He locked the door, stepped in the shower and let the warm water beat on his back until the room was filled with fog. As he dressed, he felt intoxicated as if the gates to a bizarre new world had just opened. He was pretty sure that he wanted to travel through those gates. Lily would be his guide. She certainly had his attention. Three days later, after seeing her every night, he moved in.

A month later, he still had a lot of questions. First was why had he let Lily humiliate him the way that she did? He was a guy who'd always been in control. Now he'd been reduced to a slobbering idiot around her and followed her around like an obedient dog. He had already had one appointment with Dr. Emery, his old therapist. He'd called her for an emergency session from his office. If she was shocked by Steve's story, it didn't show. She was trying to get him to figure out why Lily had him under her spell and hinted that it had something to do with his controlling mother, but he wasn't buying it.

His other question was why Lily knew about his virus project with Gerry Fox. Lily hadn't talked about the virus until just an hour before when she'd cuffed Steve in the blood-red room.

"I know what you're working on with Fox. He told me all

about it," she said, circling him like a caged tiger, waiting for meat.

"So?" Steve tried to sound nonchalant.

She took the whip off its hook on the wall and swung it. Its terrifying whoosh froze him in anticipation of pain before it bit his back with a cracking lash. Steve grimaced and groaned.

"No attitude from you. You want more?"

He didn't answer. Lily strutted in front of him and set one of her legs up on the patent leather red weight-lifting bench to her side. She was wearing her red stilettos with gold buckles all the way to her knees and only a red silk scarf wrapped around her neck. Steve had learned that she had matching boots and neck gear in every color and he'd begun to gauge her mood according to the color of the day. Red was definitely not good.

"Today, no sex unless you are a very good boy."

"And what must I do to be a good boy?" He could live without sex with her. After a month of Lily's boots, he could use a little vacation. Even *Wang Li* was bored and was watching the birds outside the window.

"I gave Fox a space for his lab, and I deserve part of his product. I already removed it from the lab. It was on my property, after all, so I own it. I want to use against my no-good ex-husband. You need to tell me how it works."

"And why would I do that, Lily? You have no idea what you are getting into."

"Okay, I will tell you. I need you to help me, or I'll release it and blame it on my ex unless he gives me the shares from Visiozyme that I am entitled to. Your fucking courts here are ridiculous. I get no satisfaction, so I must handle this myself. I have to handle everything myself."

Steve just stared at her. "This virus can hurt a lot of people. You can't just release it at your will."

"Oh? And what is it that you and Fox were going to do? Why did you even build it if it's so terrible?"

"It was a mistake. Fox hired me as a project manager to help him build it, if you must know. I never thought that it would really be an actual threat. It's like the atom bomb. Just because you have it, doesn't mean that you are going to go around and drop it on people."

"Now that we have it, I don't care. It can make me the queen of the world if I want. And my no-good ex-husband will be very sorry that he ever crossed me."

She was crazier than he thought. He was in no position to refuse her anything until he was up and dressed. Then he would see.

"Anything you want, Lily."

"That's my good boy. I knew that you would listen. Today, as a special reward, I will let you kiss me."

Still locked into his cuffs, Steve obediently leaned towards her. She stepped off the bench and stood in front of him to kiss his mouth. Her lips were inflexible and stone cold. The kiss was the worst he'd ever had. Then Lily went through her usual routine, but Steve just couldn't get aroused.

"I think you are weak, just like my ex-husband. You men are all the same in the end."

Steve shrugged. "Sorry, I'm just a bit tired."

"I will let this go today. We will see how things are tomorrow. We will have some dinner downstairs, and then I must do some work."

In the bathroom, he removed a bag of Oreo cookies that he'd

packed in his duffel. He'd taken to packing cookies since Lily never had anything to snack on and he was always hungry after one of their sessions. He opened the first cookie and scraped the frosting off with his teeth. Suddenly, he realized that it was just after he'd agreed to work on the project with Fox when Lily had spilled the coffee on him. It probably was not an accident.

Why would Fox tell her about their project? Then it hit him. He should have been paying more attention. Based on the name of the virus, she'd had her spin with him first. It figured. Fox had probably named the virus after Lily's deadly nature. But Fox had been smart enough to not succumb to Lily's dominance. Steve chided himself for being so stupid.

After he showered, he returned to his room and packed a few of his clothes in his backpack which he would take to work in the morning. He would forfeit the rest. He would not be coming back. He was unsure of how he would meet women in the future, but he didn't care.

19

OMG

In the conference room, Reinstadt quietly sorted through his email on his phone while Kylie installed OMG on her laptop. Then she ran some tests to make sure it was running properly.

After about ten minutes, Reinstadt angled his head to see Kylie's screen, "How are you doing? Is it working?" He looked at his watch.

"Yes, we're good to go. I want to rerun a search on Gerry Fox and see if there's anything else on Lily. Now that I know my laptop is at Visiozyme, I want to run searches on the execs from the top down over there too. That could certainly give us some clues. It might take a while, so I wonder if I can get something to eat? I'm starting to get light-headed. I could eat a horse about now."

"Sure. Sorry, but we don't have any horses. We had them for lunch. Would you settle for pizza?"

"Of course."

Reinstadt pushed a button on the intercom. "Jane, can you please order us a pizza?" He turned to Kylie. "What do you want on it?"

"Anything." At this point, she might even consider eating the pizza box.

"Okay, make that a pepperoni and mushroom."

He turned to Kylie. "Do you drink beer?"

"Yes."

"Jane, bring in a couple of beers from the lunchroom, please."

"Do you want the pizza delivered now?" Jane asked, now an efficient employee. Kylie smiled to herself about Jane's change in attitude.

"Yes, as soon as possible. Thank you." He switched off the intercom, removed his jacket, loosened his tie, and the top button of his shirt. Kylie swallowed hard. His looks were even more pleasing when he'd loosened up a little, the way JFK looked so charming in the charismatic photos of him sailing with his family in Hyannis. Reinstadt did remind her a little of JFK. With her help, he could be a revered president too.

"So, show me how this thing works," he said. "I never did get to see that demo."

Jane came in with the beers, not looking at Kylie. She wordlessly set them on the table with two paper cups smiling at Reinstadt.

"Thanks, Jane," said Bill, not looking up.

"No problem." She beamed him a smile. "Is there anything

else?" She fixed her eyes on him without even glancing in Kylie's direction.

"That's it for now."

"Okay," Kylie said when Jane had closed the door behind her. "It takes about 10 minutes to get a full query. Let's start with Fox." She pulled up a form on her screen. She filled in all the variables such as emails to anyone at Visiozyme and anything that included the word Lily, as well as his bank accounts and contact list, searching for anyone with Lily in her name. "While it's thinking, let's look at the Visiozyme website and find out who the major players are. I can also query connections to Gerry Fox, once we know a bit more about what to ask."

"You're a smart girl. I like the way you think," he said, flipping off the top on his can of beer and taking a sip. "Kylie, don't take this the wrong way, but with all that's happened, you can't go back to your apartment. I'm wondering if you have a place to stay?"

"I suppose if I was desperate, I could stay with my parents in Lexington."

"For all intensive purposes, are you desperate?"

She gave him a half smile and shrugged. Even if she was desperate, staying with her parents was her absolute last resort. He slid the other beer and a cup over so it was right in front of her.

"I have a spare room at my place and you can stay there for a couple of days, or until this blows over. I am supposed to be keeping my eye on you."

Kylie's face burned and she nodded, not trusting her words at first since it was as if she'd died and God invited her to stay in his special place in heaven. "Really? That's cool. I mean that's really nice of you," she finally managed. She took a long swig of beer.

"Okay, that's settled then. Let's see what we can find on OMG and then we'll head over there."

Kylie nodded. First, she found a list of all the top execs from the Visiozyme website and one by one, fed them into OMG. She received a notification that Fox's report was ready just as the pizza arrived. She loaded her paper plate with two slices and bit into one, holding it next to her mouth for easy access as she worked. It was the best pizza in memory.

Fox's report contained a long list of emails that contained the word, Lily. Many of them were between him and Simon, but several were communications with Michael Harriman, one of the names Kylie had just copied on her list and she had just learned that he was the CEO of Visiozyme. Those emails were more specific. "Sorry to hear about your divorce," sort of notes. Kylie was surprised to find that Harriman's wife was named Lily and that Fox could be so empathic. She took another bite, closing her eyes and savoring it for a moment before she spoke. "Have you ever heard of Michael Harriman?"

"Yes, he's the founder of Visiozyme, a big name in the biotech sector."

Kylie pointed to her screen. She was suddenly embarrassed to notice her ragged fingernails, adorned with black striped remnants of nail polish. "It appears that he might be a big name with Lily, as well. Can you just Google him while I go through these emails?"

"Sure. I'll get my laptop and will be right back." He was gone for just moments when he returned with his computer and two more beers. "Just to lubricate the process," he said, sliding one next to Kylie's almost empty can in front of her.

"Thanks," she said, keeping her eyes on the screen, hiding her over the moon nervousness about eating pizza with her idol. If she looked at him, he might see.

Reinstadt folded a slice of pizza into a manageable triangle and shoveled it into his mouth while he scanned the search results on Harriman. "Here's something," he said, with his mouth stuffed as a mailbag at Christmas. "Try Lily Harriman. She's the ex-wife. Here's an old Boston Globe photo of them together from some benefit."

"I know. I just saw that his wife's name is Lily. Pretty interesting."

Reinstadt angled his laptop for Kylie to see the photo of a handsome blond man with tortoise-shell glasses wearing a tux. Kylie guessed Harriman to be in his forties. He had his arm wrapped around the waist of an Asian beauty in a strapless black dress. Kylie immediately typed Lily Harriman into OMG.

"This might take a while since the program is backed up with a queue. What else did you find on her?"

Reinstadt held up his finger for her to wait. He'd just found Lily's Facebook profile. "Evidently, she's in a relationship now with a Steve Hahn. It appears that she's dumped Michael," He reported, scrolling through it.

"Oh, my God. I talked to a Steve Hahn when I was looking for a reference on Simon! They shared an office. He was like talking to a wall. This could be important, although I'm not how yet."

"Here's a photo of them," Reinstadt pointed."

"We only spoke on the phone, and I have no idea what he

looks like. Let's see." The photo showed a thirty-something guy hugging Lily with both arms. He had a full head of brown hair, parted on one side, dramatically dipping over his eye on the other side. She switched over to the Visiozyme site on her laptop and searched for Steve Hahn where she found a photo. "Look at this," she said, showing Reinstadt. She shoveled another bite of pizza into her mouth as he looked at it. "It's definitely the same guy.

"Interesting."

"Did you check to see if Lily has any connections in Chinatown? We should look up the bubble tea place, and find out who owns it," she said.

"Yes, the Bureau already sent a team down there today and they checked all that out. They confirmed that she owns the building, but I didn't put it together that she was Harriman's ex-wife."

Kylie added a query on the real Lily, requesting information on her divorce. Then she added Steve Hahn to the queue just as OMG notified Kylie that Michael Harriman's report was ready. There were hundreds of emails with references to Lily but they were mostly to his lawyer where he just referred to Lily as the EWFH (Ex-wife from Hell) and TB (*The Bitch*).

"Listen to this," she said, reading from her laptop. "What a racket. Evidently, Michael was paying her $10,000 a month in alimony!" She shook her head. "Wait. There's more. On top of that, it looks like she recently filed a contempt suit. Guess she thought that she wasn't getting enough and that she was entitled to half of his stock at Visiozyme too. How greedy can you get?" Kylie was incredulous. "They're already divorced! Shouldn't that all be settled? How can anyone be such a parasite?"

"You'd be amazed at what goes on," said Reinstadt.

"I'd never expect that. Just because a marriage didn't work out, it doesn't seem fair that one person has to keep supporting the other, if she can do it herself. Usually, it's not just one person's fault, right? How does anyone ever think that they deserve to keep taking someone's money once they're divorced? Especially, if they can support themselves?" Kylie remembered what she'd discovered about her parents. Now she was even more certain that she'd take her good old time to get married if she ever did it at all. She was also pretty sure that if it ever came to divorce, her mother would never behave like such a leech. She had more pride than that.

He looked at her appreciatively. "The laws are old-school, from when women didn't work," he said. "But times have changed, and you're right. The law needs to evolve to protect men too."

"I guess, but I don't get why people get married and how it turns into this kind of ugliness."

"People change, Kylie," he said thoughtfully.

She wondered if he was referring to himself. "I don't know, but to me, it just sounds like greed. I think that people need to feel like they have enough in life. If you never feel like what you have is good enough, you always want more and I think that must be like a big gnawing hole."

He looked at her appreciatively and smiled. "Thanks, Yoda. You are very wise, indeed."

She laughed.

"The thing is," he went on. "Some of us have more good

things than others. In public policy that affects millions of people, everyone has to have enough or you get all kinds of problems."

"I didn't mean that we shouldn't try to make the world better," explained Kylie. "I just meant that people shouldn't be greedy or vindictive. They should just be content with the good things in their lives."

"What else are finding in there?" He looked over at her computer.

"Not a lot. I searched for the name Lily, but most of Michael's results were about his ex-wife or their divorce. He didn't have a folder like the ones on Fox's or Simon's computers, which is a relief. Even though he might have a motive to do some something vile to his ex-wife, why would he release a horrible virus and kill the rest of the world? I could be wrong, but it doesn't seem to fit. I think we should keep looking."

He looked at his watch. "Look, it's already eight o'clock. I don't know about you, but I've had a really long day, and still have a bunch of paperwork to finish." He closed his laptop. "What do you say we move this over to my place? You can get settled and do the rest of your searches there."

"Sure." Nothing sounded better. It was amazing to be allowed to even bask in Reinstadt's stardust, inhale the same air, and share some beers and a pizza—never mind see where he lived. Kylie couldn't believe her luck. "Sounds good to me. I should be able to finish this batch tonight and tomorrow I'll give Stuart my results."

Kylie followed Reinstadt out of the conference room and stood in the waiting room while he got his coat and briefcase.

She was happy to see that Jane had gone home and the rest of the office appeared deserted.

Outside, the city looked like a ghost town. Just before a holiday, the street appeared especially desolate with no traffic, tourists, and Bostonians going about their business. The panhandlers had even packed it up. As they walked towards his building, Kylie and Reinstadt chatted about the cold and the unusual early snow. They fell silent as they walked past the ornate Old State House, and up a couple of blocks to Tremont Street, passing the pre-revolutionary Granary Burial Ground, dark as death, just across the street. Reinstadt touched her arm to turn again at the Parker House, and then again at Provence Street. "This is my block," he said, pointing at a building with a large gray overhang. "I bought a condo there a couple of years ago, but then, of course, you probably already know that."

Kylie grinned. Although she recalled reading his address, she'd forgotten, having been much more interested in his emails. He led her through the modern, atrium lobby, complete with potted trees, high ceilings, and gigantic abstract paintings. They rode the elevator up to the penthouse floor and he led her down a plush carpeted hallway to his door. "Welcome to Chez Reinstadt," he said, unlocking it.

He switched on a hall light, illuminating the soft gray walls and hardwood floors in the front entrance. She closed her eyes willing her threatening tears of gratitude to stay hidden behind her eyelids. The horrific events of her day suddenly evaporated as she followed him inside and shut the door.

20

Sorting it Out

Reinstadt hung Kylie's coat in a closet in the front hall before leading her into a room with massive floor to ceiling windows that appeared to be from an Architectural Digest photo shoot. "Wow," she said, drawn to the sweeping view of the Boston Common, the shimmering gold dome of the Statehouse, and Beacon Hill with its gaslights. Behind it was the slick black strip of the Charles River, with the twinkling lights of Kendall Square on the other side. Then she turned around and took in the rest of the open living area.

"Oh double wow," she said, but the word that flashed through Kylie's mind was "tasteful." Its open kitchen had the latest appliances and modern walnut cabinetry. There was a black marble breakfast bar on one end and on the other, was a large living area with a beige modular couch with earth-toned, woven decorator pillows that picked up colors from the Persian rug. An enormous brass-trimmed glass coffee table sat in front of the couch, holding neat stacks of large books arranged into perfect pyramids. Kylie wondered if he'd read them or if a decorator had purchased them for their size and placed them there for show. Nothing was out of place and Kylie wondered if he actually lived there. Behind the sofa, and in front of one of the windows was a blonde oak table where she could imagine him having a candlelit dinner with Emily Wickland, his girlfriend if in fact, they did that kind of thing. Perhaps the elegant look was Emily's doing. Kylie intended to find out more about that. She would have to remember to run a report on her.

"I hate to tear you away, but you have a view in your room too. Would you like to see your accommodations? Allow me to show you," Bill said, waving her on from where she still stood at the window. He led her down a hallway decorated with a row of photos of FDR, JFK, and Teddy Roosevelt with matching black frames, to the guest bedroom with coffee-colored walls and white furniture that included a modern four-poster bed with a blue and brown patchwork print spread.

"You have an awesome place," she said.

He shrugged. "Yeah. I suppose I do but wish that I could spend more time here to enjoy it. In the morning, you'll be able to see the harbor from your window," he noted, before walking through and switching on the light in the bathroom. There were two crackled glass raised sinks sitting on a white marble vanity with antique wooden legs. The wall-sized, gilt-framed-mirror was lit with gold and white sconces on either side. "I hope that this is adequate, Mademoiselle," he said, slightly bowing as he handed her pure-white fluffy towels from the bathroom linen cupboard. Kylie noted that the sizeable glass-enclosed shower was stocked with high-end shampoo and body wash. There were even scented candles arranged between the double sinks with a pack of matches, handy between them. She couldn't wait to try to light them and then dive into the shower.

"It's more than adequate! It's wonderful. I can't thank you enough."

"Do you need anything else? Food? Something to drink?"

"No, I'm fine. I think I'll just take a shower and dive into some the reports until I can't keep my eyes open."

"Okay, I'll leave you to it. By the way, I need to be at the office early tomorrow, so just make yourself at home. Have some breakfast and then I think you should call Stuart and take your findings over to the Bureau."

"Good plan," she said, watching his eyes, which she found remarkably bright and intelligent, as well as a gorgeous shade of a Mediterranean blue. There was a hint of humor in them, too, like he had some private joke. Kylie realized how much she wanted in on it. He was out of her league, and she felt a pang of loss for what she could never have. Being with him was like visiting a club that she would never be able to join.

"Should I take my stuff with me then?"

"If you want, but you should give it another day or so, in the hope that this can get wrapped up. Then you can go back to your apartment when we know that you'll be safe. I'll tell the concierge to let you in when you get back if you want to stay?"

No problem. Kylie would stay there forever if she could. Kylie looked at the ceiling for a moment, not wanting to appear as excited as she felt. "Yes, sure. That's awesome, and I can't thank you enough."

"It's the least I can do," he said. "Stay in touch."

After Reinstadt said goodnight and closed the door, Kylie headed into the bathroom. She planned first to light the candles...step one to relaxation. As she struck the match, she noticed that the matchbook was from Francine's, a beach dive that she'd seen near Fox's house on Plum Island. She shrugged it off as a coincidence. Lots of people go to Plum Island.

She sat and on the bed and texted Stuart: *staying in Reinstadt's guest room. Will come in tomorrow morning with news.* She peeled off her clothes and showered, scrubbing off the nastiness of her day with the lavender scented soap and shampoo. She then slipped on a clean t-shirt and crawled into bed with her laptop, anxious to see what OMG had generated on Lily Harriman and Steve Hahn. First, she read Lily's email to Michael:

I am sure that you are aware that you have violated our agreement. You need to resolve our contempt case and give me my 50% of your shares of the Visiozyme stock that you sold without telling me.
This is a huge issue since I was supposed to be notified of the sale of any stock.

It appeared that Lily refused even to have a phone conversation, only responding with hard-nosed notes and letters from her lawyer to see what else she might be able to extract from Michael. He replied saying he only owed her money from stock sales up to the time of their separation, but it appeared that Lily wasn't accepting that. In her last email to him, she demanded interest, finally telling Michael that if he persisted in resisting her, she would be forced to take more dramatic measures than court, which took too long and wasn't productive anyway. AHAH. Suddenly Kylie sat up at attention. She read faster.

She found hundreds of emails with Steve Hahn, proving that when she wanted, Lily could be exceptionally communicative. Many were explicit and shocking, but what made every hair on Kylie's forearms rise, was finding the encrypted Lily folder on her hard drive. Misha would have to open it to be certain, but Kylie was pretty sure it contained the plan for the virus release.

Steve Hahn's other emails were even more interesting. Kylie quickly scrolled through his many back-and-forth notes with Gerry Fox planning meetings, which she'd evidently overlooked before, thinking they were just Visiozyme business. Now she noticed that Simon had been copied on a couple of them. The most damning email to Fox had mentioned using their new *little one* to permanently free Lily from Michael Harriman. It had been dated three weeks ago. When? Fox had asked. We're telling Harriman that it's a Black Friday Release, he'd answered.

Did Harriman know about the virus? If he did, why hadn't HE gone to Homeland Security? It didn't make sense. Kylie took another look at his hard drive, and again, she could not find the Lily folder. She then searched Steve Hahn's, and there was the Lily folder, sitting on a top corner of on his desktop.

She found that Steve was living at Lily's home in Newton. A Google Maps photo revealed a graceful English Tudor house, situated on a long block with similarly styled homes. They all had identical shrubbery and curved walkways to the driveways, but Lily's house stood out with a huge 3-d relief of a dragon carved on her front door.

Kylie felt satisfied finding so much information and couldn't wait to present the resolved case to the FBI. Her impulse was to run out to tell Bill, but she was afraid to intrude on him any more than she already had. She thought about calling Misha, but it could all wait until morning. Her heavy eyelids begged for sleep, but she willed them open long enough to do one more search on Emily Wickland. She would let OMG do its thing and check it out tomorrow. Unable to fight sleep any longer, Kylie closed her laptop and the lights, curled up in the heavy quilt and silky cotton sheets, and fell asleep with a smile on her face.

21

Bubble Tea

Kylie sank into a bottomless sea of disturbing dreams where she was relentlessly chased, caught, and then suffocated. She awoke with her heart pounding. At first, she was unsure of where she was with the dazzling sun streaming in the windows, but when she remembered, Kylie bolted up and leaned against the headboard. When her breath return to normal, the corners of her mouth curled into a grin. Looking around at the beautiful room in Bill Reinstadt's apartment, she momentarily forgot about the Lily virus. She stretched and wiggled her toes with delight. Just as he'd promised, she could see Boston harbor from the window. True, it was in the distance, but never the less, it was twinkling in the spaces between the financial district's tall buildings. Then she remembered why she was there. She collected her thoughts, hopped out of bed, and poked her neck out of the bedroom door.

The condo was quiet, and it appeared that Reinstadt had left. She pulled on her jeans and sweater, then padded to the kitchen where she nosed around and found coffee, cereal, dishes, and utensils. She was pleased with his cereal choices of three separate types of organic granola; one with bran, one with flax, and another with oats. Of course, he would choose to eat healthily! In the refrigerator, she found a carton of berries as well as a quart of milk and a pitcher of orange juice. She chose the flax granola and dotted it with blackberries in a happy face, poured some milk, and scrolled through Emily Wickland's report on her laptop as she ate.

It appeared that Emily was omnipresent in all the local magazines and newspapers. Her PR clients were mostly hospitals. She was in countless photos taken at benefits. In every image, she was tucked under the arm of Bill Reinstadt, flashing her splendid white teeth and showing just the right amount of cleavage. Kylie had to admit that Emily was an excellent choice for a politician like Bill. With her all-American, tawny looks and model-lean build, she'd be the perfect complement to his movie star persona. Kylie was a world apart from her: a marginally cute, geeky MBA with two-toned hair, stubby fingernails, and a dwindling trust fund. She couldn't imagine that Emily was being stalked by a murderer who also planned to destroy the world. But her self doubt was not enough to stop her from being curious about Emily's personal life with Bill...not that she'd have a chance with him. Reinstadt was indeed too old and established ever to be interested in her—two years of celibacy must have demented her brain to even have any interest in him. She'd better stick to business, but first, she was compelled to check Emily's calendar.

There were Saturday night dates with Bill, but he didn't appear on her weekday schedule. Her apartment was in Charlestown, so it was not likely that they would automatically see each other. Kylie was no expert in the relationship department, but it seemed odd and struck her as a very ho-hum romance.

She thought about Reinstadt's apartment; perfect as if for show, with no mess or signs of real life. She was a little surprised that he had food in his refrigerator, so apparently, he lived there. Kylie swallowed her curiosity with the last of her cereal. Right now, there was a murderer and a deadly virus to stop. She loaded the dishwasher and padded barefoot down the long hallway to her bedroom. She planned to make her bed and get ready to leave.

She paused momentarily in front of the president's photos in the hallway, imagining that one day, Reinstadt could be one of them. She brightened with the thought that if anything ever happened with him and they got together, she could be the first lady! She recalled the easy way they'd been with each other last night. It felt like some kind of a fairy tale. It was a long shot, but maybe it was possible. As far as him getting elected, he certainly had enormous charisma. He'd risen this far, so he seemed to have enough political pull to win any tug of war; a star on the rise. She still couldn't believe that he was allowing her to stay at his place.

When she reached his closed bedroom door, she stopped, dying to know what it looked like inside. For a long moment, she stood as if glued to the floor. She knew that she had to get to the FBI, but Reinstadt had said he was leaving early. It was already eight thirty. Undoubtedly, he'd already gone. What would the harm be in taking a peek? After a heated internal debate, her hand gave into temptation as if it had a life of its own and reached for the door handle. She but couldn't get herself to turn it, thinking that it was possible that he could still be in there. She would die if he found her snooping. She removed her hand as if the brass knob was hot. Suddenly, the door opened. Kylie gasped. She was face to face with Bill Reinstadt. She wanted to sink into the floor.

He stepped out through the narrowly opened door and pulled it shut, bumping into her shoulder. "Is everything okay? Did you need something?" Reinstadt stared at her. His eyes were fiery with both amusement and disdain. He stood close enough for her to smell his mint-fresh breath. He was wearing a suit, a tie, and a smirk.

"No, everything's fine. I was just getting up enough nerve to knock. I wanted to see if you were still here. "Actually, I was hoping to tell you what I found last night."

"No problem. I was just on my way out, though. I'm running late." He said as he side-stepped around her.

"It looks like the virus was being used to blackmail Michael Harriman into giving Lily more money," she blurted to his back.

Reinstadt stopped and turned around. He straightened the knot on his tie as if it was choking him. "Interesting. Listen, I have to run, but you need to take this over to the Bureau right away, okay? It sounds like a start. Who knows? Maybe you solved this."

"Yes, maybe. I'll go over there now. I'll keep you posted." She watched him saunter down the hallway. "Have a good day," she added, then cringed at how ridiculous that sounded. Still mortified, she stared at her feet thinking that what she'd really wanted was to hug him or maybe reach out and tousle his perfectly combed hair. She wasn't sure if was gratitude, lust, or adulation. This new Reinstadt persona was not approachable, and his cold brusqueness stopped her cold. He certainly didn't seem very impressed with her findings as if he was a different person. Maybe he had just been angry because he knew she was going to snoop in his room.

Once the front door had closed behind him, Kiley willed her feet to move back down the hallway to her room with her face was still burning. She would call Misha, collect her things, and leave. Just before she reached her door, a thought stopped her. Why not look in Reinstadt's room now? He'd never know and what would it hurt to take a tiny peek...unless her luck was worse than she thought. There was always the possibility that he might have unexpectedly forgotten something and return to the apartment. What if he found her in his bedroom? She would die on the spot. She was sure of it.

Still, the prospect of seeing his private space was so irresistible that she tiptoed back to his room as soundlessly as if the walls would call him back if they knew she was snooping. This time, she turned the handle, but with no luck. The door was locked, but there was no keyhole. She hadn't seen Reinstadt lock it, so she was surprised. It must have been secured from the inside!

She was puzzled but oddly relieved. The fates just were keeping her out. She was about to turn away and return to her room, when suddenly, the door swung open. A fortyish man with spikey blond hair and startling aqua eyes loomed over her. In his black turtleneck and jeans, he had the lanky look of David Bowie or an androgynous male model, or maybe an Aryan poster boy. Whoever it was, or what he looked like, she was horrified.

"Can I help you?" He flashed a broad smile of perfect pearly whites. He looked familiar, but she was sure that she'd never met him. Maybe he just resembled a model or a rock star she'd seen, but she was sure she knew him from somewhere. He'd left the door ajar, and Kylie had a clear view of the bedroom beyond him. She was stunned.

The wall-sized window was covered with tightly-drawn black drapes, creating a dramatic backdrop against the charcoal grey walls. In the center of the floor was an unmade, oversized round bed covered with rumpled black satin sheets, illuminated by colored spotlights, just above it. Magenta accent pillows were strewn around on the grey satin comforter. She winced when she noticed the natural sheen on what undeniably was a real zebra rug on the floor. So much for Reinstadt's animal advocacy. The walls were covered with huge framed black and white photos, lit by strategically placed track lights on the ceiling. From her brief impression, each photo depicted a gorgeous naked boy. She'd never seen this coming.

Suddenly dizzy, Kylie sucked in a quick mouthful of breath. "Oh, so sorry!" She stammered and turned, about to flee.

"You must be Kylie," said the man, detaining her flight with his words. His voice was so normal...friendly and patient, almost as if he'd expected her. "Bill mentioned that he had a houseguest. I'm Emile. Just on my way out. I didn't mean to scare you."

Kylie stammered, "I had no idea that anyone else was here."

"Obviously." He flashed his neon-bright smile again. It was the kind of smile that could transform the grey of dawn into an impressive, gorgeous sunrise. She'd never seen such unusual eyes, the color the Caribbean Sea.

"So, do you like it?" He gestured towards the interior with a long arm. I'm Bill's decorator." Emile's eyes twinkled with amusement.

"Nice to meet you," Kylie managed, nodding. "It's really something. Sorry, but I can't chat. There's something I have to do."

Her face felt on fire as she rushed to her room like a scared rabbit. She shut the door and tried to get her breath back to normal before calling Misha, telling herself that were more important things to worry about than Reinstadt's bed partners. Who was Emile— just the decorator, or was he more? What did she care? She wasn't the first lady type anyway. She knew she never had a chance with Reinstadt, but still, she was still confused. If he was gay, why hadn't he come out publicly? So much for his transparency as a politician. The image of the rug in Reinstadt's room disturbed her. She felt bewildered, but mostly, she felt betrayed. She'd researched him so thoroughly. How could she have missed this? Once again, she'd been disappointed. Could she trust anyone anymore? Until she sorted it out, Kylie decided not even to mention it to Misha. She sat down on the bed and called him.

Misha's phone rang for a while. Come on, Misha. Pick it up. When he finally answered. His tone was wary. "Allo?"

"It's Kylie." She was surprised to find herself flooded with relief at the sound of his voice.

"Hey *pchelka*. I didn't recognize the number."

"I know. I have a new phone."

"You can't seem to hold onto them, can you?" She could hear the smile in his voice. "What's happening?" he asked.

"A lot. I'm supposed to go over to the Bureau office with everything that I've found, but we might need you to open some more encrypted folders. Can you meet me there?"

"When?"

"Now. I'm already downtown, so I thought I'd just walk over."

"Do you want to meet first and fill me in?" he asked.

"No, I think I should just go."

"Okay. Suit yourself. I'll see you in about half an hour."

"By the way, what's a *pchelka*?

"It means little bee in Russian. It's a nice name, like calling someone honey in your country."

"Oh," she said, oddly pleased.

When Misha arrived, Kylie was already seated with Stuart in what she now thought of as the interrogation room, explaining why she'd left Janice. Misha threw his jacket on an empty chair and took a seat across from them.

"Kylie, you don't seem to get that you're in danger," said Stuart sounding stern. "You shouldn't have left Janice. It's our job to protect you."

"So I've heard. Look, I'm all right." She shook her arms, hands, and twinkled her fingers. "See? I'm fine. It's done. I can take care of myself, okay? Can we move on? I have to tell you what I've found."

Stuart turned to Misha. "As for you, we will deal with you later. I haven't heard from you. You have a lot of explaining to do."

Misha's face paled, but there was no time for that now. Kylie blurted out her thoughts.

"Since Fox was killed and my place was ransacked, and it's pretty obvious that he wasn't working alone. I ran searches on my program for the top execs at Visiozyme and found out that Michael Harriman, the CEO, was married to a woman named Lily, and it looks like they are still going through a nasty divorce. She's now in a relationship with Steve Hahn, from Visiozyme. Hahn actually shared an office with Simon Whitehead. Steve and Lily each have the folder with the virus on their computers."

Stuart stared at her open-mouthed, and then pushed a button on his phone. "Kilpatrick, come in the conference room please," he said.

Misha beamed at Kylie. "Good work. Now the question is, how to find the virus."

"I have an address for Lily in Newton, and I think Steve could be living with her. Maybe they took it there."

Stuart laughed. "I think we should give you a job."

Kylie's pulse raced as she shot him a quick look to see if he was kidding, but Stuart had already turned to greet a young officer with a solid build and blond buzz-cut. She felt a surprise stab of disappointment, realizing how vital she'd felt working on this case.

"We have some new information on the Lily virus," Stuart told the officer. "I need you to get two SWAT teams together; one for Newton and the other for Visiozyme in Kendall Square.

We need two search warrants. I'll get you the addresses in a minute. I will meet you and the team in fifteen minutes for a briefing."

"Yes, sir. Right away." He left abruptly.

Stuart turned to Kylie. "At this point, I have no cause to keep you here, other than for your protection. Again, I strongly advise you to take advantage of it. You're free to go, but it might be a good idea for you to hang out here."

"No thanks," said Kylie, giving him a pained smile. "Honestly, we don't need to be babysat. We'd just be in the way and probably bored silly. At least if I leave, I can get some things done."

"That's what I'm afraid of. Listen, you need to keep me informed of your whereabouts, or I will bring you in."

"We will, but I feel like I should be doing something to help."

"Believe me, you've done enough. More than enough." He rolled his eyes at her. "Do you have somewhere to go?" asked Stuart.

"You could hang out with me at my apartment in Brookline," Misha broke in. He turned and wiggled his eyebrows at Kylie.

Ugh, thought Kylie. Was that supposed to charm me?

Stuart turned to Kylie. "That works for me. How about you?"

She offered him an apathetic shrug and a face like she'd sipped vinegar. "Not so much."

"Okay, then. Look, wherever you go, stay close. Update me your latest contact information. And for God's sake, stay out of trouble, will you?"

Kylie and Misha nodded vigorously.

"Do you want Misha to open the other Lily files?" asked Kylie. "So far, they've all contained the same information."

"Yes." Stuart looked at his watch. "Come back around one and I'll have you work with our tech department."

They agreed, gave him their phone numbers, and left. "I'm parked over there," persisted Misha, pointing to the Government Center garage. "So, *do* you want to hang out? We could do stuff."

"Like what?" Kylie looked at her watch. "I don't know, Misha. It's ten thirty, and we don't have tons of time. Do you have any other ideas besides going to your apartment?"

"Not really, but I thought that was an excellent idea," he grinned. "I think we should do what Stuart said." He put on his sunglasses and slid them up his nose with long fingers. "You know, maybe you want to go out sometime?"

Kylie frowned. Part of her thought that he was clueless, but there was another part. She was uncomfortable to admit it, but he was pretty nice, and in some weird way, she liked having him around. She could barely remember the last time someone had asked her out. She was either hideous, or she'd been giving out the wrong vibe for two years. This guy must be desperate since he was ignoring her don't bother me signals. "That's sweet, and you're potentially a nice guy, but you're not my type."

He looked at the sky. "Potentially? Okay then. On the other hand, I could always use another glass of bubble tea," he said.

Kylie laughed. "Interesting thought, but I don't think we should be going to Chinatown."

"Why not? They already raided the lab, and the virus was gone. We can just hang out and see if anything else turns up that's interesting. Who knows what might happen. Yes?"

"Okay, I guess it wouldn't hurt."

"By the way, what IS your type?" He shot her a devilish grin.

"I don't know, Misha. I suppose it's someone who isn't a player. Someone who doesn't have a glove compartment full of condoms. Maybe it's someone who will help save the world?"

"That's tall order, but I'll see what I can do."

As Misha drove the Porsche towards Chinatown, Kylie told him about the financial aspects of the Harriman divorce.

"That's terrible. Don't judge me," he said, driving along the Greenway. "But I have a joke."

"Okay, let's hear it." She gave him a skeptical look.

"What do a hurricane and a woman have in common?"

"I don't know. What?" Kylie turned to look at his profile awaiting the punchline. She did have to admit that he was pretty attractive. She could certainly use a laugh.

"They both come really loud and messy, and they both leave, taking your house and your car."

"Hah, hah, hah," she said sarcastically. "You're such a sexist pig. Thank you for illuminating that point for me. If you want to know the truth, that's why I won't go out with you."

"What? You don't think that's funny?"

"If I did, I wouldn't tell you." She looked out the window.

At a red light, he looked over at her and smiled. "Just so you know, *pchelka*, you illuminate me too."

"Whatever."

"Sorry if I offended you."

"If you say so," she said, but she was secretly amused.

As they approached Chinatown, Misha swerved the Porsche into the right lane, jerked it into reverse, and backed into a parking spot on Kneeland Street, just around the block from Lily's Bubble Tea.

"What's our plan?" he asked, opening the glove compartment. He removed the gun and slipped it into his jacket pocket. Some condom packages fell out of the glove compartment onto the floor, and Kylie shook her head and threw them back in, but not before reading the label, "Hung." She shook her head. *Perfect.*

"Is that thing loaded?" she pointed to his pocket, bug-eyed.

"Of course."

"Look, let's get one thing straight. I thought we were just going to look around and no matter what, it's not going to involve a gun or condoms. Not that I foresee any problems, but promise me you won't use that thing. That is, of course, unless we're in trouble."

"Which thing are you referring to?" His voice was deep and suggestive.

She rolled her eyes. "The gun, you dope."

"That's why I got it. I'll just use it if we're in trouble. It's not like I'm killer."

"I MEAN it, Misha."

"Okay. We'll just scope it out. Maybe Lily stored the virus in the refrigerator with the fruit. Argh."

"You're an idiot," she said as they got out of the car.

Misha paused as he shut his door. "How about we say that we're from the Health Department and we have to inspect the place?"

"Listen to me," said Kylie, waiting for him to meet her on the sidewalk. "This is reality, not some stupid TV show. IF the virus is real, you more than anyone, know that it can kill you within an hour. If Lily has it there, I certainly do NOT plan on drinking her bubble tea. And what will we do if we FIND the virus? We can't carry it away. What if it leaked? The FBI should be doing this. I think they have special forces for these things. They even have special outfits so that they won't get contaminated."

"FBI was down there already, right? They already checked the lab and it was cleaned out. They probably already have a watch on the place. If Lily's involved, she wouldn't show up there, unless she's crazy. We'll just go and be customers and see. We can call the FBI if we need them. Okay?"

"Okay," she agreed, but she didn't feel okay. She realized that she hadn't felt okay for a long time.

22

Meeting Lily

Weaving around the filthy slush on the narrow sidewalks, Kylie and Misha headed up Beech Street, the main drag in Chinatown, toward Lily's Bubble Tea. The street was lined with restaurants, bakeries, and herbal stores that displayed exotic-looking dried plants in rows of glass jars. Even in the late morning, the air was thick with the aroma of soy sauce and garlic and was awakening Kylie's appetite. She paused momentarily, gazing hungrily at the bakery windows with the glazed fruit-topped pastries inside. The closer they got to Lily's Bubble Tea, the louder her blood pounded in her ears. By the time they arrived at its bubble-gum pink door just a few moments later, her pulse was roaring like the ocean in her ears. Kylie held Misha back with her arm. "Wait. What are we going to say?"

He shrugged and looked skyward as if the answer was up there. Kylie waited and noticed an old Chinese man leaning against a restaurant wall across the street, apparently reading a newspaper.

After a long moment, Misha said, "I think we first see who is there. It's a small place, but they may have a back room. If Lily's in there, we just talk to her,"

"Really? Just what do you think we're going to say? Hi, Lily. Do you have any good lethal viruses today?"

"Maybe could say that we're from the newspaper, and we're writing an article about bubble tea," Misha offered. "Do you have a notebook and a pen?"

Kylie frowned at him as if he were an imbecile. "No, and I'm sure that she'd see through that. She sounds pretty devious, but who knows? Yeah, I'm sure that she'd just *love* to discuss her bubble tea with you. Why don't YOU try it? Do you have a recording app on your phone?"

"Yeah, I do. I could take pictures of Lily too and say it's for the article."

"Oh, of course. For a smart guy, you're a dork. Look, I was just kidding. I don't think that she'd fall for that. And, I'm positive that she's not going to want you to take her picture. She's too shrewd."

"That word, shrewd. Is it like the word shrew? Maybe related? I'm still not super great with English. I had it in school growing up, and it's gotten better, but there's still lots of words I don't know."

Kylie laughed. "Your English is good, but yes, they might be related. Based on her divorce, I'd say that she's both."

"Okay, whatever we do, I think that you should do the talking," said Misha.

"I thought you were going to go in there first and scope it out."

"Yes, but your English really is so much better. We make a good team, yes?"

"I think you're just scared," teased Kylie, enjoying the crack in his bravado.

"Me? No way. I just think that we should do it together. You ready?"

"I don't know. I think we should call Stuart and tell him where we are, just in case there's a problem."

"Kylie, it's you who's chicken shit. If we call Stuart, he's just going to tell you to leave."

"So? What if I *am* chicken? You don't seem to understand that this is very serious. Not to mention that since yesterday, I've already been kidnapped and escaped. Then my apartment was ransacked and I had a wild car chase with an FBI agent. I don't really have the stomach for any more." She wasn't ready to mention what happened with Emile.

The man across the street glanced up from his paper and then down again.

"I'll tell you what," she added. "You go in there if you're so brave, and if you don't come out, I'll call Stuart."

"Hah. No problem. Just in case I get killed, I have to do this before I die." He leaned in and kissed Kylie, his mouth a warm surprise on her lips. She slightly lost her balance, but he wrapped his arm around her back and held her firm. She liked his clean scent of soap, and his kiss was both warm and electric. She astonished herself by leaning into him and enthusiastically kissing him back, until she remembered where she was, and what they were about to do. She broke away. Had she lost her mind?

"God, nothing like using a situation to your advantage," she said, pushing him away, shaken. She had to admit that she liked his kiss— like tasting a small piece of dark chocolate that left her wanting more. Given the right circumstances, she might find his overactive case of testosterone pretty hot. But there was no time to think of that now. "Go," she commanded, but she realized that her voice sounded a bit more flirtatious than authoritative.

"Okay, okay. Now I can die a happy man," he said. As he smiled, his cheeks dimpled.

Kylie gave him a little shove towards the door and noticed the man across the street glance up from his paper. He was definitely watching them and she didn't like the feel of his scrutiny. Once Misha had gone inside, she pulled her phone from her parka pocket and called Stuart. She got his voicemail and left a message. "It's Kylie. Don't kill me, but I'm standing in front of Lily's Bubble Tea, and Misha just went inside. It looks like there's this old Chinese guy watching me from across the street and it's kind of giving me the creeps. I just thought you might want to know." The Chinese man took his phone out of his pocket. He stared at it, as if waiting for it to ring.

She fiddled with her own phone for a couple of moments, half-watching the man and sneaking a few photos of him when he was reading. Occasionally he looked up at her. She emailed his picture to Stuart with a caption, *This guy is acting suspiciously.* After a few minutes, Misha still hadn't come out, but two Fords turned down Beech Street. One of them blocked traffic at the far end, parking the car across the intersection, and the other one sped down the street and parked in front of Lily's near Washington Street. The driver's side door opened and Janice got out. She ran towards Kylie, who was so relieved that she could have hugged Janice. A moment later, Kylie noticed the man with the newspaper make a call on his phone. He talked to someone, threw the paper on the sidewalk, and disappeared inside the herb store.

"Get in the car, Kylie," Janice yelled. "I thought you were told to stay out of trouble."

"I called, didn't I?"

"Yes. Now get in the car, and do NOT come out until I tell you."

"Okay, Fine. Misha's in there. You should know that he's carrying a gun, just in case something happens."

"Oh, that's just great," Janice said sarcastically and pointed to the car. "NOW, Kylie."

"Alright, alright. By the way, did you see that guy across the street? He's been watching me. He just called someone and then went into that herb store."

"NOW! I am NOT kidding," she screamed.

Kylie panicked from the urgency of her voice and ran to the car. She climbed into the back seat and knelt so that she could see out the rear window. She watched Janice say something into her phone and then reach under her coat, probably for her gun. The determined glint in her eyes looked fierce. There was no doubt that she was in control. At the same time, an officer ran from the car down the block towards Lily's. Suddenly, there were four more men standing outside Lily's Bubble Tea, all wearing black suits, helmets, and carrying guns.

Janice turned toward her squad and said something. She pivoted towards Lily's Bubble Tea and went inside, leaving the men on the sidewalk. Kylie had to help. If something happened to Misha, she would never forgive herself. Why had she given him such a hard time? It looked safe enough with so many agents running around. She didn't even know for sure if Lily was in there, so this could all be a big fuss over nothing. She'd feel so foolish. But why hadn't Misha come out? She was desperate to know what what happening.

She swung herself around on the seat, opened the car door, and hopped out. Hidden by the car, she casually strolled away, unnoticed. She reached a narrow street and turned, only to find an alley that ran behind Lily's. After she'd passed a few dumpsters and back doors of some of the restaurants, she reached a wooden door with a pink stenciled sign above that read, Lily's Bubble Tea. Loud crashing sounds from a violent fight came from inside. A woman's shrill voice shouted, sounded hateful and shrill, but her actual words were muffled. She heard Misha's indistinct shouts too and it didn't sound good. She had to help. She ran to the door.

"Freeze!" Kylie heard Janice scream from inside just as the door opened. A beautiful Asian woman sprung outside. She stood about a foot from Kylie and was carrying a molded plastic cooler. Her red-lipstick scowl, painted cat eyes, looked frightening, but her knee-length, bottle green, boiled wool coat gave her a strangely stylish appearance. The color offset the blanket of black hair that draped down her back. In her thigh-high, spike-heeled boots over black tights, she was the same height as Kylie. Stumbling behind her was Misha. He had a bleeding gash on his forehead and his leather jacket ripped to shreds.

"She's got the virus in the cooler. Be careful!" he yelled. Janice stood behind him; her gun was drawn on Lily.

"Stay away, you Russian idiot," Lily hissed. Then she turned towards Kylie, holding the cooler in front of her like a shield. "Hello, Kylie. I'm Lily. I've been expecting you. Our mutual friend, Gerry Fox and I have been watching you, and I understand you've been looking for me? You think you're the only one who knows things? It's not a good thing for you to do so much snooping. You should take better care of yourself. Too much snooping can be very unhealthy." She set the cooler on the ground between herself and Misha and secured it by stepping one high-heeled boot on top of the cover.

Even in her stilettos, Lily's body was stable in what Kiley recognized as a perfectly balanced horse stance. Before Kiley could prepare for what she knew was going to be a serious fight, Lily extended her thumb and index and grabbed Kylie's larynx, her fingers clamping down like a vise. Using just her this deadly grip and the element of surprise, she slammed Kylie into the brick wall on the back of Lily's Bubble Tea, as easily as if Kylie were a sheet of paper. The impact of Kylie's head upon the brick was horrific. She bit her lip to keep from crying out from the pain. Lily extended her index and middle fingers like chopsticks. Her fingernails were filed into long ruby-colored daggers and she aimed them at Kylie's eyes in an attempt to blind her. As the daggers approached, Kylie shut her eyes and kneed Lily in the stomach. In the "Ooof" of Lily's astonishment, Kylie was able to loosen the deadly clamp from her throat with her elbow and hammer it up into Lily's chin.

Misha pulled out his gun and slowly inched closer to Lily, as she stepped off the cooler. Lily whirled around as if she had eyes in the back of her head and kicked his face. She then kicked his gun to the ground.

"*Suka*!" he swore in Russian, holding his jaw in shock.

"Back off, Lily," screamed Janice, who had run out the back door and was aiming her gun at Lily's heart. "Leave the cooler or I will shoot."

From deep in her muscle memory, Kylie recalled her punches, blocks, and kicks. She wound her hand into a mighty fist and delivered a blow underneath Lily's jaw. Lily staggered backward for a couple of steps. When Lily regained her balance, she snapped a perfect front-ball-kick with her spike heel onto Kylie's cheek. Kylie screamed in pain. She tasted the warm salt of her blood. Somehow her moves began flowing from muscle memory as easily as the rhythmic turns she'd made on her black diamond ski runs. Right. Left. Dodge. Turn. She whirled a roundhouse kick into Lily's chest.

"You are a nosy little bitch, Kylie. You think you are better than everyone, but you are going to die, just like everyone else. You think I took stole this virus so that you could take it?"

"I don't think I'm better than everyone. But I am better than you. You're an evil parasite."

Lily whirled around, the force of her kick from her momentum delivered a painful smash to Kylie's mouth. Kylie screamed with agony. Warm fluids gushed from her lip, and she realized that her front tooth was hanging by a thread. She looked down and saw her blood dripping onto her parka.

While Janice shadowed Lily with her gun, Misha inched towards the cooler that was left unattended on the ground. As he reached for the handle, Lily turned and delivered another kick onto his head. He staggered backward as Kylie lunged towards the cooler. Lily spun around and grunting, propelled Kylie's face into a metal dumpster. Kylie screeched from pain, but when she opened her eyes, she noticed that she'd landed an arm's reach from the cooler. With her head reeling, Kylie stretched her hand the extra inch needed to reach the handle and grabbed it, using it to momentarily steady herself. If the cooler contained what Misha said it did, she had to prevent disturbing or releasing its deadly contents.

With her head throbbing as if there a pipe bomb was exploding in her temples, she pushed the cooler into the melting snow to stabilize it. Woozy and confused, she shut her eyes, thinking perhaps she'd hit a tree on the way down a mountain. When she opened them, she knew this was no ski accident. There was no mountain. There was only Lily standing defiantly over her. Misha leaned against the dumpster, panting. Kylie looked over at him and bugged out her eyes.

"Step back Lily. This is your last warning," shouted Janice.

Ignoring her, Lily turned to Kylie and spat her words. "Here, my little entrepreneur. You want what's inside? I'll give it to you, no problem."

Still feeling dazed, Kylie pushed herself up to a seated position with her hands. From somewhere deep inside of her, her rage summoned a reserve of strength and a deep kiai rose from her diaphragm, a shout that came out like a triumphant, explosive HUH. The sound was both guttural and fierce, surprising Kylie as she pulled her legs up underneath her into a squat and sprung at Lily. The force of her weight pushed Lily back a foot further from the cooler, but it was still within her reach. Lily lunged for it, just as Misha grabbed his gun from the snow. He held it steady on Lily. "Don't move," he yelled.

Janice stepped closer to Lily, gun in hand. "FREEZE, Lily. Step away from the cooler," she shrieked.

"Come any closer, and I'll open it. What's inside will melt you down like an ice cube in July." Lily picked it up and backed away towards the alley, holding the cooler out in front of her face like a shield.

"You don't have that choice," said Janice. She sidestepped to the right to get a better sightline and avoid shooting the cooler. Lily reached down in an attempt to open its lid.

"DON'T MOVE," Janice screamed and fired a round into Lily's heart. The acrid smell of gun powder stung Kylie's nose. There was a surreal cloud, reminiscent of the air after Fourth of July fireworks. Through it, she saw Lily sprawled in front of the dumpster. Blood quickly sopped through her green coat, creating a brown stain that spread across the front. Her threatening persona had melted into a lifeless, but nasty ragdoll. Her red-lipsticked scowl was frozen into a permanent grimace and her legs flopped in front of her. One of her hands was still gripped around the handle of the cooler. Janice unclenched Lily's slender fingers, and they slid down to the melting snow, their jewel-like tips gleaming like her red blood that streamed into the snow.

Some other officers rushed in the yard with their guns drawn. Carefully picking up the cooler, Janice handed it to one of them. She doubled over and threw up in the snow.

"Donaldson, take this down to the Bureau and for God's sake, be careful."

"Your first?" he asked Janice.

She nodded, her face an unusual shade of pea green. She surveyed Lily, laying in the snow. "That's a pity," said Janice. "It was a gorgeous coat." She stepped toward Kylie. "And as for you? I TOLD you to stay in the car." Then, even though the blood gushed from Kylie's face, Janice hugged her.

23

The Wrap Up

Kylie heard the whoop-whoop-whoop of the approaching ambulance and then a strange silence when it stopped just outside Lily's Bubble Tea. An EMT rushed through the back door, while another one ran through the alley, pushing a stretcher. They looked Kylie over and sat her upon it. "I'm okay," Misha told them when they approached him. Although he was bleeding too, he was able to walk into the ambulance.

"You kids be good," Janice waved them off. "I'll see you later at the Bureau, assuming that you're all right. I'll call and check on you."

The shrieking ambulance wound around Chinatown's one-way streets, giving the EMTs just enough time to clean their wounds and dress them. A ferocious headache throbbed through Kylie's entire head. She closed her eyes, wanting to blank out and forget all of it, but within minutes, the EMT's rushed her into the ER with her tooth dangling by a thread. A young female dentist led her to a chair where she reinserted and bonded Kylie's tooth. She slept as the dentist worked. When the temporary crown was in place an hour later, Kylie's phone, still buried in the pocket of her bloody parka, began to ring. Kylie opened her eyes and pointed to the parka, hanging on a hook on the wall, her mouth too numb to form her words well.

"Seriously? You want to answer it?" asked the dentist. Kylie nodded, and an assistant retrieved it.

"Heywoh?" answered Kylie as best she could with her lips feeling like slabs of leather.

"Kylie, it's Bill Reinstadt. Stuart called and told me what happened. Are you all right?"

"I'm finh. Just having twouble talking, and I've got a big bandage on my face, but I'm okay. I just got my toof stuck back in." She wasn't quite as enthusiastic about talking to him. There were so many questions.

"That's good. Sorry that you're having all this trouble. How's Misha?"

"He's okay. He's got a gash on his face. We bowth have to buy some new coats, though."

"You did it, Kylie! Not only have you exposed a horrible crime, but you've helped to solve it, hopefully, plenty of time to prepare for Thanksgiving. I'm very impressed. You guys should get your new coats and then come into the Bureau. Stuart has Steve Hahn down there now, and he wants to talk to you both about the Lily folders. I'm tied up at work, but I'll stop by as soon as I can get away. Remember, you can still stay over tonight again if you need to. Just have the concierge let you in if I'm not around. Hopefully, it will be okay for you to go back to your place tomorrow."

"Thanks, Bill. I appreciate that. I guess I'll see you later."

"I did want to mention that I heard you met my decorator. I suppose I should have warned you that he was there. I know you must have a lot of questions, but for all intensive purposes, how about we keep this as our little secret?"

Emile was his decorator? She doubted it. She didn't care if Reinstadt was gay, but she did want his honesty. Still, he had been so good to her. She was going to let this go for now. Kylie's numbed lips stretched, trying to smile. "Sure. Of course. I did wonder about your zebra rug though."

"Oh, that. That was Emile's idea. Evidently, it's very old. He didn't kill any zebras to get it. I understand how gross that is." He sighed. "For all intensive purposes, I suppose I should reign him in a little."

Kylie seemed satisfied. When she was finished with the dentist, Misha was waiting in the lobby, engrossed in a game on his phone. He had a full gauze bandage across his forehead. Kylie stood in front of him, and he looked up, startled. "Oh, my goodness. Wook at you. How're you doing?" she asked, trying to refrain herself from touching his face.

"I'm okay. Man, we look like we were in a war," he laughed ironically, taking in her bloody coat and bandaged cheek. "Your tooth looks good, though," he added when she smiled. "*Pchelka*, you okay?" he asked softly.

"I'm fine, except that I can hardly twalk and have a headache. We *were* in a war. I just heard from Reinstadt and Stuart has Steve Hahn. Stuart wants us to come in and help with the Lily Folders. They're bringing Michael Harriman in too. First, though, I think I need to go shopping since I might scare people looking like this. It's pwetty bad, even by my standards," Kylie said, pointing to her stained parka.

"We're in middle of big bust, and you want to go shopping?" chortled Misha, as if this was the funniest thing that he'd ever heard.

"Yes, I do. And it wouldn't hurt for you to look more normal either."

"I never look normal," he grinned.

"Gwad you find this so amusing. I'm going to wok down and pick up some Vicodin at CVS." She waved her prescription at him." Then, I want to buy a new parka at Macy's. You can come, I suppose, or if you think this is so funny, I'll meet you there."

"I guess I could pick up something. Quick, right?"

Kylie still felt a little stunned, but she was already walking out the door, urging him to hurry by rotating her hand. As they crossed Kneeland Street, Misha craned his neck towards where he'd left his car. Satisfied that he could see the bright blue Porsche shine amid the dreary colors and the slush, Misha shoved his hands in the pocket of his tattered jacket. He would pick up the car later.

They headed up Washington. For the first few blocks, they felt invisible as they walked unnoticed among meandering homeless people and older Chinese women maneuvering their grocery carts. Apparently, they weren't interested or didn't think it unusual for two young people to stroll by with bandaged faces and bloody coats. They stopped in the CVS, a drugstore nearly as plentiful in Boston as Red Sox fans, and came out with a bottle of twelve little tablets which Kylie counted on to get her through. She popped one in her mouth as they continued on past the more upscale blocks lined with luxury apartments, theaters, and restaurants. Here the people that passed gave them curious stares and then politely looked away.

"Let's go in," said Kylie heading to the door at Macy's. She left him in the men's department. "Give me ten minutes. I'll meet you back here," she said, hopping on the escalator. She headed right to the coats, tried on the first plain black parka she found in her size. Delighted that it fit, she promptly bought it.

"I'll wear this," Kylie told the clerk when she paid. She transferred the contents out of from her old pockets into the new parka before handing the bloody jacket over to the clerk for disposal. The woman held out a trash can, scowling as if Kylie was giving her a dead rat.

The Novocain began to wear off as Kylie rode the escalator down to the main floor. As she rode, she spotted Misha sporting a new leather motorcycle jacket, preening in a mirror among racks of overcoats. He'd combed his hair over his bandage and was already wearing his aviator shades. Maybe the Vicodin starting to kick in, but Kylie had to admit that he certainly was good looking. Too bad that was too full of himself, even if he was a good kisser. She was still convinced that he was a player, just having an adventure. She was NOT going to let herself fall for this guy. "I see you're ready," she said joining him at the mirror. "Shall we?'

Kylie zipped up her new jacket and tied the fur-trimmed hood under her chin. She led the way out of the store and they walked the short blocks on Washington Street, realizing that together, even in their new coats, they probably look like they'd escaped from a hospital or a mental institution. "So, tell me happened with Lily," Kylie asked.

"I asked the girl behind the counter for bubble tea. While she was making it, I asked if Lily was there, and she said no. So, then I asked if I could look around at place since I was going to write an article on bubble tea establishments and wanted to see what it looked like, but Lily came out from the back room, very suspicious. She asked me what I wanted, although she obviously had heard me. I guess she didn't buy my story," he shrugged as he talked. "She told me to get out, and I told her that she wasn't very friendly and then she took one of the kitchen knives and tried to slice me. When I started to reach for my gun, she kicked my forehead with one of her frigging high heels. Not nice. Then she ran into a back room and out the door. I followed her outside, and that's about when you were kicking the shit out of her and when Janice came in."

"Yes, and the rest is my dental history," said Kylie, touching her new tooth.

Within moments, they arrived at the Bureau, where an officer at reception sent them through a security scan and after making Misha leave his gun. He directed them to the conference room that Kylie had begun to think of as her satellite office. Stuart was waiting for them, filling out paperwork.

"Kylie! Misha!" Stuart greeted them like old friends. "You two just can't stay out of trouble, can you?"

The Vicodin was definitely working. Kylie was starting to feel great and gave him a wide grin. She touched her bandage and gave him her best smile, still a tiny bit cockeyed from the Novocain. "Just trying to help, Stuart."

"Are you guys okay otherwise?"

They nodded.

"Good. So, here's the thing," Stuart said, as they sat down. "We've got Steve Hahn in another room, and I need to see your evidence."

"No problem," said Kylie. "Problem is that I don't have my laptop here, but Misha can log in through his computer. You still have his laptop, right?"

Stuart picked up his phone and called someone. Within minutes, there was a polite knock on the door and a young agent laid Misha's computer on the table.

"That should work," said Misha, sounding thrilled to reconnect with his computer. He sat down at the table and logged into OMG with Kylie leaning over his shoulder.

Kylie directed him to the report on Hahn. "Here, she pointed. Hahn's has the encrypted folder right here on his desktop. When Misha cracks this open, it's most likely going to be the same one that Gerry Fox and Simon had, as well as Lily Harriman. This folder probably has everything on the lethal virus."

Misha broke in, "Yes if it's like the other ones, it will have the formula, all the drug sequencing, and the release plan. Everything."

"We've got the vial that was in Lily's cooler. I also want to make sure that there aren't anymore," said Stuart.

Kylie nodded and moved to another chair where she would still have a clear view of what Misha was doing.

"This may take me a minute," said Misha, who was focused

with laser attention on Steve Hahn's desktop files. He found the Lily folder and began typing in series of numbers and symbols, that made no sense to Kylie.

After about five minutes, Misha looked up. "If this is right, Boston is a test. It looks like Lily had another vial and planned to auction it."

"Let's see," said Stuart.

Misha scrolled down a bit. "Here," he pointed. "Looks like they plannned is to demo it in Boston so that buyers will see its power."

"If there's another vial, we're still not safe. Does it say where they're going to release it? When? Is anyone else involved?" Stuart asked.

"It doesn't," said Misha. "Hahn's here, so why don't you ask him?"

"That's the plan. I'll need my laptop back, if I may?" Stuart picked up the computer.

"Sure," said Kylie. "Or, if you want, we can put the report on a thumb drive, and you can have it."

"I have a better idea," he said. How about you put the whole program on a thumb drive and you show our tech team how to use it?"

Kylie gulped. OMG was her baby that she'd paid with a good chunk of her trust find and six months of her life to produce. Did Stuart expect her just to hand it over? Reinstadt had already agreed to pay $250,000, but then he hadn't signed anything yet. "Of course, I'm happy to help," she said, but you should that it cost me a small fortune to get it developed. Is there any chance of getting reimbursed?"

Stuart's eyes danced with amusement. "And the sky is going

to start raining unicorns. You should know that you could be looking at a jail sentence for hacking, my dear. Are you sure you want to go down that road? We are still watching you both very carefully. You are very lucky that I haven't locked you up."

"Stuart, it's obvious that we're trying to help here and NO, I don't want to go down any road that leads to jail. I'm just saying that it would be really nice to get something for it. After all, I developed this program, and you obviously see its value for solving crimes."

"Kylie, don't you read the news? If you are going to invent something, it needs to be so far beyond anything that's out there. I mean, we have international hacking events now on a regular basis."

"I know that, but that isn't technology that's available to most people. I didn't design this for espionage, although it's not bad, is it? And, it's obviously better than anything that you have now, or you wouldn't want it. Without it, I wouldn't have been able to give you all this information, right?" she managed a grin, which she hoped was appealing.

"I suppose, you do have a point, but a minor one." Stuart rolled his eyes towards the ceiling as if consulting someone upstairs. "God help me, I doubt it, but I'll see what I can do," he said. "Meanwhile, let's table the money thing. I want you to talk to our tech director."

"I have it on a thumb drive already," she said, retrieving it from her wallet and waved it in the air. "But can we be there when you interview Hahn?"

"Nope. You two monkeys sit tight. I'm going to send Jason in here to get you and can work with him and install this thing so that you can have your laptop back."

"Gee, thanks," said Kylie.

Stuart left Kylie and Misha, and Kylie set her elbows on the table and sunk her head into her hands, feeling her gauze bandage between her fingers. I can't believe that they're just going to walk away with OMG."

"You don't know that for sure. It might be okay. The thing is that it worked and we helped prevent a horrible disaster."

"All I wanted was to help people make good decisions. I never intended to get involved in this kind of craziness. Do you realize how much money I put into developing this program? It's all from my savings. Well, actually, my trust fund. I didn't want a regular job, but it looks like I blew that too, since now I am going to have to get one so that I can support myself. I planned this as a lean start-up, but this one is anorexic. I always dreamed of doing something exciting and meaningful. I don't think I'm asking a lot, do you?"

Before Misha could answer, a portly man in mid-forties rushed into the conference room, his belly bulging over his khaki pants. "Hi guys," he said. "I'm Jason. Come with me and bring the program. We'll get this baby cooking."

Kylie and Misha followed him down a hall to a dark room filled with five guys intently working at their desk computers with one oversized monitor on the wall. Jason sat them down at his desk with large double monitors. His red face and balding head glowed from the screens. "You have something for me?" He held out a pudgy hand to Kylie.

"Indeed." She presented the thumb drive with a slight bow. Jason installed it and Kylie walked him through the program.

"Great job on this," he said, clicking around to the different functions.

"It was supposed to be able to open encrypted folders but it doesn't always work. That's where I come in," said Misha.

"Okay, let's take it for a spin," said Jason.

Kylie and Misha spent the next hour training Jason. When they were done, Jason returned Kylie's thumb drive to her and marched Kylie and Misha back to the conference room. "I'll let Stuart know that you're here," he said. I hope you kids have a good Thanksgiving."

"Thanks, you too," said Kylie.

She turned to Misha when Jason closed the door. "What are doing for Thanksgiving?"

"Not much. I don't have family here. I came for school and stayed, so it's never been something I did."

"That's too bad. Have you ever gone to a Thanksgiving?"

"Not really." He looked at his shoes, appearing boyish and vulnerable.

Maybe it was the Vicodin, but underneath Misha's bravado was something melancholy and sweet that suddenly appealed to her. He wasn't as tough as he pretended to be. And what if she'd lost him to Lily's viciousness? Before she knew what was coming, Kylie blurted out an invitation to Thanksgiving with her parents.

"Just as a friend, of course," she rushed. "And, I should warn you, my family is pretty strange."

"It's fine," he said, with a slight bow. "It would be my honor. Anyway, how strange could they be if they produced you?"

"Hah. Just be prepared," she said.

They were discussing details when Stuart returned. "You kids are free to go," he said. "We have a confession! And, by the way, they found your laptop in Hahn's office at Visiozyme."

She turned and high-fived Misha. "Fantastic!" She sat back in her chair and closed her eyes, as if saying a silent thank you. She felt jubilant, but then remembered that there could be more of the virus out there. "Did you find any more vials?"

"Possibly. It turns out that Lily stored the virus with her uncle. He has an herb store just across the street from her bubble tea place. Your instincts were right to sense something was off and your photo was useful. You were right. He was the man who was standing across the street from you. She'd gone down there to retrieve the vial from her uncle. We got her cell phone log, and the uncle had called her just minutes before you encountered her in the back of the shop. He must have been standing watch and was trying to warn her. Some of our officers were still down there and they found him, getting into his car. What we don't know is if this was all of it. We're searching his place."

"I knew he was involved by the creepy the way he was watching me," said Kylie. "So, it's possible that we're still not safe?"

"We're not sure if there's anyone left to release it or if there, or if the uncle has hidden it, or if there's really any more of the virus." Stuart knotted his brows.

"What did Hahn say?" asked Kylie.

"At first, he was Mr. Innocent and denied everything. Then we showed him the folder that we had from his computer, and we got a full confession."

"What a relief! Did he say why he did it?"

"Yeah. Fox hired Hahn to do the project and Hahn brought Simon into it to do some of the coding. Later, Lily stole it and it somehow got tied up with her divorce from Michael Harriman.

She'd told him that if he didn't give her what she wanted, she was going to do something diabolical and blame it on him. But it was much bigger than just something to blackmail her ex-husband. Fox planned to release it in Boston as a test, to demonstrate its muscle so that he could sell it to foreign governments. Hahn said that as far as he knows, there were only two vials, but we aren't ruling out the possibility that there might be more. He didn't work in the lab. He only helped design the virus.

"If they planned on selling them, why would they make just two? Are you sure there was no one else involved?" Kylie asked.

"No, we're not sure. It is a possibility, especially if there's more. As far as Fox, we do know that a while back, there was also some sort of stock takeover going on at Visiozyme. There must have been something going on between Fox and Lily if he named the thing after her. Hahn thinks that Fox was trying to buy the company to make it a leader in chemical weapons, instead of prescription drugs. Your poor buddy Simon was just a flunky who knew too much. Unfortunate."

"What about the ex-husband?" asked Misha.

"We've got him in for questioning, and he's filling out a statement now. It appears that Lily gave him a really rough time. She sounded like a piece of work. Although he wasn't involved in any of this, he wasn't exactly displeased about the outcome. I've never seen a guy so happy to see his ex-wife dead. There's going to be a press conference later. Are you two up for coming for a photo?"

Kylie and Misha looked at each other. "Sure," they said in unison.

"But are you going to say the case is solved? What if there are other vials?" asked Kylie.

Stuart extended his chin and scratched it. "We'll work on the spin on this. There's no proof that there's more of the virus floating around so I'm pretty sure that this is the end of it. We can't be scaring people unnecessarily, although we have to be cautious, of course. I'll see you at three at the Statehouse."

Kylie shot Misha a worried look. He raised his eyebrows in response as they filed out to the lobby where Misha could retrieve his gun.

"Do you want to hang out with me until press conference? I have to go back and get my car, so maybe you could come too," he asked.

"Sure, but no bubble tea, thanks."

24

The Clean up

Supposedly the Lily case was resolved, but Kylie had a nagging feeling that something wasn't quite right about the story on Emile. It would be nearly impossible to run a search on him since she didn't know his last name, but she had to try. There was also her ransacked apartment waiting to be reassembled, so as they left the bureau, she asked Misha to drive her home.

"You want some help?" he asked.

"It's a disaster. I don't want to impose."

"No problem. I have to hang out until the press conference anyway," he said.

"Sure, but you're warned," she said, directing him to her building.

When he found a parking space in front, he grinned. "Good omen. See?"

Even though she already knew what to expect, Kylie's heart sank when she opened the door and saw the shambles of what she'd called home. Besides having her belongings trashed, her space would forever be tainted by the indelible image of Fox sitting on her couch.

"You weren't kidding," said Misha. "This is terrible. It looks like you had a tornado."

Kylie shuddered, remembering the shock of Fox sitting on her couch and was grateful for Misha's company. The search on Emile could wait.

They started in the kitchen, where the contents of the cupboards had been tossed onto the counter and floor, and the food that had been ousted from the freezer lay defrosting in puddles next to empty ice cube trays on the linoleum. The refrigerator had been swept clean. The caps were off all the bottles and if their contents had been emptied into a marbled glob in the sink.

Kylie began to clean the counters as Misha anticipated her movements, nimbly dancing around her as he swept her tiny kitchen with a broom. He played some French jazz on this phone which helped Kylie's mood. Within an hour, they'd cleaned and put the kitchen back together and Kylie was on her way to feeling more put together too.

As the last broken glasses and dishes were thrown away and what was salvageable had been washed and returned to their proper places, It helped, but Kylie still felt pretty glum. "I guess it's a good excuse to clean my apartment. I never liked those dishes anyhow. It should feel good to get this back in order, but honestly, I feel like I've been decimated. First, my place was ransacked, and then I had to buy a new computer, and a phone. Oh, and I had to pay for a helicopter ride, a new coat, and a new tooth. Now it looks like I need to buy all new food and even dishes too. I'll probably need a new couch too with the cushions slashed. That doesn't even touch what I lost on paying Simon and having to give OMG away. I hate to sound like a complainer, but it's too much.

"Go ahead, cry if you need to," he said. "You're allowed. You have a lot to complain about. Tell you what. How about I refund what you paid me? Let's just say it's my contribution to solving this crime."

With Misha's permission that she hadn't even allowed, Kylie's tears rolled down her cheeks. She leaned against the kitchen counter hugging herself while Misha put away the last of her packages of ramen noodles. After all of this, she didn't even know if she could afford Ramen anymore. But she knew her tears were not just from feeling sorry for herself, from gratitude. She'd received so much kindness for from Reinstadt, Janice, and now Misha.

After a few moments, Misha noticed her crying. He walked over to where she was leaning against the sink and touched her shoulder gently. "*Pchelka*, It's going to be okay." He lifted her chin and wiped her tears with a finger. His simple gesture opened a floodgate, and Kylie's shoulders shook as sobbed. Misha opened his arms and enveloped her, rocking her slowly her in her arms until her tears subsided. She couldn't recall having been held like that before. In fact, except for his kiss earlier that day, it had been way too long since anyone had even touched her. She was afraid to move. She could hardly breathe and drank in his embrace like an infusion of a vital nutrient that she'd been lacking.

Misha spoke softly. "I know it might be hard for you to think of anything good in this, but you have lot to be happy about and things to be proud for. You had a vision and went for it. Not everyone does that. You were brave and smart and survived all of this. Best, you solved a terrible crime, and you're getting your apartment clean. As a bonus, you met me! Arrrrghh!"

The edges of Kylie's mouth curved into a smile as she snuggled deeper against his wool sweater. A long-frozen part of her began to thaw, and that part wanted to kiss him. But Kylie was afraid that part couldn't be trusted. She felt too shaky, too vulnerable, and just said, "Thanks, Misha. You've been great." She was sorry when Misha raised one of his arms and looked at his watch.

"We need to go back soon for the press conference. Maybe you should get ready?"

"I guess." She broke away and looked at him, but his face was blank. Maybe he thought she was just a charity case. She probably was.

"What does one wear to a press conference?" she asked.

"I have no idea."

She looked down at the dirty jeans and rumpled sweater that she'd been wearing for two days. "Probably not this. I guess I should change."

In the bathroom, Kylie took the contents of her medicine cabinet that had been dumped in the sink and set them on the counter. She splashed cold water on her face, careful not to wet her bandage. Her skin looked dewy in the mirror, except for the grotesque gauze covering a good part of her left cheek. She dreaded seeing the scar that would always be a souvenir from Lily, that she also considered it a badge of honor. She freshened her messy ponytail and applied a pink lip gloss. Next, she rummaged through a pile of clothes on the floor in her bedroom put on a pair of black dress pants, a clean turtleneck, a blazer, and boots.

"I'm ready," she said. She would have to run the report on Emile when she got home.

Misha turned from where he'd been staring at her MBA on the wall. "You look good except for that white little pillow taped to your face, but not much that you can do about that. It's kind of sexy."

"Yeah, right."

"You're fine. Really. It's your badge of courage. We should go."

They hiked up to Charles Street and unto Beacon Hill. In less than twenty minutes they stood at the yard that was once a cow pasture for John Hancock's cows. Now it was the site of the historic Massachusetts statehouse, the jewel of Boston, with its burnished gold dome shimmering in the sunlight. They climbed the wide steps. Inside, the walked through the cacophony of voices echoing in the main rotunda to find Stuart and Janice in one of the hearing rooms. There was a flurry of activity with members of the press milling and media techs setting up tripods and microphones at a podium.

"I see that our little trouble-makers are here," Janice said to Stuart as Kylie and Misha came in. She turned to Kylie and smiled, "You clean up nicely."

"Kylie, I'd like to talk to you privately for a minute," Stuart said, ushering her over to a corner. "I realize that we got off to a bit of a rough start and never really thanked you for what you did here. True, you are a law-breaker and a world-class butinski, sticking your nose everywhere you shouldn't, but if you hadn't, a lot of people might have died. Not everyone would have done what you did. We wouldn't have had the confession from Hahn without your evidence. You stuck with it and put up with a lot. I think you've got the makings of a good FBI agent, if you have the stomach for it."

"Wow," she grinned. "I was terrified that you were about to arrest me. Honestly, I've been a wreck through this whole thing. All I wanted was to do was start a business, and I thought I had an awesome idea."

"Yes, I suppose you did, and if it was applied to legal means, I would have applauded you. But you have had some good insights and pretty great instincts. You can work with us in that capacity. You don't have to be out in the field. You would work with Janice and help to investigate crimes with technology. You two would work as a team. Would that be more to your liking?"

"How does Janice feel about that?"

"She was the one who brought it up."

Kylie grinned as if she'd won the lottery. She'd come to realize that this was her dream—certainly not a boring desk job that she dreaded. She had to admit that she liked Janice. But she had to play it right. "Yes, I might consider it. Have you thought about how I might be compensated for OMG? After all, you do have my program now, and you must admit, it saved the day."

"Spoken like a true entrepreneur. I'm looking at our budget, but it's doubtful."

She frowned. "Please remember that I paid Simon a hefty

sum to build it, and had no income for six months while we were working on it, so it's not fair for me to just give it away."

Stuart stroked his chin and gave her an ironic laugh. "Life isn't always fair, is it? You haven't been arrested for hacking and perhaps that's your fine and your ticket to freedom. You can probably kiss that money good-bye, but look, tomorrow is Thanksgiving. Why don't we meet on Monday after the holiday and I can tell you what's involved and make you a formal offer? That is if you're interested?"

Kylie laughed, "I'd never considered this kind of work, and strangely, I'm surprised to say that it does."

"Excellent. I think you'd be a terrific addition."

"One thing though," said Kylie, tilting her chin chin. "What about Misha? He's not being deported is he? He's a good guy and was an enormous help. I think he wants to apply for citizenship. Maybe there's something you can do to help?"

"I'll see what I can do. Meanwhile, let's set a time to talk after the holiday."

As they were setting a meeting time, Bill Reinstadt slowly navigated through a gaggle of news-hungry reporters shouting questions at him. He held a hand up to stop them, finally making his way over to Kylie and Stuart's corner of the room. Although Kylie smiled in greeting, her confusion had knocked him off his pedestal. Evidently, Reinstadt was just another flawed person like the rest of them.

"Kylie. Stuart. Glad to see you both. It's much better under these circumstances than the last time we met," said Bill. I have to hand to you for cleaning this up so quickly."

Kylie motioned for Misha to join them from across the room

where he was leaning against a wall. "Misha was an important part of this too."

Misha shook his head no, as if to say, this is your show. Enjoy it.

Janice rejoined them. "How's my little crime fighter?" she asked Kylie.

"I'm fine, now that this is over. That is, *if* it's over. I only wish I'd had time to finish your omelet."

"Another time," Janice laughed.

They chatted for few moments until the press secretary came in. Reinstadt excused himself and followed him up to the front of the room. The hum in the chamber quieted as he took the podium and began to speak. "Thanks for coming this afternoon. We have an extraordinary statement about a crime that threatened the lives of our entire city. I'm happy to say, that it's been both detected and thwarted. I would like to introduce Bill Reinstadt to you who had a pivotal role in this by bringing it to our attention. Reinstadt stepped up to the podium. As usual, his confident air exuded his unique blend of vitality and optimism.

Kylie still thought he still looked presidential, but his dishonesty about who he was fed her doubts which had rooted and started to grow. Who was Reinstadt really? And that zebra rug? Could she believe anything that he said after seeing that?

He cleared his throat and began, "Less than a week ago a young local entrepreneur reached out to me. She's a recent Harvard MBA who created a database tool and wanted to demo it. Then, before she could even show it to me, she'd uncovered a sinister plan to release a deadly virus into the atmosphere on Black Friday. Through no fault of her own, she found herself embroiled in it. We immediately pulled in the FBI and Homeland Security to intervene. Through her program, we found the perpetrators and the virus. Everything is fine now, and it was her program that helped solve the case and get a confession from the perpetrator. Her name is Kylie Maynard, and she is resilient and courageous. You'll meet her in just a minute. I want to thank both the FBI and Kylie for their outstanding efforts in preventing a devastating disaster. In the meantime, three people died during this investigation: Simon Whitehead, Gerry Fox, and Lily Harriman. Kylie was kidnapped by Gerry Fox but escaped and later had a life or death battle with Lily Harriman, trying to save the virus from being released. I am sure I speak for all of you when I say how proud I am of her. But before you meet Kylie, we have a word from our governor."

There was applause as the governor came in and stood next to Bill who introduced him. His wooly grey hair peeked around his ears in what was otherwise cue ball bald. He looked old school and tired standing next to Reinstadt. "I want to thank Bill for handling this and of course our government agencies, forever vigilant in caring for our welfare. But most of all, I would like to present this award of recognition for valor to Kylie Maynard, who evidently endured a lot in this ordeal, and without her, we would all be at risk. Kylie, can you please come up here?"

Kylie's face felt as hot as if she'd been sitting in a sauna. She sandwiched into her place between the governor and Bill Reinstadt. The governor shook her hand, then presented her with a framed certificate of valor. "Kylie, please accept this certificate as a token of our appreciation. You're an outstanding citizen, and the people of Massachusetts are forever grateful to you."

"Thanks, so much." Kylie accepted it, smiled, and held it up for the press. The governor asked her to say a few words.

Kylie leaned into the microphone bouquet on the podium. "Thank you Governor Kelly and the people of Boston. I never dreamed that I'd ever be involved in anything like this, but evidently, life can throw some curve balls. Anyway, I'm pleased that my program turned out to be such a useful tool. It was a heck of a ride, and I'm grateful to Bill Reinstadt, to the FBI, and to Simon Whitehead who built the program and then was killed, and Misha, my programmer, for working with me to help solve this." She held up her certificate. "This means a lot to me. Again, thank you very much."

Afterward, Kylie stood near the podium, not ready to join the large noisy crowd on the floor. She was interviewed by reporters from the Boston Globe, The New York Times, and three local TV stations. When almost everyone had left, Reinstadt suddenly appeared at her side.

"Congratulations," he said. "I meant what I said. I'm so proud of you."

Kylie involuntarily warmed in the glow of his smile. For just a moment, she forgot about Emile and she touched the bandage on her cheek, hoping it had magically disappeared. The plump wad of gauze was still there, cottony-soft under her fingers. "It wouldn't have happened without you. Looks like I have a job interview with the FBI next week."

"So, I heard. If you need a recommendation, just say so. Do you need to stay at Chez Reinstadt again?"

"Thanks, but I think I'll be okay at home now, even though

it's a mess. Maybe you could leave my bag with your concierge, and I can get it on Friday?"

Reinstadt nodded thoughtfully. "Of course. Hopefully, your decision doesn't have anything to do with your meeting Emile. I really am sorry about all of that, but you know, you shouldn't have been snooping. But I guess we both know that's what you do, right?"

Kylie sighed. "Mea Culpa. Look, I'm beyond embarrassed. Honestly, I am so sorry about that."

He gave her a knowing smile. "Come on, Kylie. You are impossibly nosy. We both know that you'd do it again if you had the chance, wouldn't you? And if you hadn't, eventually, you might have nosed around a little more with OMG and found out anyway."

She nodded ruefully. "I suppose you're right. It's true that I'm sorry though."

"I know. I never know if people are really sorry that they did something, or just sorry that they got caught. I'm not trying to make you feel bad. I'm just trying to make a point. The truth is that people are what they are, and they do what they do because of it. We can't help it. I am not going to judge you and hopefully, you are not going to judge me. Quid pro quo. We are just going to keep this quiet. Agreed?"

"Of course. Look, I don't care if you're gay. What I do care about is that you don't let anyone know who you really are. There's lots of gay politicians. What do you care if people know? It just seems so dishonest. It's about who you are as a person, and the fact that your whole platform is about transparency makes this feel like a betrayal. Don't you have to live transparently too? If this a lie, what else are you lying about?"

"Of course, I 'd love to live openly, but just like you are using OMG, which is really a spying platform, to do some good, I feel that the end justifies the means. I'm going to get further, and do more good in the world if most people think I am like them. I think who I sleep with is private, and I plan to keep it that way. It has nothing to do with my ideas about I want to run the country. Can you understand that?"

"I suppose, but I'm not sure that I agree. And the rug? You're supposedly an animal advocate." Kylie threw her hands in the air. "I know what you said, but a zebra rug? Really?"

"Emile gave it to me a long time ago. If I just threw it out, the poor zebra would be wasted. At least this way, I can sort of honor him."

"Walking on the skin of a dead zebra is a weird way of honoring him."

"Look, we can talk about this more another time. I can tell that you are the girl who is going to keep me honest. I just want you to know that I have a lot of respect for your spunk and your energy. If you don't like your offer at the FBI, please come and talk to me. Okay?"

"I will. And thanks for everything. But can I ask you one more question?"

"If it's quick. What?"

"It seemed like it was inevitable that I'd encounter Emile. Did you want me to find out?"

"No, not really. I'm a little embarrassed that it happened like that. It was just unfortunate timing. My guess is that perhaps Emile wanted you to know that he was there. Maybe he was just letting you know how things stand so that you wouldn't get any ideas."

"Oh, I see," she blushed and surprised herself by throwing a hug around his neck. It was good that he could be so honest with her. Perhaps she could trust him after all. His skin felt warm under her clammy hands. Her fantasies about him weren't entirely buried since she felt a small stab of disappointment that he was gay. But what had she expected? He was never attainable anyway.

He backed off so their bodies didn't quite touch and patted her back as if he was burping a baby. "Have a good Thanksgiving."

"You too. Are you celebrating with Emile?" She was amazed at her boldness.

"Yes, we're just having dinner at Chez Reinstadt."

"Well, don't eat too much turkey." Kylie waved him off and turned headed towards Misha. He had been patiently waiting for her, amusing himself with his phone from a chair on the sidelines. He was startled when she approached, flashed his widest dimpled smile. Suddenly, Kylie sucked in her breath. She was elated to see him.

Kylie had planned to pick up a couple of slices of pizza at Sal's, across from the Common, then head home and relax with a movie, but when Misha suggested a celebration dinner at Stephanie's on Newbury Street, her plan sounded pathetic. Enough of being a hermit.

"Sure," she said, surprising herself. "I'll meet you there. How's seven thirty?" That was just enough time to go home, log into OMG, and find out more about Emile. She was only sorry that she'd never learned his last name. No matter. She would find it and then have a lovely, relaxing celebration with Misha. They deserved it.

* * *

Even though she had worked hard with Misha putting her apartment back together, Kylie was dismayed when she unlocked her door and the first thing she saw was the shredded couch cushions. She ignored it and got to work, opening her laptop on her table. Running the new searches on Emile was like shooting in the dark since she wasn't entirely sure what she was looking for. She'd started by searching Reinstadt's email, hoping to find Emile's last name. Nada. Frustrated, she realized that perhaps OMG wasn't as powerful as she'd thought. She'd have to dig up some information from the usual places available to everyone else in the world. She Googled Bill Reinstadt, hoping to find some photos of him with Emile. There were hundreds of articles with photos to sift through and she began clicking through them, one by one.

As in many of the photos, he was flanked by his gorgeous, supposed girlfriend, Emily Wickland, but there was one color close-up that stopped her cold as Emily's aquamarine eyes stared out at her. They were the same shade as Emile's...unforgettable. And her perfect smile? It was exactly like Emile's too. No wonder he'd looked so familiar. She had already seen many photos of Emily!

Kylie shook her head in disbelief and then leaned in to study the photo more closely. Bill and Emily appeared to be the perfect political couple, with the glow of movie-star glamour. What would Reinstadt's supporters think about being duped like this? Kylie felt betrayed. She didn't care that he was gay, but this was nuts. She was shocked. What would his adversaries think? She could imagine what this might do to his career if this got out. No wonder he was so interested in accessing OMG, her spying machine. He needed to monitor what was being said about him.

But perhaps she was mistaken. She carefully re-examined Emily's perfect, light-up-a-room smile that beamed at her from her computer screen. Unless he had an identical twin sister, it was unmistakably Emile. Evidently, he owned some very good wigs and hairpieces, not to mention a fashionable and very flattering wardrobe. Kylie couldn't tell if he was just a cross-dresser or if he was transgender. It didn't matter. She intended to find out more.

She filled in the query fields for a new search on Emily Wickland. This time, she would look at more than Emily's calendar for dates with Bill, still uncertain what she was looking for. Within ten minutes, she had thousands of emails, Emily's financials, texts, and access to her hard drive. Kylie had a couple of hours until it was time to meet Misha and she dove in.

Kylie already knew that Emily owned *Making Faces*, a PR firm. It was registered under Emily's name, not Emile's. Kylie suspected that the company was an arm of Bill Reinstadt's political ambitions since it appeared that he was her best client. Kylie wondered why Emily hadn't just run the company as Emile, but it appeared that there was no public Emile. He seemed to be invisible. But why? She searched the emails but didn't know what she was looking for. Her instincts told her that everything she would find under the name of Emily

Wickland, would be squeaky clean. She desperately wanted to find out who Emile really was. She looked at her watch and sighed. Even though she knew it was gnawing at her, this would have to wait until she returned from dinner.

* * *

Stephanie's was one of Kylie's favorites restaurants, just a few blocks from her apartment. Its prime location was on the corner of Exeter and Newbury among chic boutiques, restaurants, and galleries. People went to be seen in the outdoor café in the summer, and in November, it was still crowded inside and a reliable place to get a good meal. Misha was already seated in a tufted leather booth when Kylie got there.

Unsure if this was a date, Kylie wasn't sure if she wanted it be one. It was fine with her if this was just two friends celebrating. But just in case, she'd taken a tiny bit of extra care in getting dressed, and part of her was hoping that the dinner wasn't just as colleagues. She had been so involved running the search on Emile, there was no time left to fuss. Just as well. She wanted to look nice enough, but not like she was trying too hard. Still, something told her to free her usual ponytail, and she quickly brushed it out, letting the blonde ends grazing her shoulders. She quickly applied some blush to her non-bandaged cheek to give herself a healthy outdoor glow. She dabbed some gloss to her mouth, that seemed to have a little smile on the corners, despite her nagging anxiety about Emile. She wore the same turtleneck and pants from the press conference, but added a thin leather belt around her waist, some gold hoop earrings and put on her high heeled boots.

Misha rose as she came in. His face was flushed and Kylie noticed that he'd changed into a nice sweater and wool pants.

"You look hot," he said.

Kylie got that this wasn't a dinner for colleagues and was a little surprised to be warming to the idea. They ordered margaritas and lobster guacamole to start.

"That was amazing today," Misha commented. "I do encryption all the time, but never for anything so life and death."

The waitress set their drinks on the table.

"I know. In case I never said it, you did a great job," said Kylie.

Misha raised his glass. "Here's to us. It's a crazy world out there and we make a great team."

"Yay team!" Kylie wasn't sure what that meant exactly but seemed neutral enough. She clinked his glass and took a sip. The drink warmed her as it went down like drinking a glass of summer.

By his warm eyes and smiles, she realized that Misha was flirting and she had to admit that part of her was on high alert. And that part of her liked it. But something was locked up inside her, making her feel like a prudish, born-again virgin. What was the matter with her? She remembered his glove compartment full of condoms. He was obviously a player. Maybe in time, she'd feel safer once she got to know him…

The weight of her worries about Reinstadt and Emile were part of it too, but she held back in that department as well. She'd promised Bill, after all, that it would be their secret, but something nagged at her that there was something that wasn't quite right. This seemed like it was bigger than about Reinstadt being gay. It was about totally deceiving the public. She would wait just a bit longer since if there was something else to investigate, she could probably use Misha's help. Knowing so many secrets about people had turned her into a holding tank of information and she wasn't sure how much she could absorb without exploding the tank.

The waitress set the guacamole on the table. Kylie scooped up a huge mouthful of lobster bits and mashed avocado onto a chip and ate it. She shut her eyes, enjoying the flavor. When she opened them, Misha was grinning at her.

"You look like you're enjoying," he said.

"It beats ramen or pizza," Kylie said, smiling. But mostly she was enjoying Misha's company. If only she wasn't anxious that something was wrong and wanted to get back and solve the Emile mystery. They ordered hamburgers and more margaritas, but as Kylie guzzled the last of her second drink, she fought to keep her eyes open. "I'm exhausted," she yawned.

"Hey, so you want me to stay over your place to make sure that you're okay? I'll be like your bodyguard."

She surprised herself by nodding yes. "I've got some reports that I have to finish, but I have to admit, it would feel good to have you there. The place still gives me the creeps after Fox's evil aura slimed up my couch." Even though Kylie had already been home, done some work and gotten dressed, sleeping there alone felt frightening, since she still saw Fox pointing a gun at her. "But, you'll sleep on the couch, if that works," she added. "Maybe you can neutralize his bad vibes."

"Of course. Not to assume, but I took the T down here, just in case, so that I don't have to worry about my car."

They walked down Exeter, past Commonwealth Avenue, where the small white Christmas lights lit the center mall like a fairyland, and up a block to Marlborough Street where they turned towards her apartment. Happy to have Misha there, she dug up some blankets and a towel for him. They said goodnight and Kylie stumbled into her bed and into a deep sleep, comforted that Misha was snoring softly on her couch and his gun was sitting on her coffee table.

25

An unexpected source

On Wednesday morning, Kylie awoke and tiptoed out to the living room. Although not nearly as bright as her room at Reinstadt's, it was the brightest time of day in her apartment with soft morning light streaming through the living room window. Soundlessly, she stood behind her couch and watched Misha sleep. She liked the way his dark lashes fringed his flushed high cheekbones, reminding her of old paintings she'd seen of sensuous-looking Italian youths picking grapes, their ruddy cheeks offset by their black curls, looking earthy, yet irresistibly innocent, just like Misha. Except for her confusion about Reinstadt, she'd hardly noticed a guy in a long time. Seeing Misha so sweetly asleep opened her heart.

After some moments, Misha's eyes fluttered open, as if he'd sensed her there. He raised a finger and traced a line on her arm with his fingertip. "Good morning," he smiled. There was that dimple that she'd secretly come to adore.

"Hey," she said, smiling back. "I'm starving. There's no food here unless you want ramen noodles. How about we go out and get some coffee and croissants? Then I can figure out what to do about my poor slashed-up furniture."

"Sure, we can go out, if that's what you want to do. It sounds like you're busy and I should take off and let you get your work done. I guess I'll see you tomorrow for Thanksgiving." He gave her a funny look.

"Yes, but maybe you want to come back later? How are you at making apple pie?"

Misha shrugged. "Not good. In my country, our apple pie that is more like a cake; not that I ever really baked anything. I am good at making some things though." His innocent look morphed into a devilish grin.

In one quick motion, his strong, bare arms pulled her over the back of the couch until she toppled on top of him and his arms encircled her. Her legs slid down and he covered her with his blanket. She was too surprised to protest, or perhaps she loved the feel of his bare skin. Kylie hungered for his kiss as their mouths sought each other. She forgot the coffee and croissants.

She thought that Misha's skin must have been electric, since everywhere she touched him, which was practically all over, her hands tingled. Somehow her T-shirt and sweatpants pajamas had fallen off and were stuffed somewhere under his blanket. Magically, he'd already lost his boxers. *Had he slept naked?* She rubbed her hand over the six-pack she'd seen in the photo of him at the beach. He groaned as she moved her hand lower. All she wanted was his kisses and his hands all over the outside and inside of her. Misha obliged.

"Argh. My condoms are in my car." He swore in Russian.

"So much for being prepared," she panted.

"It just calls for some creativity." Misha flipped around and kissed a trail down on her stomach to her thighs. Gently, he opened her legs with his fingers and got very creative with his tongue. Not that she'd had all that much experience, but Kylie had never been touched by anyone who had really known what he was doing in that department. She started to contemplate just how many women he'd practiced on, to perfect his technique, but her racing heart overcame her thoughts. Wherever he touched her, she opened herself more to him, as if he were a violin virtuoso with each sweep of his tongue as his bow, carrying her to some rapturous symphonic finish.

"Very innovative indeed," she said, panting. This guy was as good at oral sex as he was at encryption. She definitely didn't consider herself an expert, but only knew that she wanted to make him feel good too. Kylie grinned and began licking small circles on his belly beyond. Her hands and mouth seemed to know what to do, teasing him, encircling him, kissing him, loving the way he closed his eyes and groaned, until she'd returned the favor. Afterwards, they lay in each other's arms for a long time.

It was Misha who finally remembered coffee. While Kylie showered, he made a trip to a coffee shop and returned with two steaming cups and some croissants. After they had finished, Misha covered her face with kisses which led to a repeat performance on the couch. When he finally left for home, it took Kylie a while to refocus and to finish her information gathering expedition on Emile.

Every avenue she tried was a dead end. She ran every kind of search that she could think of, but there was nothing on Emile Wickland. There was nothing on Emile, an interior designer, or a PR person either. Kylie was stumped. Perhaps his first name was not really Emile either? She so wanted it all to be okay and be over. She was ready to have a life again but considering all that could be at stake, she would have to tell Misha and probably Stuart too.

Kylie mulled this over as she did the wash, got her hair highlighted, and bought a new dress. Never much of a sewer, Kylie did the best she could to mend the gashes on her couch cushions but decided that she would christen it the Frankenstein couch and covered it with a cozy fleece blanket. Misha showed up just after she'd eaten some takeout and looked around, amazed. "Wow. This looks like a different place. And you look gorgeous."

They drove to the grocery across the river where Kylie pulled up a detailed list on her phone. After they had returned and restocked her kitchen, they rolled the dough, cut the apples, and assembled the ingredients for what promised to be two honest-to-goodness pies. Kylie even wove lattice strips on top. Proud of her work, Kylie settled in on couch and called her mother while they pies baked.

"WHERE have you been?" raged her mother. "I've been calling you for days, and you haven't answered," Allison yelled so loudly that Misha could hear from where he was checking on the pies. Kylie held the phone out from her ear as she listened to Allison go on, "Next thing I know, you're all over the newspapers and TV. Kylie, what is going on with you? Are you even my daughter anymore? I shouldn't be getting this kind of news about my daughter on TV."

"Of course, I'm still your daughter. I know that I've been hard to reach. Now you have an idea of what was going on at least. I lost my phone during all the problems that I was having, so I'm calling you on one of those drugstore throwaways. I'm fine, though. I'll tell you all about it tomorrow at Thanksgiving. Speaking of that, I'm bringing two pies and a friend. His name is Misha."

"You're just full of surprises. How long have you been seeing him?"

"I'm not seeing him. He's doing some work with me. Is this a problem?"

"No, it's fine. We will see you around eleven then."

When the pies were out of the oven and were cooling on top of the stove, Misha put on his jacket." I must do some work, so I'll go now, but I'll see you tomorrow, okay? I want to be well-rested for Thanksgiving if I'm to make a good impression."

"You're mad because I told my mother that you're just someone who works for me, aren't you? Look, this morning was fun, but it's not like I'm taking you home to meet my parents like we're um, a serious couple, you know. I mean we aren't really a couple yet, right?"

Misha studied the floor. Kylie noticed his jaw muscles tighten. "

"I guess, if that's what you think. That's fine. No problem. Will you be alright here alone?"

"Yes, I'll be fine, but I want to tell you something before you go." She spilled the story about meeting Emile, and how she thought that Emile and Emily Wickland were the same person.

"Wow. That's pretty amazing."

"I know. The thing is, I sense something really fishy there and I've been trying to find out more about Emile, but I've hit a wall. He doesn't seem to exist anywhere; especially since I don't even have his last name. I thought you might have something up your sleeve that we could use."

"Yeah, that's tough. The bad thing about databases is that you have to have some initial information to run a query before you can get any information. Sounds like you did all the right things. I should mention though, that in Russia, we have a facial recognition app that's not in this country yet. Maybe we'll integrate that into the next version of OMG, right."

"Absolutely. Please tell me you have the app," said Kylie.

"Actually, I do." He smiled, pulled out his phone, and opened the app. "Here, look. It works by matching the photos with profiles on Russia's version of Facebook, called *VKontakte*. Text me Emily's photo. We could try it."

"Yes. Of course the photo is of Emily Wickland, not Emile. But if I'm right about them being the same person, it could identify him. Give me a minute."

Kylie opened the photo she's been studying of Emily Wickland and texted it to Misha.

"Got it," he said when it came through a moment later. He uploaded it into his app and within minutes, he had a list of similar-looking Russian beauties. He scrolled down the list with interest and mumbled something in Russian.

"What does that mean?" asked Kylie.

"Where were all these women when I lived in Russia?"

"Ha ha. You have a *VKontakte* account. You can certainly contact them if you want."

"Don't be an idiot," he said as he continued to scroll down through the list. After moments of this, he slowed at a photo of an androgynous, short-haired woman.

"Look at his one," he said. "I can't tell if this a woman or a man. Do you think this could be Emile?" He handed Kylie his phone.

Kylie enlarged the image and studied the beautiful aquamarine eyes and perfect smile staring back at her. "Wow. It could be. Click on it."

Misha obliged and they both stared at the profile of a man called Emile Azarov. He had hundreds of friends. Misha clicked his friend list and found they were all young boys.

"Weird," he said. "We have no idea if this is related, but I think you should call Stuart."

"Right. No doubt about it."

"Okay, look, I'm going to go home and do some work. I'll send you a screenshot of the page to send to Stuart. Are you sure you're okay to stay by yourself?" Misha slipped the phone back in his pocket.

"I'll be fine," she said. She didn't feel fine, but she had to be alone in her place sometime. Fox had polluted her space with his intrusion, but now the new memory of making love with Misha, paired with apple pie aroma, there was a wholesome, homey feel to her apartment. This was more than that. This wasn't about Gerry Fox. She didn't want Misha to go. Kylie couldn't remember feeling so rattled by a guy.

After he'd left, she called the Bureau and left a message

for Stuart. He called her back five minutes later and Kylie explained the entire Emile story.

"So, OMG, the miracle program, isn't infallible?" He asked.

"Looks like it, but Misha used this Russian facial recognition app called *VKontakte*. We found a profile of a man called Emile Azarov, who has an amazing resemblance to Emile. I can send it to you as soon as I get it from Misha."

"Yes, please do that. It's a holiday weekend, and we are a little light staffed. It might take a while. This is more of a favor, just to satisfy your hunch."

"I think you should make it a priority. I have a weird feeling about this. What if it's related to the virus? If someone seems really solid on the outside, there's some back-room craziness going on inside, isn't that a valid enough reason to check it out?"

"Yes and no. Obviously, your world-class talent for snooping helped solve a horrible crime, and that's because you trusted your gut. So, yes, it can pay off. On the other hand, you can't just go digging up dirt on everyone, looking for things."

"This isn't everyone. This is the lover of a man who may very well get elected to the Senate, and who isn't who she seems. Or he isn't. I'm not sure which."

"Okay, Kylie. I'll look into this, but promise me that if I come up empty, you'll drop it?"

"I promise."

"Good. Now have a good Thanksgiving with your family tomorrow and forget about this."

"Thanks. You too."

She sent him the information as soon as she got it from Misha. Feeling a little unsettled, she watched the news and painted her nails with a bright red polish. When it was dry, she crawled into her bed missing Misha until she finally drifted off to sleep.

26

Thanksgiving

Kylie buzzed Misha into the building at exactly the designated time on Thanksgiving morning. Punctuality was a quality that always impressed her. When he appeared at her door looking as sharp in a slim-cut sports jacket and a tie as a model from GQ, she raised her eyebrows with appreciation. "Wow, you clean up nice!"

She'd put on her new, figure-flattering, heather-gray sweater dress and ankle boots, and laughed to herself, just imagining what her family would think when they got a load of this dressed-up version of her with Mr. GQ —not to mention that they would be arriving in Misha's Porsche. He presented a bouquet of pink roses from behind his back.

"Are those for my parents?"

"No, they're for you. You deserve them." Closing her eyes,

she buried her head in the petals and inhaled in a lungful their luscious scent. When she opened her eyes Misha was staring at her, fascinated.

"Oh, my goodness, Misha. They're beautiful. You didn't have to do that, but thank you. They remind me that there's still beauty in this world."

He shrugged. "Kind of like you, which is also why I wanted you to have them."

Kylie stood on tiptoe and kissed brushed his lips with a kiss. He reached behind her back with his free hand, drew her into his tweed jacket, and returned her kiss. She felt it down to her toes that curled inside her ankle boots, and she pulled back, a little breathless.

"We have to go," she said, giving him a tiny pout. "I'll put these in water and get my coat."

"You know, I love America, but the girls here like to play cat and mouse," he said. "Russians are different."

"I don't know what you're talking about. What were you expecting? We have to go to my parents' house."

Misha shrugged. "If you like someone, you should show it."

"I thought I showed you yesterday." Although she was a little miffed, she smiled. It was refreshing to have a guy be worried about how she felt as much as the other way around. "Anyway, you're the one who left last night, and now, it's time to go. We have lots of time to work off our dinner when we get back." She gave him another kiss, this time with more gusto, before adding, "Thanksgiving's a big deal. Plus, I'm a little spooked about spending a day with my parents. Here, please carry one of these pies." She handed him one and picked up the other.

"You're right. Sorry. Maybe I'm nervous too. So much going on. So, you do like me then?"

"Isn't it obvious?" She grabbed his spare hand and led him out the door to the landing where she turned and kissed him again before descending the stairs. "Of course I like you, you goof."

Misha's car was parked right outside. They placed the pies on the floor in the back seat of the Porsche and sped up Storrow Drive, though Fresh Pond in Cambridge, to Route 2, where she had been oh so recently with Janice.

"Did you call Stuart?" he asked, as he drove.

"Yes. He didn't sound too worried about it. It was more like he was humoring me, but he said he'd run a search on Emile Azarov."

"Great. I'm sure if there's anything, he'll find it."

Kylie nodded. She admired Misha's chiseled profile as he drove, secretly thinking that he was like having her very own, personal version of Tom Cruise. "Can I ask you a question?" she said.

"Possibly. What?"

"What's the real reason that you've got a gun?"

"Okay, no problem. When I came here, I was afraid. I'd heard about terrible things that happen here."

"Unlike your country, right?"

"For sure, we have bad things too. The truth is that I was expecting the worst, and then when I was beat-up when I was a freshman, I got the gun."

"What happened?"

"These guys came up to me on the street and they were pushing me around. My English wasn't as good then and I couldn't really talk to them. They mugged me, took my money, and my watch that was from my Dad. I swore I'd never be a victim again."

"I'm so sorry. That's terrible. Have you ever used it?"

"No, only for practice, but not in anything real, except for yesterday." He laughed ruefully. "We both saw how good I was then."

He blew air into his cheeks and Kylie thought he looked embarrassed. "Not using your gun is a good thing. Actually, I hate the idea of guns, but if I'm honest, I have to admit that I slept better knowing that you had one at my place the other night. I'd never felt afraid until all of this happened. But now, I'm thinking that I'm going to take more karate. If I take a job at the FBI, they'll probably have me learn how to shoot too."

"If you want, I belong to this gun club and can take you. Not to discourage you, but I doubt if their tech department does much shooting. Still, it could be fun and you never know if you are ever going to need it. If you want, we could go on Saturday?"

"Perfect." Kylie smiled.

"Okay, now can I ask you a question?"

"Okay, you just did," she said cautiously. "I guess you can go for two."

"What happened with Andrew?"

"How do you know about him? Oh no. You used OMG and ran a report on me, didn't you?"

"Guilty. I couldn't resist."

Disgusted, Kylie shook her head. "I guess that we're not going to have any secrets, are we? I'm considering taking some classes in computer programing. Just so you know, you'd better watch out. Then maybe I can have some privacy."

"Really? Good for you. I think you should. I can help you study."

She smiled at him with amusement.

"And Andrew?" He peered at her over the top of his aviators.

"I dated him in college, as you undoubtedly know."

"What happened?"

"We were together for three years. One day he decided that he wanted to see other people. That was it."

"That must have been hard."

Kylie swallowed and nodded.

"And after that?" he asked.

"I was a mess for a while. Then I went to grad school and had all of my startup craziness. Trust me, I've had no time to date. So, here I am."

"There was no one after Andrew?" Misha raised his eyebrows in surprise.

"Hey, you read my reports. Nada. I was done with guys."

"I hope that you changed your mind? Seems like yesterday was a good start, yes?"

"Yes, but we'll see. I'm working on it."

Kylie directed Misha to the Lexington exit, where only two days before, Janice had driven onto the shoulder of the ramp, bypassing the line of cars. Within minutes, Kylie had Misha turn onto the street where she'd grown up, and pointed out the house, a rambling white colonial with green shutters. It sat on top of a sloping hill, its driveway widening at the top to allow room for guest parking. Misha turned in, parked the Porsche and reached behind his seat, producing a chrysanthemum plant bursting with golden blooms. "For your mother," he showed Kylie as she picked up the pies.

Allison swung the door open as they approached and shook her head sadly at them. "Oh, my God. Look at you. Aren't you the pair!" She dabbed at Kylie's bandage with one of her buffed fingernails.

"Hey, we're fine. I know that we look like the walking wounded, but we're definitely okay. "Mom, this is Misha," She said, turning to Misha. "This is Allison, my mom."

"Welcome," her mother said, still shaking her head sadly at his bandage. She eagle-eyed Kylie as if she were about to zoom in on a mouse. "Well, we certainly want to hear all about what happened."

"Thank you for having me," Misha said formally. He handed her the plant. "This is for you. Happy Thanksgiving."

Allison accepted it, holding it the air admiringly. "Thank you, Misha it's lovely. Happy Thanksgiving to you, too."

"Can we please come in before I drop one of these pies?" asked Kylie.

"I'm forgetting my manners," said her mother. She stepped aside, allowing them to pass into the foyer.

Allison put the plant on a table by the front door as Misha removed his sunglasses and looked around. "Nice house," he said.

Kylie realized that she knew some facts about his life, but there was so much that OMG wasn't able to provide. What did the house where he grew up look like? That would be the next version if she only had someone like Simon to build it. In the meantime, she had a lot of questions to ask.

Allison ran the pies into the kitchen as Kylie's father

sauntered into the foyer. He gave Kylie a brief hug while sizing up Misha over Kylie's shoulder. Allison returned a moment later and Kylie made the introductions. David took their coats and then waltzed Misha into the living room with his arm around his shoulder. "That's quite a car!" he said with appreciation. "Hey, what do you say we start the festivities? What do you drink?"

"David, it's only eleven in the morning," Kylie's mother warned to their backs.

"It's a holiday, Allison," he stated flatly, without turning around.

Kylie had no idea about Misha, but she knew the day would unravel with her father off to such an early start. He'd be trouble by the time they ate. They all would be in trouble. "I'm coming too," Kylie said. "In fact, I'll make the drinks."

"Count me in. I want to hear the story before everyone gets here," said her mother, sitting down on an armchair chair across from the couch where David and Misha sat like bookends.

Kylie set out four cut-crystal Scotch glasses on the bar near the sofa and filled them with cranberry juice, club soda, and ice. Misha touched her fingers on the glass when he took his and smiled at her. Kylie smiled and then served the rest. She sat down in the matching armchair.

"What the hell is this?" asked her father, examining the contents of the glass.

"It's called a Cape Codder and it's your ticket to an enjoyable day," said Kylie. "Hang in there. You can have a Scotch when everyone else arrives." He narrowed his eyes but swallowed a cautious sip.

"Okay," said her mother. "What's been going on?"

"It all started when I thought up this platform for my business and then had this guy, Simon, build it for me."

"Is this the same Simon who was murdered?" asked Allison.

Kylie nodded.

Her mother pushed her glasses down her nose, exposing her narrowed eyes, a classic Allison move.

"It's okay, Mom."

"I'm not sure how having someone who works for you get murdered be okay."

"What I meant was that the situation is now under control. I know it's very sad. Simon was kind of a weasel though. I can only imagine what he'd gotten himself into."

"Oh, said David. "I'm sorry to hear that. But say, weren't you going to demo your program for us today? I was looking forward to seeing it."

"I was, but it's become pretty complicated. I might be selling it to the FBI, so I shouldn't be showing it to anyone until I know. Sorry, but I guess you'll have to wait a bit longer." Kylie knew she'd dropped a bomb, but was glad for the excuse not to demo OMG. She'd lost her desire to expose their hypocrisy with the damning evidence that she'd found out about each of them.

They certainly weren't exemplarily parents or flawless people, but after all, she'd been through over the past few days, and with almost losing her life, Kylie knew now that that were much worse things that other people did. Her parents weren't such terrible people. They just were flawed and clueless. Frankly, she was relieved to see them and to be back in her childhood home. She no longer saw the point of outing their sins to the rest of the family. They didn't deserve that.

"What? Excuse me?" said her mother. "Kylie, I don't hear from you for weeks and then see you on the news. Your picture is plastered all over the TV with the governor and with Bill Reinstadt, but I can't even get you to return a phone call. I think you should tell us what's going on. Now you say that you're going to be working with the FBI?"

Misha interjected, "Let's say Kylie designed a platform that will allow FBI to find criminals."

Her mother's eyes shot daggers at Kylie. "At least one of you can give me a straight answer. And what about you?" she asked Misha. "How do you fit into this? Are you Russian?"

"Yes. I'm from Moscow. I came here for school."

"And you're working with this guy?" her father asked Kylie, sounding dubious.

"Yes. Misha's an amazing encryption expert." Kylie's eyes shone, but she took a deep breath to brace herself against his inquiries, which sounded like they were headed for a world-class interrogation.

"So, you don't have any family here?" asked her father.

"No," said Misha, taking a sip of his drink. His grip around the glass made his knuckles protrude like little white-capped peaks. "No, not really. As I said, I came here for school, then just stayed."

"What does your family do back in Russia?" he asked.

Kylie expelled the breath she'd been holding. "Dad, please stop interrogating him. Misha's a good guy. What do you think, that he's a spy?" Her good intentions had quickly melted into exasperation. In the past two days, she'd been kidnapped, and almost murdered. Then she'd helped solve a sinister crime. How absurd for her and Misha to now sit and be questioned as if they were little children. She'd come home feeling thankful to be alive and happy to see her parents, but nothing had changed with them. Kylie realized then how much her life would never be the same after what she'd gone through.

"I don't know if he's a spy, Kylie. I don't know anything about this young man except that he's Russian, he drives a flashy car, and he appears to be dating my daughter. I have every right to be concerned."

"Your father is right," said Allison.

"Listen, both of you," she said. She articulated each word as if it were fizz slowly being released from a bottle. "I want you to understand something. I've had a crazy few days, and going forward, I'm going to be doing some work that I consider crucial. Maybe you have no idea, but I helped save this city from a terrible epidemic. I'd like you to trust my judgment. I'd like you to respect me and my decisions. I may not be able to talk about what I'm doing, but I ask you to honor that. And, I want you to respect any friend that I bring into your house."

Her parents stared at her, open-mouthed, too stunned to talk.

"Can you agree to that?" pressed Kylie.

They both nodded as if they were marionettes. No one said anything for a minute. The energy in the room had shifted. The storm had cleared. Act One was done. Misha loosened his death grip on his glass and set it on the coffee table. Her father slumped a little, crossed his legs, and took another sip of his Cape Codder without complaint. Her mother's anxious Type A face had softened into a look of admiration. Kylie's indignation dissipated, but she couldn't resist adding, "You know, I keep telling you to read Gibran. He said, *If you love somebody, let them go, for if they return, they were always yours.*"

"Thanks, Kylie, said her mother. We will keep that in mind. With that, I think I'd better check on the turkey."

"I'll come with you," said Kylie, following her.

Kylie sat on one of the bar stools at the marble-topped island and swiveled around as she watched her mother dart about the kitchen checking on the contents of the various pots and pans. Ordinarily, Allison wasn't what Kylie considered domestic. Kylie was fascinated, observing her mother's annual kitchen chaos that somehow magically, would produce an excellent feast. Every inch of countertop space covered with pots, pans, and ingredients, and the mess had spilled onto the table in the breakfast nook. But when her mother opened the oven door to baste the turkey, the aroma made Kylie's mouth water. Whatever shape the kitchen was in, didn't matter. Kylie loved the disarray, so much homier than Allison's usual orderly kitchen where mostly takeout meals were warmed and where Kylie had been forbidden to make a mess. She thought that this is what a home should smell like, and look like too. She realized how much she'd longed for that.

"Anything you want me to do?" she asked her mother.

"Go get the mixer for me out of the cupboard over there, so that I'll have it ready for the whipped cream for the pies." She pointed at a corner cupboard, understanding that Kylie needed a road map for the kitchen.

"Sure, but I wanted to talk to you first."

"Oh?" Her mother stood across from where Kylie sat at the island and looked at her with curiosity. The softness around her mother's mouth that Kylie had noticed in the living room hadn't survived its trip to the kitchen—it had sprouted the usual parentheses that framed her mouth.

At the risk of losing the good feelings she'd created, Kylie continued. "I wanted to tell you a little more about what I've been doing. You might have heard on the news that my product is called OMG. It's this platform that allows people to find out data that will help them make good decisions in their lives."

Allison stared at Kylie. "Go on. What are you getting at?"

Although the kitchen was well out of earshot from the living room, Kylie lowered her voice. "Well, when I was testing it, I ran a search on you and Dad, just for practice. From the results, I found out about you and Collin Anderson. I was pretty shocked. It made me feel so bad for Dad, and for me too. I mean, Mom, how could you? It's like you've been lying to everyone."

Allison ran her fingers through her hair, pushing it back from her eyes. It was thick and the same chestnut color as Kylie's. "Kylie, I'm not sure what to say. But first of all, I can't tell you how disappointed I am that you've been spying on your own parents. What kind of daughter does that? I know that doesn't excuse what I did, but I'm also I'm sorry you had to find out about me this way. I'm just not comfortable with you spying on me. It feels like a betrayal."

"Are you kidding? MY spying feels like a betrayal?" Kylie was incredulous. "What about you cheating on Dad and then treating me like you are holier than God, for my whole life? That's a betrayal."

Allison shut her eyes as she chose her words. "Kylie, I'm sorry. It's not the kind of thing that you discuss with your daughter. I don't know if you can understand this, but I've been unhappy with your Dad for a long time. You know what he's like when he drinks, and he's like that all the time now. You're not around to see it, but I live with it. He's either ranting about something or other, or he locks himself in his office with a bottle and I never see him. Collin made me feel whole. I can actually have a conversation with him."

"It sounds like you had a lot more than a conversation. It's a shitty thing to do to Dad."

Her mother nodded, looking wan and a bit lost, a new look for her. She looked older and sadder too. It was unsettling to Kylie to see her invincible mother appear even slightly vulnerable.

"I know. I certainly don't feel good about it. I realize how weak and despicable I must sound." Allison dismally shook her head.

"Yes, it's pretty disgusting. What are you going to do?"

"I don't know. I've been toying with a separation. Maybe if I do it, your father will understand that he must stop drinking and then, hopefully, things will change. It could be for the best."

"What about me? I can't say that you've exactly been a warm and fuzzy mother. You had a daughter to love and I guess that wasn't easy either? It's like you checked out everywhere. All I ever got from you and dad was expectations."

"I know. I admit that am not the greatest mother. It's true, I am driven and it's been hard for me to play mommy, but I do love you. You must know that on some level?"

"Yes. I suppose so. On some level."

Allison started at Kylie with a strange expression on her face.

Her lips slanted into a half smile. "Come here." She opened her arms for a hug — an unfamiliar gesture to them both. To Kylie, it felt like crossing the border into a foreign country, but her mother had handed her a passport. Kylie stepped in.

Her mother's slightly smaller body felt angular and rigid. It was as if Allison didn't quite know how to do it. Still, Kylie let herself be enveloped by her stiff arms and her mother began to slowly burnish circles onto her back. "I am sorry, baby girl, that you didn't know that I loved you."

Allison's hair smelled like high-end salon shampoo and Kylie buried her face into the scent. A few tears escaped and Kylie hated that she was being such a cry baby. She'd done way too much of that lately. But her mother's hug, stiff as it was, it felt as wonderful as it felt strange. After some moments, Kylie angled her neck to look at her mother. The edges of her Allison's lips, usually turned downward in determination, were curved up at the edges, as if even her lips were saying "yes." They reminded Kylie of what she used to call "sailing lips", her nickname for the mellow, happy look of blissed-out people coming back from a sunset sail.

"Thanks, Mom," she sniffled. She didn't know if she was ready to say I love you back to her mother. She didn't know if she even could utter those words — a phrase that she hadn't said even once in her life. But there was time, and something had shifted inside her, just a little. They stood there hugging for another moment and Kylie finally said, "I guess I better get the mixer for you."

When Kylie returned to the living room to rescue Misha from her father, they were having a lively discussion about cars, but even though it appeared to be going well, Misha looked grateful that she'd returned. Kylie decided that she would have a heart to heart talk with her father about his hidden bank accounts another time.

Soon, her mother joined them and the conversation flowed with a spirited and an unfamiliar warmth and ease. "Here's a toast to all of you, to your listening to me, and to Thanksgiving," said Kylie.

As they clinked glasses, Kylie's phone buzzed in her purse. She didn't recognize the number. Curious, she decided to answer. "Hello?"

"Kylie, you don't know me. My name is Candice Fox. I'm Gerry Fox's widow."

Kylie's stomach dropped to her feet. She clenched her phone. "Yes?"

"Look, I'm sorry to bother you on Thanksgiving, but it took me a while to track down your phone number, and I wanted to talk to you as soon as possible. I don't think this can wait."

Kylie's parents and Misha watched her with worried curiosity on their faces, which much have reflected her own knotted brow. "What is it?"

"Here's the thing. The press reported that this case was solved. I am horrified that my husband was involved in anything so heinous, but since he was, I want to tell you that I am afraid that it may have gone deeper than you all seemed to think."

"Really. Go on."

"I'm contacting you directly instead of the FBI because I don't want to get involved with them. I have two teenaged sons and I just want to wash my hands of this whole business. It's enough that the agents were coming around, questioning me about that woman's murder. I'd prefer you to research this first, and then you can tell them if you find anything. Gerry and I had our problems and he didn't talk a lot about what he was into, but I do know that he and Steve Hahn used to have regular meetings with a couple of other guys. They'd meet in New York. One of them was Russian. His name was Emile. I don't know his last name. The other one was Bill Reinstadt."

Kylie's blood roared in her ears. "Do you have proof of this?"

"No, not really. Gerry just told me he was meeting with these two. I do know that they met several times. It might not mean anything, just because he had some meetings, but I've given it some thought and I think there's more to it."

"Why do you think that?"

"Just a hunch. He was more secretive than usual about what this was about. I never knew what to believe after a while, so I stopped asking. But I sure didn't believe that they had to go to New York for a biotech initiative. Why would Reinstadt be meeting him in New York?"

"I see. Can you get me the meeting dates? Did he stay at a hotel?"

Kylie gave Candice her email to send her the information. She might have to do a bit of digging, but it would be a snap for OMG to come up with some answers if they were there any.

"I'll be in touch," Candice said. "Again, I'm so sorry to call you on a holiday. Happy Thanksgiving, though."

"Yes, you too," said Kylie. She hung up, flabbergasted. She blew out a mouthful of air and shook her head sadly at Misha and her parents.

"What?" asked her mother. "Who was that?"

"Gerry Fox's widow."

"Really. What did she want?" her mother pressed.

"It appears that there may have been more people involved in this than we thought. I'll let you know when I find out more." Misha touched his forehead as his eyes bulged. She bugged her eyes back at him and shook her head as her mellow holiday mood dissolved into a buzz of anxiety that was becoming all too familiar.

"Excuse me a minute," said Kylie, taking her phone into the kitchen. She called the Bureau and left another message for Stuart. "This is Kylie. Please call me right away."

"What's going on?" asked Allison when Kylie returned to the living room.

"I just left a message for an agent who was working on this case. I'm sure he'll be thrilled to hear from me on Thanksgiving, so right now, let's just enjoy the holiday. It is possible that I might need to do some work after dinner," said Kylie.

"But it's a holiday," said Allison.

"I know, but this is really important." Kylie gave Misha a knowing look, implicit with the understanding that he'd be helping. Misha nodded back, his eyes shining. Kylie narrowed her eyes at him and nodded. He was part of this now. And he had better behave.

27

Fallen Idol

Just moments after Kylie had called Stuart, her phone rang. "Hey, little crime fighter," said Janice. "Stuart just called and filled me in." Her tone sounded urgent, even though her words were casual. "We could still have a big problem if there's some virus left. If there is, it's possible that they're still planning to release it tomorrow."

"Yes, I know. I was the one who told Stuart." Clutching her phone, Kylie paced into her mother's kitchen for privacy.

"Gotcha. Anyways, Stuart wants me to bring Reinstadt in for questioning. Did he happen to mention where he's having Thanksgiving?"

"Actually, yes. He told me that he's having a quiet dinner at home with Emile, but who knows anymore if anything he says is true? Look, what can I do?"

"Nothing. What would be helpful is if for you to stay safe at home. Just enjoy your dinner. Are you with your family?"

"Yes. You?" Kylie remembered that Janice had lost her father, but realized that she didn't know much else about her.

"My parents are gone, so I'm just working today. It's a good day to be busy."

"Sorry to hear that. Do you need Reinstadt's address?"

"Kylie, this is the FBI. We're all set with that. And I mean it. Stay home and have a good holiday."

When they hung up, Kylie rushed into the living room. There was no way that she could now enjoy sitting around, eating turkey. After all, she hadn't promised Janice that she'd stay home. She and Misha could go downtown to Reinstadt's apartment in case Janice needed them, but this time, she'd make sure that they would stay out of trouble.

"Look, I'm really sorry about this, but unfortunately, Misha and I do have to leave."

Misha looked alarmed. Her mother looked stricken, but her father had poured himself a Scotch in her absence and was settled into his armchair and appeared to be enjoying his drink. "These things happen," he said.

Her mother folded her arms. "But what about dinner? It's Thanksgiving! Aunt Judy, Uncle Pete, and Andrew will be there soon. You haven't seen them in over a year. Can't this wait?" The volume of her urging increased, appearing to be linked to the noticeable vee deepening, above her nose. "What's going on? You can at least tell us."

"Mom, I'm sorry, but no. This is urgent. I promise to tell you later, but we need to go. Can we take just a bite of something for the car? I'll try to come back and catch everyone later."

"If you can wait two minutes, I'll throw something together. I won't let you starve." Allison ran into the kitchen.

In the kitchen, Kylie watched Allison slice two rolls and load the insides with some turkey parts from a pan on the counter. She speed-wrapped the sandwiches in napkins and handed them to Kylie. "Here. At least you can at least eat these."

Kylie thanked her and hurried through the hall, where Misha stood waiting by the door, holding Kylie's parka. Her mother followed and her father rushed in to say good-bye. Kylie gave them quick hugs as Misha thanked them. They barreled out the front door and hopped into Misha's Porsche.

"Where are we going?" he asked.

Kylie gave him the address. "It's Reinstadt's apartment."

What's going on?" Misha jerked the stick shift into reverse, tore down the driveway, shifted into first, and sped up the street.

"Janice is going to bring him in for questioning. I want to be there."

"Did she invite you to come?"

"Not exactly. I think we can help though. We'll stay out of the way, but if they need us, we'll be there, right?"

He gave her a worried look with one raised eyebrow. "If you say so."

Once they were on Route 2, Kylie handed him a sandwich. She took a mouthful of her own. "Bummer about dinner," she said. "This is good. I guess I didn't feel much like eating once I talked to Candice Fox, but now that we're on our way, this is hard to resist. And it is Thanksgiving."

"Yeah, I know what you mean. I was sorry we couldn't stay. Your parents are nice people."

Kylie cocked an eyebrow at him, but Misha stared at the road ahead. She took another bite of her sandwich.

Despite her nerves and her shock about Reinstadt, the turkey had awakened her appetite. She was sorry about missing the pies. But much more than regretting the abandoned pies and turkey, she was sorry about Reinstadt's devastating duplicity. How could she ever have believed in him? Kylie took another bite of her sandwich for solace.

"What's your plan?" asked Misha.

"I don't have one yet."

Deep into their thoughts, they were quiet as Misha wound the Porsche past the strip malls on Fresh Pond and past blocks of lovely older homes before turning onto Storrow Drive. With no traffic, the Porsche zoomed along the Charles River past Harvard and BU to downtown. As he neared the exit, Misha looked over at Kylie. "What exactly did Janice say you should do?"

"Stay home." She looked out the window.

"Kylie, this is crazy. Why didn't you listen? We could be sitting down to a nice dinner instead of nosing in where we shouldn't be and maybe getting hurt."

"We'll be careful. But I just couldn't sit there eating turkey with my parents while this was happening. I just have to talk to Reinstadt. What if he's arrested and I never get to tell him what I think? Besides, I think I can help."

"No offense, but do you really think Reinstadt cares what you think? And how are you going to help, anyway? You have no plan. We don't know what we're dealing with." His voice softened. "Wasn't Lily bad enough?" He reached over and touched to the bandage on her cheek.

"We had to do that. There was no choice, at least for me. Same thing now. I have to see this through," said Kylie as they neared Reinstadt's street.

"You're not trained to do this, and I'm not much better. True, I've got a gun, but I don't want to use it. And we're interfering with Janice. This is a seriously bad idea. You can still change your mind. I think we should go back."

"Maybe. Look! There's a parking space." Kylie pointed to the miraculous open spot just visible from around the corner. Misha swerved over and backed in. "See? This is a good omen," she said.

"I guess."

He opened the glove compartment and slipped his gun into the pocket of his leather jacket.

"Misha, please don't be offended, but I think I should go up there alone. I'm the one he had a connection with. I think it would be harder if you're there."

"I understand, but this could be dangerous. I should come."

"No, please stay in the car. I'll just be a few minutes. Janice will be there, and it will be fine."

He shrugged and patted his pocket. "I don't like it, but I'll be here waiting. If it takes too long, I will come up."

There was no going back. She needed to hear the truth from Reinstadt. Determined, Kylie marched past some small jewelry shops and restaurants before rounding the corner to Reinstadt's building. She entered the lobby and waved at the concierge, who she recognized from her stay at Bill's apartment. She put on her best smile. "Happy Thanksgiving," she said gaily. "I'm here for dinner at Bill Reinstadt's." Kylie was that she was dressed up enough to pass as a probable guest.

He nodded in recognition. "Go on up. Have a nice Thanksgiving."

She rode the elevator to Reinstadt's floor. Kylie knocked with a sweaty hand. She still had no idea what she was going to say. When no one answered at first, she put her ear to the door to listen. Everything seemed to be quiet inside. If Janis were there, she would have heard some sort of conversation through the door. She knocked again, more loudly.

After a few more minutes, Reinstadt opened the door. He looked like a very different person, slouching in his faded black tee shirt and jeans. His eyes widened. "Kylie, what a nice surprise. And you're all dressed up! What can I do for you?"

"I never picked up my backpack and I was in the neighborhood, so I thought I'd grab it. Can I run back into the guestroom to get it?"

"I already left it with the concierge for you."

"Oh, I'm so sorry to bother you. I'll get it on the way out. But since I'm here, can I talk to you about a couple of things? Would it be okay if I came inside for a minute? I know it's Thanksgiving. It won't take long." She struggled to erase any signs of her contempt for him that might appear on her face.

"I guess if it's just a minute. We're in the middle of preparations." He stepped aside allowing Kylie inside the hallway. Kylie expected him to lead her into the living room, but Reinstadt's feet in black sneakers appeared rooted in the hall. Kylie was surprised that no Thanksgiving aromas were wafting from the kitchen. Instead, it smelled of cigarette smoke. She wondered what preparations he was making.

Reinstadt angled his head towards the living room and yelled, "It's Kylie. I'll be right there."

"Hi, Kylie. Sorry, but we're not really up for company at the moment," a man yelled from back in the apartment. Kylie assumed that it was Emile.

"So, what's up?" Reinstadt crossed his arms. He seemed distracted and his left eye twitched.

Kylie's best hope was that this was all a misunderstanding. Perhaps Candice Fox was setting him up for some reason, but his nervousness fueled her anxiety. "I'm pretty concerned about something and thought maybe you could clarify some things."

"I'm listening." He leaned against the wall. His normally well-kempt hair fell over his forehead and looked like it needed washing. All he needed was a toothpick hanging out of his mouth to complete his edgy James Dean look.

Kylie spoke softly. "Earlier today, I had a call from Gerry Fox's widow. She told me all about your meetings with Fox in New York. I thought you didn't know him. You told me you'd met him at a fundraiser. Why would you lie about him? What were those meetings about?"

He held up his hand like a traffic cop to stop her flow of words. "Whoa, just a minute here. You're a nice kid, Kylie, but you have a real knack for sticking your nose into other people's business. Do you really think this concerns you? You've got a real problem with boundaries."

"Actually, I have a problem with wanting to know the truth. If there's more of the virus out there and if you're involved, I want to know."

"You're jumping to conclusions. I think your playing at being a detective has gone to your head."

"Maybe you should answer my questions," said Kylie.

There was another knock at the door. Reinstadt shook his head in disbelief. "Excuse me," he said, slipping around her to answer it.

It was Janice with a male agent, both dressed in street clothes. Janice rolled her eyes and frowned when she saw Kylie. "FBI," she said, flashing her card. "Hi, Mr. Reinstadt. May we come in and ask you some questions? We have a search warrant." Janice showed him the paper.

"No problem. Seems like we're having a party. What would you like to know?" His voice had become magnanimous as the Reinstadt Kylie had known.

"More company?" Emile's irritated voice boomed from inside the apartment.

"Yes," Reinstadt answered and then turned to Janice. "Please, come in."

He led the group into the living room where Emile sat on the couch smoking a cigarette. Kylie glanced over at the kitchen, but there was no sign of any Thanksgiving dinner preparations...it still looked as neat as if it were staged for a photo shoot. Reinstadt introduced Emile, who didn't look very happy for the company. He snubbed out his cigarette into an overflowing marble ashtray and nodded hello.

"Excuse me for one minute please," said Reinstadt and he headed down the hall towards the bedrooms.

Janice started to follow him but Emile reached under one of the decorator pillows and produced a gun. He jumped up and pointed it at them. "Don't go after him. Listen, I'm really sorry, but I need to leave. Please, don't try to stop me." He sidestepped towards the front hall, his gun aimed at the group.

"Stop right there!" Janice reached for her gun.

In a quick pivot, Emile turned around and grabbed Kylie around the waist. His bony hand dug into her ribs so hard that she felt the clamp-like grip through her coat. He held his gun to her ear.

"I hope you folks don't mind, but my friend Kylie and I are leaving. If you stand in our way, I will shoot her. Now step aside and let us through. If you even think about following us, she's dead." Emile's tone was polite as if he was excusing himself to squeeze in a row of theater seats. Kylie was afraid to move.

Reinstadt emerged from the back hallway, carrying a paper cup. He narrowed his eyes at Emile, who returned his look, giving Bill a slow nod. Reinstadt unceremoniously swallowed its contents, crumpled the cup and threw it on the floor.

Kylie glanced at Reinstadt to see if he would help her, but Reinstadt's eyes were on his shoes. His face looked as stricken and as much in shock as she felt. Emile led her towards the door. Kylie's heart pounded. She couldn't remember one karate move in her limited repertoire that would help. All she had to do was squirm, and Emile might shoot her.

"Stay here and don't even think about coming after us, if you want to see Kylie again," he told Janice.

Emile tightened his vise on her ribs and forced Kylie out the door. He marched her down the hallway to the elevator, all the while, keeping a close watch on his apartment. He pushed the down button. Within a minute, the door opened. He shoved her in and pressed a button. "Poor little Kylie," he said mockingly. "You're always getting yourself into trouble, aren't you?"

"You won't get away with this. Janice will catch you," Kylie told him once their elevator was heading down.

"Maybe so, but if anything happens to me, you're going to die too."

"You know, the concierge just might notice that you've got a hostage. He'll call for help. By the way, Candice Fox told me that you and Bill were involved with Fox. I can only assume this was about the virus. Why would you do this? Why kill random people?"

Kylie winced as Emile dug the tip of the barrel of the gun into her head behind her ear. "Maybe you should shut up, or I will kill you now in this elevator. But since you asked, you should have a little imagination. Don't be so naïve. You live in your safe little MBA world, and all you know is what you know. Just think about the power that comes with possessing a virus like this. With power, comes money. Put that in your Harvard business plan."

Kylie's turkey sandwich was threatening a reemergence. The elevator doors opened into the parking garage.

"Walk quietly with me out the door, and don't make a fuss," said Emile.

Kylie gritted her teeth and as he led out a door that leads to the street. She'd been counting on the concierge helping her but that wasn't an option since Emile had bypassed the lobby. The street was strangely empty. Where was everyone? Emile pushed her out the front door, in front of him as if she was a human shield.

"Where are you taking me?"

"Don't worry. You're not going far." Emile pulled her into a nearby alley, close to where Misha was sitting in a parked car.

She prayed that Misha saw them. Emile still had her in his grip but was facing her now.

"Why did you get Reinstadt involved in this? You ruined his career, you know," she yelled.

Emile laughed. To Kylie, he sounded marginally hysterical. "What career? He owed everything he was to me. I invented Bill Reinstadt. Just the way I invented Emily Wickland."

"Who are you, anyway?" she asked.

"Let's just say that I'm a businessman. I'm here because one always has to be creative about funding to grow a business into new markets. As an entrepreneur, you can appreciate that, right?"

Kylie nodded. "Within limits."

"We had a nice little plan. Fox would get the product made, I'd help sell it, Reinstadt would get elected on its funds, and wield its power."

"I see. Your ticket to world domination. Too bad it didn't work."

"Don't be so sure." He dug the gun deeper into her head.

Kylie shut her eyes. She had no choice. Without too much trouble, she leaned her head towards him and heaved a yellow liquid version of what had been her turkey sandwich onto his shirt. Emile pulled his hand up from her ribs to cover his face in horror.

"You stupid girl," he yelled.

Kylie snapped a punch under his jaw. As the blow connected, a loud HUHHH came from deep inside of her, releasing all of her anger at Reinstadt and her fear. Emile reeled from the shock. As he stepped backward, Kylie had just enough room to knee him in the groin. He cried out in pain and doubled over. With another loud rush of air, she expelled an even louder kiai and kicked the gun from his hand. She quickly pivoted and dove for it when it landed just a few feet away. She pointed up it at him "Don't move," she screamed. Kylie had no idea how to use a gun, but hoped that all she had to do was pull the trigger.

Emile straightened up, panting. "You're quite the little street fighter. I could use you in my business. Why don't you put the gun down and just come with me? We'd make a good team."

"You're joking, right? No thanks. I don't think you're going anywhere, except maybe to jail."

"She's got that right," yelled Misha running into the alley, pointing his gun at Emile for extra cover for Kylie. "Don't move."

A moment later, Janice ran in. "I can take it from here." She cuffed Emile. "Thank goodness you were so loud, Kylie. It helped us find you," Kylie still aimed the gun steady upon Emile as Misha slipped his gun into his pocket.

"I think Interpol will be pleased to have you home," Janice told Emile. "First though, you need to tell us where we can find rest of the virus"

"I have no idea what you're talking about." Emile's light blue eyes danced with contempt.

"We'll see about that. You can tell us now or we can find out later. It will be harder on you if you want to play it that way."

Emile shrugged his shoulders, his cuffed wrists rising up his back.

"You okay?' Misha asked Kylie. "You can drop the gun now, by the way."

"Oh. Yeah. I threw up all over Emile, but I feel much better now," she grinned.

Janice held out her hand to Kylie. "Give me that gun before you get into even more trouble."

Kylie obliged and followed Janice as she walked Emile to her car and guided him into the back seat. She turned towards Kylie and Misha. "The other agent's still upstairs with Reinstadt. I called for backup and they'll be bringing him in."

"Can I talk to Reinstadt?" Kylie asked Janice. She wanted to tell him what she thought. Reinstadt was a total sham. How could she have been so duped?

"Not if the virus is up there. I'll don't know if I'll be able let you talk to him down at the Bureau right after we bring him in, but at some point, you can visit. Why don't you two go home for now and I'll keep you informed?"

Kylie and Misha exchanged a look. "We still could catch dinner," said Misha, hopefully.

Kylie was crestfallen. "Look, I'll be working at the Bureau soon," she protested. If it weren't for me, none of the Lily virus would have been discovered. Hundreds, maybe thousands of people could have died. I'm not officially working for the FBI yet, but I've certainly helped solve this crime. Don't you think I've earned some membership into the inner circle here?"

"I know, Kylie and I'm sorry. I'll call you when I find out anything that I can share with you. You're not working there yet. No offense, but God knows you've already stuck your nose in way too much."

"Okay, okay," Kylie conceded.

"Come on," said Misha. He took her arm and led her around the block to his car. Kylie reluctantly got in.

Feeling shaky, Kylie settled into her seat at stared out the window as Misha headed back towards Lexington. She didn't understand how Reinstadt, her idol, could be involved with this. He was unworthy of all that she'd bestowed on him. If he had gotten elected, it would be a disaster. Didn't she deserve some credit? But she was too disheartened and battle-weary to fight this final exclusion. Tears began to roll down her cheeks.

"I know how tough this is for you," said Misha.

"Yes. The whole reason I wanted to produce OMG in the first place is so that I would *know* who to trust. It's so ironic that the one person trusted the most, was just some manufactured persona. I have no idea who he really is."

"Yeah, it's always it takes time to know if you can really trust anyone, but I just wanted to say that you can trust me. I'm an open book. I've never lied to you and I never will."

Kylie gave him an appreciative look and fell quiet. She was jarred from her thoughts when her phone rang. It was Janice. At first, Kylie could hardly grasp the meaning of Janice's torrent of words. "They found the virus in the guest bathroom in Reinstadt's apartment. There was a vial in a cooler that was just sitting there, open. Evidently, Reinstadt took a dose while we were there. While they were taking him in, he started looking ghoulish. He'd sprouted red blotches of rash all over his face and arms, and then it exploded into tiny blisters before they got to the bureau. They took him to Mass General instead, but he was dead by the time they got there."

"Oh my God," said Kylie, sickened with grief and disbelief. "We were standing right next to him. Plus, I used that bathroom when I stayed there. I was probably just a foot away from it."

"I know. I just questioned Steve Hahn about it. Evidently, if you don't have it by now, you're not going to get it. You have to ingest it or touch it and the symptoms start within minutes. You'll be okay."

"My God. I can't believe it. Did you find out why he did it?"

"Yes. He talked before the worst symptoms kicked in. He seemed eager to tell his story, actually. The poor guy must have been holding it in for years. It seems that Emile met him while he was still in high school and became his sugar daddy—put him through college and law school. Everything. It turns out that Emile ran a gay child porn ring in Europe, but he wanted Reinstadt for himself. He groomed Reinstadt to be everything that he finally became. It was Emile who convinced him to use the virus to fund his campaign."

"Thanks, Janice," she said and hung up. Kylie felt the sting of grief and disappointment. Were there no heroes left? She hung her head and sobbed.

"What's the matter?" asked Misha.

She told him. He shook his head sadly.

No one that Kylie had been close to had died until Reinstadt. Until today, she'd loved every pearl that he'd spoken, every policy he'd endorsed. She'd loved the way he looked, his energy, and what she'd thought was his integrity. How could anyone fake all of that? She felt duped. She might have well idolized a fictional character like a Mr. Darcy or a James Bond. At least if it had been one of them, she'd have known that he wasn't real. The Bill Reinstadt she thought she knew was just an illusion. Now she had no idea who he was. She suspected that he didn't either.

Weeping, Kylie looked out the window as Misha drove

towards Lexington. Once they turned off Route 2, she dried her eyes. He reached over and held her hand as they drove. Within minutes, they reached her parents' house and Kylie rang the doorbell for the second time that day.

Allison answered the door. "You're back!" Come in, both of you. We just sat down to eat." She looked at then closely before herding them into the foyer where they removed their coats. "You both look like you're coming from a wake."

"Pretty much we have," said Kylie and she told her what had transpired.

Allison opened her arms and held Kylie. "Oh my God. My poor baby. What a thing to go through. I'm so sorry." Misha examined his feet.

Then Allison opened one of her arms and invited Misha into their embrace. Kylie thought perhaps an alien had inhabited her mother's body, but she didn't care. They stood there for a long moment. Kylie realized that OMG had brought her to this juncture. She could never have imagined hugging her mother, never mind twice in one day. She'd helped solve a heinous crime and had been offered a job by the FBI. There would be other cases. She didn't care about the money she'd lost anymore. She would earn it back over time. And maybe there would be other heroes—real ones. It had been a crazy yet remarkable journey.

The corners of Kylie's mouth curled with pleasure as if someone had poured a bucket of butterflies into the room. She was keenly relieved that the case was solved. There would be other cases. Maybe there would even be other heroes. She was thankful to still be alive, for her family, and her excitement about the future. And, she felt grateful for Misha, although, she would have to see about that. She took a step back and looked at her mother. "Thanks, Mom. You have no idea how grateful I am to be here."

"Me too. Let's go eat some turkey," said Allison.

The End

Thank you for purchasing *OMG* and I am extremely grateful for your interest. I hope that you enjoyed it. If so, it would be really nice if you could share this book with your friends and family by posting to Facebook and Twitter as well as taking a moment to post a review on Amazon.

Your feedback and support will help me improve future projects. I'd love to connect with you!
Web: jennypivor.com
Instagram: jennyp_art_photo
Facebook: jennypivorwritingandart
Email: jenny@jennypivor.com

Other books by Jenny Pivor

The Closing
Boston Dogs
The Official Loving Boston Coloring Book
Dates Outta Hell

42768258R00189

Made in the USA
Middletown, DE
20 April 2019